# HITTING THE GAP

## LAUREN FRASER

# CONTENTS

# BLURB

**Hitting the gap is easy compared to falling in love with your best friend.**

For a smart girl, Bailey Reynolds has terrible taste in men. How else can she explain why she agreed to move halfway across the country with her fiancé? Her now ex-fiancé. The lying, cheating, jerk. Now she's not only in a new city, but homeless, and needing her childhood best friend to come to her rescue. Good thing she stopped believing in fairytales a long time ago because they sure don't happen for curvy girls like her.

Fun-loving, Hawks third baseman Ramon (Gonzo) Gonzalez enjoys his single life. Who wouldn't? He's got no commitments and his pick of women. But he'd do anything for the people he cares about, including giving up his spare bedroom. When he insisted Bailey move in with him, he'd thought sharing his space might take some getting used to. What he didn't expect was the late-night conversations and seeing her sleep-rumpled face over coffee to make him re-evaluate everything he thought he felt about their relationship. Now he's lusting after his childhood friend. And that was never part of his plan.

Getting girls has always been easy. Finding one he wanted to keep? Not so much, until now. But Bailey's fears and insecurities run deep. And it'll take all his skills to convince her a life with him is so much better than any fairytale ever could be.

Sign up for Lauren's newsletter and receive a free copy of Undercover Attraction. Join my mailing list for news of my latest release and sneak peeks at upcoming books and special newsletter only content.

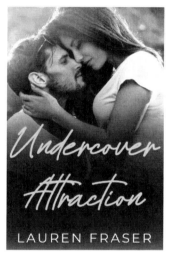

Sign up at http://www.laurenfraser.com/newsletter

# CHAPTER ONE

N ope, not a chance. There was no way anyone he cared about was living in this dump, especially not a woman. Maybe that made him sexist, but at this moment he didn't care.

Gonzo eyed the run-down apartment complex with the overflowing dumpster, the peeling paint, and big pieces of broken concrete on the path. The place looked like it should have a "condemned" sign slapped to the wall instead of "for rent".

What had Bailey been thinking, wanting to move here? This was possibly the worst neighborhood in the city. Even if money was tight, there were safer places to live.

He glanced down the street, looking for her vehicle.

Where the hell was she? She'd told him to meet her here at 1:00 to help her unload the moving truck. It was 1:30 and there was still no sign of her. But then, did he really expect anything different? His childhood best friend was notoriously late. Heck, it was such a well-known fact that his parents had let it slide when he'd missed curfew on more than one occasion because they knew he was out with her.

Finally, he heard the distinct rumble of a U-Haul truck that was a few too many moves past a repair. He couldn't see much of the driver, but from the size, he guessed it was a woman. When the truck got closer, he spotted Bailey's smiling face and red hair behind the wheel. Only Bailey would look happy pulling up in front of a shithole like this.

She double-parked the truck in front of the building and hopped out of the cab. Her feet barely hit the cement before she launched herself in his direction. Her movement didn't stop until she crashed into him. The forward momentum nearly knocked him on his ass, and he took several steps backward to keep them upright as Bailey's arms wrapped around his neck. Lush female curves filled his hands. It had been a couple years since he'd seen Bailey in person, but he sure as hell didn't remember her hugs feeling like that.

Whoa. Whatever curves she had were irrelevant. This was Bailey.

"Hey, Bay." He chuckled as he pulled her in tight for a hug. The familiar smell of citrus and something that was distinctly his childhood friend filled his senses. It was good to have her here. Until this moment, he hadn't realized just how much he'd missed her.

When Bailey had said she was moving to San Diego for a job, he hadn't known what to expect. He wasn't a fan of her boyfriend at all, but when she'd called last week to ask for his help with the move, she said they'd broken up and she was coming alone. Now that he didn't have to worry about her dick boyfriend, he was really looking forward to spending time with his childhood best friend.

Bailey glanced at the building and wrinkled her nose. "Hmm."

"You can't be serious about living here," he said.

She chewed her bottom lip, and a wave of nostalgia filled him. How many times had he seen her make that exact same face growing up?

"It looks a little different from the online picture." Her brows knitted together. "This is Sunnyvale Apartments, right?"

Gonzo eyed the graffitied sign with the word 'Sun' peeking through the paint. "That's what it says."

Bailey pulled her phone out of her pocket and swiped it open. Her lips pursed tightly, and she looked back at the building, then down at her phone and back at the building again. The lines of confusion on her face grew.

"You okay?" he asked.

She thrust her phone toward him. "Is this even the same building? I mean, even brand new, this place wouldn't have looked anything like that?"

He eyed the picture on the screen. "What the fuck? Is this seriously the ad?" The building in the ad looked modern, with clean lines and beautiful landscaping. The one in front of them looked like 1970 threw up. He could already picture the snot green shag he was gonna see inside the apartments. "There's no fucking way you're living here," he told her.

"Maybe it's better inside than out." Bailey chewed her bottom lip as she eyed the building. Even for an optimist like her, the comment was a stretch.

"It couldn't possibly be worse."

Bailey studied the building and sighed. "Let's go find the manager and look."

"The only thing we're finding the manager for is to tell him you aren't moving in here."

Bailey bristled. "Don't even start with that macho bullshit, Gonzo. I didn't let you boss me around as a kid, and I'm sure not letting you do it now." She squared her shoulders, and he bit back a groan. Damn it. He should have known better. If there was one thing destined to make Bailey dig her feet in, it was telling her she couldn't do something. The woman took independence to new heights.

"All right, let's go look." He swept out his arm to gesture she go first. He needed to have her back to make sure he could protect her if anything happened. As they stepped across the broken path toward the building, he scanned their surroundings, ready for anything.

"Hopefully we don't get shanked," Bailey mumbled.

"No shit." The hairs on his neck stood up and he looked behind him. A group of young men leaned against a car, watching them. He rolled his shoulders to loosen his neck in case he needed to get into it with these guys.

Bailey stopped and scanned the area. She turned toward the men and called, "Do you know where I can find the super?"

What the hell was she doing drawing more attention to herself?

One guy pushed off the car and sauntered toward them. His New York ball cap tilted sideways on his head. The guy couldn't even cheer for a good team. New York. Come on. As the guy scanned Bailey appreciatively,

Gonzo stepped in front of her to block the other man's view.

"You moving in?" the guy asked Bailey.

Bailey nodded. "Trying to."

Just as Gonzo said, "No."

"Super's in 101. If you need anything once you're moved in, gorgeous, you come find me."

"Thanks," Bailey said.

The guy licked his lips, and his gaze trailed slowly down her body. The leer was so disgusting Gonzo needed a shower and it wasn't even directed at him.

"She won't," Gonzo growled.

The guy eyed Gonzo, then nodded to his friends, and the other four guys started walking toward them. "You look like you got somethin' to say." The guy stepped toward Gonzo.

Fuck. He flexed his hands. The last thing he wanted was to get into it with these assholes. He liked his odds one-on-one. Hell, even two-or-three-on-one. But five-on-one? Those weren't great odds. Factor that at least one of these guys probably had a piece and he was fucked.

"Holy shit, you're Ramon Gonzalez," one of the newcomers said.

"Yeah."

The guy lifted his sweatshirt to show off the Hawks T-shirt he was wearing underneath. Thankfully, the other men stopped posturing and Gonzo breathed a sigh of relief. Looked like he might get out of here unscathed yet.

"What the fuck are you doing in this neighborhood?" the guy asked.

"Just need to talk to the super for a minute."

The guy tilted his head as he assessed him, looked at his boys, then back at Gonzo. "She your girl?"

"Yeah." He felt Bailey tense behind him. What was he supposed to say? If the guys were fans, Bailey was as a hell of a lot safer if they thought she belonged to him.

The newcomer eyed Bailey speculatively and nodded his head. "If she moves in, we'll keep an eye on her."

"Thanks," Gonzo mumbled. There was no way Bailey was moving in here. When he felt her fingers wrap into the waistband of his jeans as she pressed closer to him, he was pretty sure they were on the same page.

"So how's the team looking this year?" the guy asked.

"Pretty good."

A scrawny guy walked around the side of the building and pulled up short when he saw them. The Hawks fan glanced over, then said, "That's the super."

"Cool, thanks," Gonzo said. He reached around and grabbed Bailey's hand and pulled her to his side so he could protect her if needed. Once they got a few steps from the group, he whispered, "Bay, seriously, you didn't move to some Podunk town where you sit and have lemonade on the porch with the neighbors. People here have guns."

"I know," she whispered back. "That's why I was being nice. If anyone was going to get us in trouble, it was you."

Unfortunately, she probably wasn't wrong about that assessment. "You can't seriously be thinking of moving in here." He pointed to a hole in the wall by the staircase. "That's a fucking bullet hole, Bailey."

Her eyes widened and she cringed. "Really?"

"Yes, really. Now, can we please get out of here?"

"I can't. I put down a deposit to hold the place."

Gonzo pinched the bridge of his nose. "Guess we're talking to the super." He cupped her elbow and propelled her toward the super.

"You Bailey Reynolds?" the man asked.

"Yes."

"You're late." He glared at her.

Gonzo rolled his eyes. Nice customer service. Clearly, the manager matched the shithole exterior.

The super turned on his heel. "Follow me."

Gonzo and Bailey fell in line behind him. Bailey's head swiveled from one side to the other as they walked. If she was thinking anything close to what he was thinking, they should run, not walk, to the nearest exit.

They stopped in front of apartment 213. The super pushed the door open and coughed slightly as he stepped into the room. Gonzo hadn't even taken a step and he could already see the disgusting carpet. He hadn't been far off in his guess. It was more of a mustard puke color rather than snot, but equally disgusting.

Following Bailey into the room, he pulled up short when the smell punched him in the face. Bailey's head snapped back a second before she retched, then slapped her hand over her mouth. "Oh my god, what is that?" She plugged her nose. "It smells like death. But not like good death."

"Good death?" he asked. What the fuck was good death?

Bailey's mouth gaped like a fish as she tried to suck air into her lungs. It was like the stench sucked out the oxygen from the room, making it hard to breathe. Fuck, the smell was so bad he could taste it. What was that?

Bailey flapped her hand in front of her face. "God, it's like decomposing smelly feet doused in parmesan cheese and cat piss."

That was a pretty accurate description.

She tilted her head back, then retched again. "Nope, I can't." She covered her mouth and bolted for the front door.

Gonzo walked to the door, turned, and blocked the super from leaving. "We're gonna need that deposit back."

The man narrowed his eyes and sneered. "No, she agreed to live here. If she wants to back out, that's her choice, but she's not getting the deposit back."

Gonzo stepped into the other man's space and took a great deal of pleasure in watching him back away. "We both know that ad you placed was a load of shit. That's false advertising and there's not a court in the world that would honor that bullshit." He let his derision for the little weasel show on his face. "And when my lawyer gets done with you, this place will look like a luxury condo compared to what you'll be able to afford if you don't give her back her money."

"You can't sue me."

"Watch me." Gonzo stared at the little man. He crossed his arms over his chest and continued to block the other man from leaving the apartment. Finally, the guy sighed.

"Fine, follow me to my office and I'll transfer her the money back."

Gonzo grunted in acknowledgement and stepped out of the room. He sucked in a breath of air but couldn't smell anything except the apartment. Great, that stench now lived in his nose. *Like when you puked on yourself and that's all you could smell.* He turned to Bailey. "He's gonna give you your deposit back."

The super pushed past them and stormed down the hallway. Bailey eyed the apartment and chewed nervously on her bottom lip. "I don't have a lot of options, Gonz. I gotta live somewhere."

"Well, it sure as fuck isn't going to be here. Let's get your deposit and we'll figure it out."

# CHAPTER TWO

B ailey sat at the outdoor picnic table and stared at the U-Haul parked in the mostly empty lot. Gonzo's SUV was the only other vehicle around.

Getting out of her lease had been the right move. There was no way she could live in that crappy apartment, but now where was she supposed to live? Ugh, it was a good thing she didn't have a knife and her ex nearby, or she would not be responsible for her actions. Fucking Brad.

She clenched her jaw and took a deep breath to keep the tears at bay. This was not how her life was supposed to be. She had a plan, and until recently, she'd been on track. Now it felt like her life was a flashing neon sign of missteps and mistakes. How could she have been so stupid? Resting her elbows on the splintered wood table, she dropped her head down and dug her fingertips into her tense scalp.

She felt someone approach and looked up as Gonzo set a tray with burgers and fries on the table.

"Eat, you'll feel better." Gonzo pushed the tray toward her then grabbed a burger off the tray for himself.

Bailey opened the foil wrapper and stared at the greasy burger in her hand. She could practically hear Brad's voice condemning her for even looking at the burger let alone thinking about eating it. She swallowed past the lump in her throat. When was the last time she'd allowed herself to eat fast food? Her stomach rolled and she set the burger down on the tray.

"What's the matter? Did I fuck up your order?" Gonzo asked.

She eyed the foil wrapper. "What? No, of course not, it's fine."

"Then what's going on?"

"Nothing." There was no way she was about to admit to Gonzo that the idea of eating the greasy burger made her feel sick. He wouldn't understand. She looked up to find her friend watching her closely.

Gonzo's eyes narrowed. "Please tell me you haven't become a vegetarian or something."

"No, no, nothing like that. I'm just not very hungry." She pinched the bridge of her nose and sighed. "What am I supposed to do, Gonz? I've got nowhere to go."

"Move in with me."

Bailey's head snapped back. "What?"

"Just move in with me," he said, then picked up his burger and took a large bite.

How could he throw something like that out so casually and then just stuff his face? He couldn't be serious. "Yeah, right," she mumbled.

He wiped the edge of his mouth with his napkin, then took a sip of his drink. "Why not?"

"Oh, I don't know. Because I can't," she scoffed.

"Why? You need a place to live. I've got a spare bed-room. It's not like you have a ton of options at the moment, Bay."

"Yeah, but, come on, we've barely seen each other in the past ten years. I can't just move in with you."

"Bailey, don't be stupid. I've known you since I was five years old. The shit that matters doesn't change."

If only that were true. The girl he knew would never have allowed a man to treat her like she let Brad. She barely recognized herself. "People change, Gonz."

"Ok, how've you changed?"

"I don't know, I just have."

The man sitting across from her barely resembled the boy she remembered. Sure, he'd always been confident, maybe even a little cocky, but now everything about him screamed he could back it up. Whereas all her confi-dence had disappeared the moment she'd found out her ex-boyfriend had cheated on her with her best friend. Her petite, perfect size zero best friend. The one she'd stupidly convinced her fiancé to hire as his assistant. God, she'd been so stupid. No, the Bailey he knew was gone.

"Did you become a serial killer?" Gonzo asked as he took another bite of his burger.

"Of course not," she scoffed.

"You develop one of those weird home shopping net-work addictions and that entire U-Haul is filled with porcelain dolls?" He tilted his head toward the U-Haul.

"No, smart-ass." She rolled her eyes. "But people change, Gonzo."

"Jesus, Bailey. You clogged my toilet in high school."

"Ugh." She gasped. "Rude. You don't need to bring that up."

He laughed. "Bay, seriously, I gave you my favorite sweats when you got your period at school. I've held your freaking hair while you puked. You've snotted all over me when you cried over some loser."

"Hey, I don't think you can talk about my bodily functions, dude. I touched your 'special sock'." She shuddered. She could still picture the mortified look on Gonzo's face when she'd picked up the offending sock off the side of the bed so she could sit down. Why boys used socks to masturbate she'd never understand.

"Exactly," Gonzo agreed. "Kids are fucking gross and we remained friends through all of that. I'm pretty sure we can handle living together now."

"Gonzo, come on. I follow you on social media. I know how active your social life is. There's no way you want me cramping your style."

"Bay, I have four bedrooms. You being in one of them is not going to cramp shit. You can be my wingman and get rid of anyone who clings on and doesn't want to leave."

"You're disgusting."

"Yep, but you love me anyway." He tossed a fry in his mouth and winked when he caught it.

"Mmm, sometimes I wonder why," she muttered.

"I'm being serious, Bay. It's not a problem at all for you to move in. During the season, I'm barely home, so you'd practically have the place to yourself. You can stay as long as you like. Learn San Diego, get the lay of the land, figure out where you want to live. Wait till you find something you actually like so you don't have to move a bunch of times."

It would be nice to actually look at a place in person before she committed to moving there. Maybe she'd even be able to find something closer to the university, so she could walk to work and she could hold off on buying a car.

She chewed on her bottom lip and looked at Gonzo. "You sure you wouldn't mind?"

"Nah, not at all." He took a sip of his drink. "Why don't we go check out my place? If you like it, we go find a storage unit and put your stuff into that so you can return the U-Haul. If you hate it, we start calling around to see if we can find you someplace to move. Either way, you need someplace to stay tonight, and my place is free." He threw his garbage onto the tray.

"Free's good."

"Figures." Gonzo snorted. "See. You haven't changed that much after all."

Twenty minutes later, Bailey walked into the apartment and scanned the open layout. Good lord. She knew Gonzo made a lot of money, but this was ridiculous. She wandered over to the row of floor-to-ceiling windows that covered the entire living room and looked out. The ocean spanned out for miles in front of her. The unobstructed view made it feel like her own private sanctuary. "Wow. That view sure beats looking at old man Peter's lawn full of cars."

"No shit." Gonzo snorted. "Does he still have those?"

"Of course he does. Not much has changed in the old neighborhood."

Bailey glanced back at the ocean view. "Seriously, Gonz, this view is amazing!"

Gonzo walked up beside her and nudged her with his hip. "It's not bad, huh?"

"Yeah, you could say that."

"You remember when we were kids and dreamed about seeing the ocean someday?" he asked.

"Yeah." She smiled at the memory of the two of them sitting in the tree fort in her backyard, talking all big about what they were going to be when they grew up. She was going to be an astronaut and fly to the moon and Gonzo was going to be a professional baseball player. Over the years she'd changed her mind a million times, but Gonzo's dream had never wavered. Looking at this apartment with the view of the ocean and the TV that took up an entire wall, it was like he'd gone down the dream list and checked off every box. Whereas her list had been lost years ago. As happy as she was for her childhood friend, she couldn't deny there was a little part of her that was jealous. She'd busted her ass doing everything she was supposed to do and where had it gotten her? Alone in a new town, without a car, without a home. Honestly, it was kind of humiliating.

She glanced around the apartment. Even if she hadn't broken up with Brad, she'd never have been able to afford to live in a place like this. And in her current situation, her budget ran more toward the apartment she'd just turned down. As nice as it would be to have a free place to live to give her a chance to save up some money, she couldn't take advantage of Gonzo. He'd always been the kind of guy to bend over backwards for everyone else, even when he didn't want to. Offering her a place to crash was just another one of those times.

"So you wanna see your room?"

She eyed the gaming system in the entertainment stand. This place screamed bachelor. Rich bachelor, but bachelor. "I appreciate the offer, but I can't stay here."

"Why?"

"Come on, Gonz, you're off the hook. We both know you made that offer just to be nice, and I'm not going to hold you to it."

"I wouldn't have offered if I wasn't cool with you staying. Come on, Bay, there's no fucking way I'm going to let you move into some shithole just so you don't feel guilty about crashing in my place. I've got lots of space. I'm barely here, anyway."

She'd seen the way girls threw themselves at Gonzo growing up. She could only imagine it was worse now that he was a professional ballplayer. And Gonzo had never been one to shy away from attention. "Yeah, but I don't want to cramp your style when you are home."

"How are you gonna cramp my style?"

Heat ran up her face. She could practically feel how red her face was. Damn Irish genes. "I don't know. Girls?"

"You'd have your own room, Bay." He looked at her and grinned as she shifted uncomfortably under the scrutiny.

"I promise to control myself when it comes to sex."

She snorted. "Right, so you're just not going to have sex?"

Gonzo's eyes widened in horror. "Jesus, no. Of course I'm going to have sex. I just promise not to do it some place that will make you uncomfortable."

"Geez, thanks." She rolled her eyes. "Seriously, you don't think having me sleeping in the next bedroom is gonna cramp things when you bring some random woman home? Most girls wouldn't like it."

"Not really worried about whether or not they like it, honestly."

"Oh, my god. Please tell me you have not become that guy."

"What guy?"

"A player who doesn't give a rat's ass about the girl's feelings."

"Bay, I don't want to offend your sensibilities here, but the women I bring home aren't like you."

"Obviously," she muttered.

"They know the score. They're here for one reason and one reason only. Because we both want to have sex. That's it. Once we're done, we're done. There's no reading the paper over breakfast or shit like that." He ran his hand through his dark brown hair. "They aren't here in the morning, Bay. It's not something to even worry about. As soon as we're done, they leave."

Was that seriously how his sex life was? No emotion, like a contact sport, just a fun way to end the evening. That seemed pretty empty. "Don't you ever date?" she asked.

"I don't have time for that during the season." Gonzo wandered over to the fridge and pulled out two bottles of beer. He held one up in the air and she nodded in acceptance. "And it feels like too much work the rest of the time." He handed her a cold bottle of beer.

"Don't you get lonely?" she asked.

"Come on, let me show you the spare bedroom."

Apparently, he wanted to avoid that conversation. Bailey followed him through the lavish apartment. "Did you decorate this place?"

"I picked out the TV. Does that count?"

"Not really, no." She ran her hand over some kind of sculpture. The metal felt almost alive beneath her touch. She had no idea what it was supposed to be, but it was beautiful nonetheless. "Did your mom or your sisters help?"

"Does this look like my mom's style?"

Bailey paused in front of a large painting that filled the wall facing the foyer. "No, not really. But then it doesn't really look like yours either."

"Eh, it's an investment piece, or so I'm told. The colors are cool."

He continued down the hall then turned right at the first doorway. Bailey followed him into the room. She sucked in a breath when she saw the ocean view. "Oh my god, this is your spare bedroom?"

"Want to stay now?"

"Little bit, yeah." Tearing her eyes off the view, she scanned the room. A queen-sized bed covered in pillows took up one wall of the room. She ran her hand over the plush, deep purple comforter. How did they make a blanket feel like that? She'd never felt anything so soft in her life. A beautiful abstract stormy seascape hung on the wall over the bed. The slash of purple in the skyline perfectly matched the comforter. She touched the bedside table. "I love these. They look like driftwood."

"That's the idea."

"If this is your spare bedroom, I gotta see yours."

Gonzo walked out of the room and she rushed after him. Bailey sucked in a breath when she saw the view from his bedroom. A huge king-sized bed took up one wall, facing the expansive ocean view. "Wow."

Gonzo rested his hip against a large dresser, one foot crossed over the other as he watched her.

"Wow, you really have everything you ever dreamed of, don't you?"

A look crossed so quickly over his face she almost missed it. "What?" she asked.

"No one has it all, Bay."

She looked around the bedroom. Her gaze landed on a picture of Gonzo with his family on what looked like a Hawaiian vacation. She picked up the picture and smiled. "Looks like you're pretty damn close."

He walked over and glanced down at the photo. "Mom always dreamed of going to Hawaii. She said when she moved to the States that was the place everyone said you had to see."

"You took your whole family, nieces and nephews and everyone?"

"Yeah. There was no money for our family to do something for my parents' twenty-fifth, but I managed to do it for their fortieth."

She smiled down at the photo. "I'm sure it was everything they could have ever dreamed of."

Gonzo snorted out a laugh. "Not even close."

"What happened?"

"My niece had seen this restaurant on social media. I don't know, some celebrity or something had been there, so she insisted we all go." Gonzo cringed. "We all got food poisoning."

"Oh my god, no."

"Yep, then a few days later, my mom got stung by a jellyfish." He shook his head. "The whole vacation was just one clusterfuck after another."

"Well, you got a good family photo out of it at least," Bailey said.

"Thank god we took that the first night because we sure as hell didn't look like that when we went home."

"Still, it's very sweet that you took your whole family on vacation."

"Yeah maybe. Raul and I got into it as usual about how I was showing off by being a big spender, taking his family on a trip he couldn't afford."

"Guess some things never change, huh?" Bailey said. Gonzo's brother had always been jealous of his younger brother.

"Didn't stop him from accepting the trip, though." Resigned annoyance tinged Gonzo's voice.

"He's always wanted whatever you had."

"Including you," Gonzo said.

"Yes, well, once he found out you weren't interested in me, he quickly realized he wasn't either." Bailey cringed. "Ah well, his reasoning was messed up, but at least he saved me from graduating high school without ever being kissed."

Gonzo turned. "Hang on. Are you telling me my brother was your first kiss?"

"Afraid so. First and only kiss in high school. How'd you not know that?"

"How's that even possible? I remember you going into the closet with what's his name, Jeff ... um ... Clark, in eighth grade."

"Mmm, yeah, he was afraid you'd punch him if he copped a feel."

"Yeah, and I would have. Big difference between a little kiss in the closet and grabbing your boob."

Bailey snorted out a laugh. "And you wonder why no one wanted to kiss me. Even now, more than a decade later, you still sound annoyed about it."

"I just think you deserve more respect than that."

"Well, I appreciate that, but in high school I have to admit I wished someone, anyone, liked me enough to risk pissing you off." She sighed. "Probably why I let your brother kiss me, even though I knew it would cause issues between you two because I stupidly thought someone finally liked me." She set the picture back down on the shelf. "Ah well, it was a long time ago." And yet somehow the humiliation of how that time in her life felt was still alive and well.

Brushing off the wave of embarrassed nostalgia, Bailey walked over to the window and looked out. Gonzo stepped up beside her and bumped her with his hip. "So what do you say? Want to be my roomie?"

Her gaze lingered on the waves crashing against the shore. How amazing would it be to wake up to that every day? She'd never dreamed of living anywhere so luxurious. Would it be wrong to stay and enjoy it just for a little while? Things with Brad had ended so crappy, she hadn't thought they could get much worse until she'd seen that apartment. What if that was all she could find? Or afford? She glanced at her childhood friend. What would she do without him? "Yeah, I want to be your roomie."

# CHAPTER THREE

"Last one." Gonzo dropped the box on the bedroom floor and glanced around the spare bedroom. Boxes of Bailey's belongings lay strategically near the closet and the bookcase. He counted seven boxes, well eight if he included the one he'd placed on the bathroom counter. That's it? She'd agreed to stay here for the next couple months at least, and she only needed eight boxes? His sister needed more than that for a weekend visit.

"Do you have a knife or something I can use to cut the tape?" Bailey asked.

"Yeah, one sec." He left the bedroom, grabbed a pair of scissors from the cutting block on the kitchen counter, and made his way back to the room. He stopped at the nearest box and deftly sliced open the seam. "You opening them all?"

"May as well. There's not that many."

He walked up to the next box, sliced it open and continued around the room until all the boxes were open. Now what? Did he help her unpack? Was that an invasion of her privacy? Was he a dick if he didn't help? Shit.

"Thanks. I appreciate all your help today."

"No problem." It wasn't in his nature to stand and do nothing, so he crouched down and flipped the lid of the box closest to him. "Is this all books?" That seemed safe enough to unpack.

Bailey grimaced. "Maybe."

He chuckled. "You only wanted a handful of things out of storage, and one of them was a box of books?"

"Two boxes of books," she replied. Her cheeks flushed the cutest pink color, making her freckles more pronounced, as she glanced over at him.

She had nothing to be embarrassed about. He just couldn't imagine needing one box of books, let alone two. "Wow, we definitely have different priorities." He pushed the box over to the bookcase. "You want any of this stuff left on here or get rid of it all?" he asked, pointing to the knickknacks and book stacks his decorator had artfully displayed on the shelves.

"Umm, maybe see how much space my books take up and you can leave whatever fits."

"All right." Flipping open the lid, he pushed the flaps down so he could start emptying the box. He picked up a textbook and eyed the title. *Introduction to Sociology*. Made sense since she was a sociology professor.

He scooped up a handful of books and placed them on the bottom shelf next to the textbook. His gaze snared on the next book in the box. *Algorithms of Oppression.* Geez, nothing like a little light reading.

Growing up, Bailey had always been the brain and he'd been the jock. She'd helped him with school and he'd kept her from being a social pariah. As odd as it was, their friendship had just worked.

He was well aware of the fact that he'd gotten more out of their friendship than she had. If it hadn't been for her, he wouldn't have graduated high school and he sure as hell wouldn't have made it through university. Without Bailey, he never would have figured out he had dyslexia. And that diagnosis had made all the difference for him. Suddenly, he wasn't just some dumb jock. But as he eyed her reading material, he sure felt like one.

As he finished loading the books from the first box onto the shelves, he could hear Bailey in the walk-in closet hanging her clothing up on the rack. He pulled the second box of books toward himself and flipped it open. A book with a half-naked dude displayed on the cover rested on the top of the box. Interesting. He reached in and pulled out a stack of books and flipped through them. They all had half-naked men on the cover.

Hmm, not so academic, now. He picked up the book on the top of the pile and flipped to a dogeared page. The word clit jumped out at him, and his eyes widened. What the hell was this? He continued to read. Ho-ly shit.

"Busted," he yelled. "Bailey Reynolds, you're a perv." He practically hooted as he looked down at the book in his hands.

Bailey poked her head out of the walk-in closet. "What?"

He couldn't keep the glee out of his voice. "The first box was all textbooks and academic shit. But this one" — he pointed at the second box he'd pulled up beside him — "this is your lady porn."

"I don't have lady porn," she mumbled.

"Oh, no?" He raised his eyebrow then cleared his throat and read. "Flattening his tongue, he made one long, slow swipe of her pussy. He swirled his tongue around her clit then sucked the hard nub into his mouth, and she bucked off the bed."

Bailey's eyes boggled. "Why are you reading my books?"

"Should I not be?"

She covered her mouth and giggled. "No, it's fine. I have nothing to be ashamed of."

"Except you like porn."

Bailey rolled her eyes. "It's not porn, it's spicy romance."

"I'll say it's spicy," he mumbled. Jesus, the thing described how the guy went down on her, in detail. The passage had been way hotter than anything he'd ever read before. "One girl's spicy is another guy's porn, I'm just saying."

She placed her hands on her hips and glared at him. "Are you seriously being all judgy about my choice of reading material?"

"Me? No. Fuck. Read away." Who knew his little Bailey liked to read dirty books? In high school she'd blushed practically every time he took his shirt off and now she was reading this kind of thing. "It just surprised me, that's all."

"Mmm-hmm," she mumbled. She turned on her heel and headed back to the closet. "You can borrow it if you want," she called over her shoulder.

He eyed the book. Even though he'd learned a bunch of tricks to make reading easier, he still didn't really love to read. Having to make the effort for something that came so easily to everyone else still made him feel stupid. "Any chance they have an audiobook, because I could definitely get behind that."

Bailey popped her head out of the closet and glanced at the book in his hand. "That one doesn't, no. But that one does." She pointed to the pile of books sitting beside his leg.

"I'll keep it in mind."

She ducked back into the closet, and he pulled out the next handful of books. As he held the books, he looked back into the box. His gaze landed on a long wooden box. He was just lifting the lid of the wooden box when Bailey whipped out of the closet like the room was on fire. "Don't open that," she yelled.

Too late, he'd already lifted the lid. And there was no way he couldn't look. Jesus. Bailey had a box of sex toys. His head snapped up as Bailey dove across the room. Her palm crashed against the lid before she ripped it out of his hands and held it against her chest.

Bailey closed her eyes. Her normally freckly white skin turned as red as her hair. "Please tell me you didn't see what was inside the box."

"What? You mean your little erotic toy box? Nope, didn't see a thing."

She shoved the box in the bedside table and stood with her back to him.

"That's where I'd keep it, too," he added helpfully.

"Oh my god, shut up," she groaned.

"What? I saw your books. Of course, you need a little wank while you're reading," he teased.

She flopped onto the mattress and covered her face with her hands.

Shit. He pushed himself off the floor. Was she really upset he'd found her sex toys?

Her shoulders started to shake, then Bailey made the most unladylike snort he'd ever heard. She slapped her hand over her mouth and continued to giggle.

With a laugh, he dropped onto the mattress beside her and slung his arm over her shoulder. "Bailey, Bailey, Bailey," he chanted.

She glanced over at him, tears streaming down her face because she was laughing so hard.

He squeezed her shoulder, pulling her body against his side as he did. "I've never been more proud of you."

Bailey threw her head back and barked out a laugh. "You are the only person I know who'd be proud of me for having sex toys."

He grinned back at her. "With the shit you gave me in high school about wanking, how could I not be thrilled that you finally admit to doing it?"

"I didn't use to do it." She laughed.

"You didn't sell that story back then and now that I've seen all this, you sure as shit aren't selling it now." He eyed the bedside table. "So you gonna let me properly look in the box?" he asked and wiggled his eyebrows up and down.

"Nope." Bailey giggled, then dropped her head against his shoulder. "God, Gonzo, I've missed you so much."

He pressed a kiss against the top of her head. "I've missed you too, Bay." He took a deep breath. This felt nice. Too nice. It was Bailey. He cleared his throat. "What about now?"

Bailey shoved into his shoulder with hers as she sat up. "No. A girl's got to keep some secrets."

"Yeah, that ship has sailed," he snickered.

Her tooth dug into her bottom lip as she glanced over at him. "You really don't think it's weird I have a box of sex stuff?"

"I think it's fucking outstanding." That was kind of the problem. He wasn't supposed to think about Bailey and sex at the same time. He'd worked hard to keep them separate in his mind. Now he couldn't.

"Really?" She seemed so unsure when she looked back at him.

"Of course. Why wouldn't I?"

She worked her tooth into her bottom lip so hard he was worried she was going to break the skin. "Bay?" he pressed.

"Brad just thought it was wrong to have toys when I had him. It pissed him off when he found out I had them."

Gonzo snorted. "What a dick." He looked over at Bailey. It pulled at him how she suddenly looked so unsure of herself. "I'm just gonna throw it out there that any guy who's confident about what he brings to the bedroom doesn't need to be jealous of a toy."

"Mmm, maybe," she mumbled.

"Not maybe. I'd love it if a girl I was fucking wanted to bring in some toys."

"Really?"

"Fuck yeah."

Bailey licked her lips and suddenly he was painfully aware of how close they were sitting and how close that box of toys was to him. He cleared his throat, then pushed off the mattress. "I'm getting hungry. You want to order pizza?"

She watched him for a second. "Umm, yeah sure."

"Cool." His head bobbed up and down like a freakin' bobble head. He clenched his jaw and forced his head to stay still. "What kind do you want?"

"I'm good with anything but ham."

"Still don't like it, huh?"

"No, it's a weird texture." She scrunched up her face. "Blech."

"Got it, no ham." Needing some space, he walked toward the door.

"Thanks for all your help with everything."

He rapped his knuckles against the doorframe twice. "No problem." Once in the hallway, he paused. What the hell was that? Bailey was his friend. She needed a place to stay. He didn't know why she'd broken up with Brad, but it was clear she was feeling vulnerable, and he wasn't going to be some dickhead who took advantage of that. It would be fine. He'd always managed to keep it in his pants with Bailey before. This wasn't any different. His dick twitched as he thought about using the toys on Bailey. Except it was. Fuck.

# CHAPTER FOUR

Gonzo eyed the empty pizza box in the middle of the kitchen island. Why did he always eat so much? He leaned back on the couch and rested his arms on his stomach. Man, he loved pizza, but he was going to pay for today's shitty diet. Looked like there was an extra-long run in his future tomorrow. Damn, it always seemed like such a good idea in the moment. He eyed Bailey as she set her plate down on the coffee table and sat back in the opposite chair. "Did you ever learn to cook?" he asked.

"Of course I can cook. Well, sort of, it's not like I can whip up duck confit or anything, but I can get by."

"It's not that hard. You just have to make sure you cure it long enough in the spices and then roast it slowly," he absently replied.

"Oh my god, do you seriously know how to make it?" Bailey gaped at him like he'd just admitted to being a flat earther or something.

"What? I like to cook, you know that," he mumbled.

"Well yeah, but there's like I make cookies when I can't sleep and there's people who make duck confit." She blew a raspberry. "I can't even wrap my head around you being all Julia Child."

He rolled his eyes. "I'm not all Julia Child, I just find cooking relaxing."

"Does that mean you're gonna cook for me?" She leaned forward and placed her hands under her chin and fluttered her eyelashes.

"Maybe, if you're nice."

"I'm always nice. It's my middle name."

"Uh-huh." He grabbed his water glass and took a sip. "I like to cook on my days off and I meal prep for game days, so if you want me to cook when I'm home just let me know."

"Are you kidding? You just said you can make things like duck confit. Of course I want you to cook."

He chuckled. "All right, well, I do up a shopping list for meals and stuff when I'm home and I have someone who goes shopping and stocks the kitchen for me."

"Ooh fancy."

Ignoring the way she teased him, he continued, "Anyway. The schedule and shopping list are always on the fridge and Sylvia comes by twice a week, once to clean and once to restock the fridge. The game schedule kind of determines when each happens."

"You have a housekeeper?"

"I do. She's a single mom from this program Pete's a part of." When he'd found out about the program, he'd wanted to help and employing one of the moms seemed like a good way to do that. "She helps us all out with shopping and stuff and it lets her have a flexible schedule around her son's appointments."

"So she does this for multiple players?"

"Yeah, some of the guys hate cooking, so she cooks their meals, does meal prep and grocery shopping, dry cleaning that sort of thing. I hate grocery shopping and no one wants to clean a toilet on their day off, so Sylvia takes care of all that for me. I just didn't want you to be surprised if you saw some random woman in the apartment."

"I appreciate that."

"I'll give her a call while I'm home and let her know you're here as well, but feel free to add anything you want to the grocery list."

"I'm not going to put my groceries on your shopping list, Gonzo."

"Why not?"

"You're already letting me stay with you for free. I'm not going to start adding my food as well."

"Up to you, but I'm telling her to double everything when I'm home if I'm cooking."

"That's fine. Just let me know what I owe you each week."

"Yeah, that's not happening."

"Gonzo." She glared at him, making it very clear she was not happy about him paying for stuff. Well, tough, it wasn't up for discussion.

"I could use a soak in the hot tub. You want to come?"

"You have a hot tub? Where?"

"Up on the roof. I have a little private rooftop patio thing up there that's perfect for the hot tub."

Bailey nervously chewed the inside of her mouth. "I don't really love wearing a bathing suit in public."

"It's not public. I'm the only one who has access to it. No one can even see you in there. Fuck, I go naked half the time, but I'll cover the goods for you."

"Gee thanks," she mocked. "Still, I ju—just," she stammered.

"Bailey, I've seen you in a bathing suit a million times."

"Yeah, but not recently."

"Bailey, I've examined your butthole as a kid. I'm pretty sure any kind of changes to your clothed body are a moot point."

Her eyes bugged out. "You did not just say that?"

"Yeah, I did. It's true."

"We were five," she screeched.

"Still counts. I've seen all your naughty bits in detail, so seeing you in a bathing suit isn't going to shock me."

She mumbled something that sounded a lot like, "That's what you think."

"Don't be a prude. Put your bathing suit on and come soak off the shitty day."

"I'm not being a prude," she grumbled.

"You kind of are. It's a body, Bay, we've all got one."

"Fine, but no laughing." She pointed her finger at him.

Why the hell would he laugh? He placed his hand on his heart. "Promise. If it makes you feel more comfortable, I won't even look."

"Okay then," she agreed.

"Go get changed."

He quickly put on his swim trunks and grabbed a couple of towels out of the linen closet. He slid his feet into a pair of flip-flops because the idea of having bare feet in the elevator grossed him out.

As he waited for Bailey, he loaded the dishwasher with their dinner plates. He'd just finished wiping down the counter when she appeared. His gaze swept over her oversized T-shirt and down her bare legs. She looked back at him and his abs flexed like they had a mind of their own when it seemed like her gaze lingered on his naked torso.

"Let me just grab shoes," she said before she quickly disappeared.

A moment later, she returned. "I'm ready."

He walked to the front door, pulled it open and stepped back to allow Bailey to go first. At the elevator, he tapped his fob against the control panel and pushed the button for the roof. "I'm the only one who has access," he told her.

When the doors opened, Bailey gasped as she stepped outside. She scanned the rooftop and a wave of pride slid over him. He'd spent a boatload of money on his rooftop patio to turn it into something relaxing. He hadn't realized how different his vision was from his designers until she'd started working on it. After a few adjustments, it now felt perfect.

"You have a basketball hoop?"

"Just a little one. You can shoot empties from the hot tub right into the recycle bin."

"It's very you."

He walked over to the hot tub and flipped off the lid, then set the towels down on one of the lounge chairs. "You getting in?" he asked.

"You turning around?" she countered.

"You were serious about that?"

"Yes." She crossed her arms over her chest.

"Geez, okay, let me get in and I'll close my eyes." He put his foot on the bottom step and then flung his leg into the hot tub. As his second leg hit, he sighed. Damn, that felt good. He moved over to the far side of the tub and dropped into his favorite seat. Once positioned, he dropped his head back and closed his eyes. "All right, I'm not looking."

The water splashed as he felt Bailey step into the tub. He really wanted to open his eyes, but he forced them to remain shut.

"Okay, you can open them," she said.

He blinked as his eyes adjusted. The top of Bailey's full breasts bobbed in the water. Damn. Her tits had not looked like that the last time he'd seen her in a bathing suit. Maybe she'd been right to make him close his eyes. The last thing he needed to be doing was leering at his houseguest.

Bailey shifted her body and the water sloshed around her, drawing his attention back to her chest.

Stop it. He looked over at his basketball hoop to distract himself.

They sat in silence for several minutes before Bailey finally spoke. "Are you sure you don't mind me waiting a bit to look for an apartment?"

"Yeah, of course. Like I said, I'm hardly here, so it's no big deal."

"I'll be out of your hair before school starts."

"Not a problem if you aren't. If things go well, we'll be in the playoffs, so you'll mostly have the place to yourself until mid-October."

"I can't stay here that long." She looked toward the railing that faced the ocean view. "I can't get over this apartment. Thank you for letting me squat here. It might be hard to get rid of me now that I've gotten a taste of the good life."

"A hot tub is the good life?"

She leaned her head back against the edge of the tub and sighed. "It's certainly not the bad life. God, this feels amazing."

He shifted himself deeper into his seat as he angled the jets against his lower back. "It's one of the reasons I picked this place. I was looking at another condo that was a bit nicer but didn't have the rooftop patio."

"I can't even imagine what a nicer apartment would look like. This place is gorgeous."

He pulled his arm out of the tub and rested it along the edge. Glancing over at Bailey, he smiled. "You awake over there?"

"Mmm-hmm, just enjoying the quiet."

"Does that mean shut up?" he teased.

Bailey popped one eye open. "No, not at all."

"So you gonna tell me what happened between you and Brad?"

He cringed when her entire body tensed. Nice job, Gonz, way to ruin a perfectly good soak. "You don't have to tell me if you don't want to."

"It's not that I don't want to." Bailey shifted in her seat. "Okay, yes, that's part of it, but..." she paused and looked up at the sky. "Today just really sucked, and I don't have the mental capacity to think about Brad and all that shit." She brought her head back down and glanced at him.

The sadness in her eyes made him want to pull her into a hug. He'd always been protective of Bailey. It killed him that the situation with Brad had obviously hurt her and there was nothing he could do about it. "I get it. No one wants to rehash shit about a breakup."

"Thanks for understanding. I promise I'll fill you in on everything that went down and how I ended up here. Just not tonight, okay?"

"Sure."

They might not be talking about it, but the mood had shifted. He could practically feel the tension radiating off of her from across the hot tub. He was an idiot. He never should have brought it up. Needing to change the vibe, he searched for something neutral to talk about. "So you want to come to the game on Sunday?"

Bailey lifted her head. "What?"

"Sunday, you want to come watch? You can sit with the WAGS, have a couple beers, get to know some people."

"I'm sorry, WAGS? What the hell is that?"

"Wives and girlfriends. Although since you'd be sitting with my buddies' girls, it would technically just be the girlfriend section. Although my man Max will be there, so..."

Bailey shifted her body so she angled toward him and rested her head on her arm. "Who's Max?"

"He's Smitty's kid."

"Oh nice. So besides Max, who would I be sitting with?"

"As far as I know, Peyton, Kendall, and Kia are all attending Sunday. That's why I thought you might want to go. Kind of get it out of the way and meet them all at once."

"So I'd be sitting with three girlfriends?"

"Yeah, is that a problem?" He didn't have a clue why it would be, but she looked a little unsure about the whole thing. "It'll be fun. We can all go grab a beer or some food after," he said.

"What are they like?"

"The girls?"

Bailey rolled her eyes. "Obviously."

He chuckled. "They're cool, you'll like them. And Max is a riot." He stuck out his foot and pushed against her leg. "Stop overthinking shit. Come to the game, have fun, have a beer. If you hate them well..." It would be awkward as shit if she hated his friends. "You'll still have to hang out with them because they're like my family here, but you won't have to sit with them at games anymore."

She chuckled. "Well, that's comforting."

"You'll like them. They're all really great."

She sighed. "Whose girlfriends' are they?"

"Kendall is Pete's girlfriend and Ryan's sister."

Bailey's eyes widened and her mouth formed a little O. "Wow."

"Yeah, it was interesting when they got together. But I couldn't imagine anyone better for him."

"So Ryan's sister and I'm assuming one of the other women is Ryan's girlfriend?"

"Yeah, Peyton. She's cool, really sweet, barely swears."

"Seriously. And she hangs out with you guys?"

"I know, right?" He chuckled. "And Kia is Smitty's girlfriend and Max's mom. And she tries to keep it clean because of Max, but it just doesn't happen most of the time."

Bailey smiled. "Now, her, I might be able to relate to." She pursed her lips out like she was trying to decide.

"It's not that complicated, Bay, it's a ballgame. You used to love watching them live. Come on, you know you want to."

"I can come watch you and not sit with your friends."

"Why would you want to? It's way more fun to sit with people. Trust me, you'll like them. This isn't like when I made you sit with Ozzie's girlfriend at home opener first year of college. She was a bitch."

"Oh my god, she was awful." Bailey shuddered. "I didn't think girls like her actually existed in real life, until that game."

"She was unhinged too. Did I ever tell you what she did to our dorm room when they broke up?"

"No, what'd she do?" Bailey leaned forward, her eyes wide as she waited for him to talk.

"She took stalking to like a whole new level." That woman was the reason he didn't bring a girl back to his place the entire first year of school. He'd been terrified to have anyone know where he lived. "Having her show up everywhere we went was concerning, but fuck..." He shuddered. "The first time Ozzie brought a girl back to our place it was whole other level whacked. Somehow, she got into our apartment and took a shit on his bed. Then there were fucking used tampons stuck to the walls." Even now, just remembering it he felt nauseous. "Disgusting. That chick was disturbed."

"Oh my god." Bailey recoiled. "How'd you know it was her?"

"She wrote this fucked up message on the mirror. I don't know some kind of inside joke or some shit." He cringed. "To this day I still don't know how she got the key to our place since Ozzie swore he didn't give her one. It was messed up."

"Geez, that's..." Bailey shook her head. "I don't even know what to say about that."

"It was fucked up," he said.

"Obviously," she agreed. "I thought she was just a bitch, but wow, she had some mental health stuff going on."

"I guess that's one way of looking at it." He shook his head to clear the memory. "But I promise my friends are nothing like her."

"Well, geez, I would hope not. My god." Bailey laughed. "You sure know how to sell it, Gonz," she teased. "My friends are nice, they're normal, trust me, they don't take shits on people's beds, you'll like them," she tittered in a goofy high-pitched voice then flopped back against the side of the tub holding her belly as she laughed.

He snorted. "Shut up. I wasn't doing a sales pitch."

"Oh, okay, Gonz," she mocked.

"Shut up." He flicked his hand in the water and sent a spray toward her.

"Gah," she squealed when it hit her in the face. Glaring at him, she sat up, narrowed her eyes, and held her arm above the water like she was going to hit him back.

"You don't want to start that shit, Bay," he warned.

"Don't I?" Her hand sliced into the water, sending a tidal wave toward him. The spray hit him square in the face.

"Oh, it's on." He sat up and pushed water toward her as she shoved it back at him. He turned his head to avoid the worst of it in the face.

Bailey squealed and began rapid-fire hitting her hands against the water. He pushed off the seat toward her. The spray pelted him in the face. He reached out and grabbed her arm, yanking her toward him. Off balance, her body collided against him, and he had to adjust his weight to keep them from toppling over.

Wrapping his arm around her waist, he held her captive against his side with one arm as he used his other to flip water at her. Bailey squirmed against him. And he wrapped his arm tighter so he didn't lose his hold. Her ass dragged across his dick as she wiggled.

Suddenly, he became very aware of the fact that he had a half-naked woman squirming in his arms. The fabric of their bathing suits was not nearly a strong enough barrier to keep his dick from firing to life.

Their eyes met. Bailey gasped and held still, like she was holding her breath. Fuck. Instantly, he dropped his arms and jumped back, putting as much space between them as possible.

The awkward silence hung in the air. Should he say something? But what? *Sorry, my dick's a fucking perv and doesn't have boundaries.* Jesus. First, his mind took a dirty turn this afternoon when he saw her toy collection, and now he fucking molested her in the goddamn hot tub. Yeah, great friend he was turning out to be.

"I think I'm just gonna—" Bailey flicked her wrist and pointed toward the stairs.

Cool, so looked like she wanted to just pretend that didn't happen. That sure as hell worked for him. "Yeah, sure, of course. I'm gonna soak a little longer." He dropped back onto the chair and sunk deeply into the water.

"So, I'll see you tomorrow?" Bailey asked.

Trying to feign a nonchalance he definitely wasn't feeling, he tilted his head back and closed his eyes like he didn't have a care in the world. "Yep, see you in the morning."

The water sloshed as Bailey moved out of the tub. He forced himself to keep his eyes closed. After that shit show, the last thing he needed to do was get caught checking out her ass as she climbed out of the tub.

When he was sure he was alone on the rooftop, he banged his head against the tub, hoping it would knock some fucking sense into him. "This is Bailey, dude," he mumbled, like somehow if he said it out loud it would make it feel like less of an issue.

He'd had a warm, curvy woman's body in his arms, rubbing against his dick and he'd had a physical response, that was all. It didn't need to mean anything. It wasn't the first time he'd had a woody in front of Bailey. Shit, when puberty hit, he pretty much lived at half-mast. Bailey had bought him a package of socks as a joke, for Christ's sake. He relaxed his shoulders. It was fine. She probably barely would have noticed if he hadn't freaked out and made shit all awkward.

He groaned. Who was he kidding? His dick had pushed against her ass. Of course, she would have noticed. He bashed his head against the tub again. Fuck.

What was wrong with him? Lately he just hadn't been feeling the whole one-night stand thing for some reason. Probably because his friends were all partnered up and he saw what that looked like.

And now Bailey was here, in his apartment. Even all rumpled from moving, she was sexy as shit and his brain just fucking short circuited for a minute. That's all. What he needed to do was just pick up some random girl. Reset the wires and he'd be back to normal. Bailey was here to get back on her feet. She had shit to figure out and that didn't include whatever the fuck was going on with him.

# CHAPTER FIVE

S hit. Bailey's pulse jumped as she tried to decide if she had enough time to dart back to the bedroom before Gonzo finished unlocking the front door to let himself into the apartment. Before she had a chance to decide, the front door snicked open and Gonzo stepped in. She took in the sneakers and sweaty workout gear. "You've got to be kidding me. You worked out already. It's like 7:30 in the morning."

"I like to get an early start on game day." He raised an eyebrow as he watched her tie up her shoelaces. "Where you off to?" he asked.

"I'm just running to the store."

"Like that?" he asked.

She looked down at her T-shirt from yesterday and fought the urge to touch her hair. She hadn't bothered to pull it out of the messy bun she'd put it in last night to sleep, so she could just imagine what it must look like. But when a girl needed tampons, she needed tampons. She shrugged. "Yeah."

He wrinkled his nose as he looked her up and down. "As one of your oldest friends, I'm just going to be brutally honest. You kind of look like you're just coming off a weeklong bender. I know you didn't really want to talk about all this, but clearly you need to."

She raised one eyebrow in challenge. "Why do I clearly need to?"

"Bay, come on, you've let yourself go a bit and I have to wonder why."

She reared back. "Oh my god, did you just call me fat to my face?"

Gonzo's eyes widened in shock. "Jesus. No. Fuck. I would never say that. I was talking about your hair and the way you dress. You used to spend half the day fucking around in the mirror, playing with hairstyles and makeup and shit. The Bailey I knew would never leave the house without making sure she was fully decked. Now you're going to the grocery store in your pajama pants."

"I was moving. Not going to the freaking opera."

"I know that, Bay, but you have to admit not that long ago, even moving you would have had some outfit all planned out. Now you don't seem to care. The sunny girl I knew seems gone."

"Well, that sunny girl woke up to her period, so you get what you get." But he wasn't wrong. Before all this shit with Brad, she would never have left the house looking like this, even in a tampon emergency. Normally, she'd have at least combed her hair and thrown on a pair of cute yoga pants or something. But this morning, she honestly just couldn't be bothered. What was the point?

"I'm coming with you and we're grabbing breakfast and you're gonna fucking talk about what happened with Brad, whether you're ready or not."

"And if I don't want to talk?"

"I'll just hold your caffeine hostage. You'll be singing within minutes."

Bailey huffed out a breath, then looked him up and down. "How is it okay for you to go out in public all sweaty and gross and that's fine, but me going out like this is somehow offensive?"

"First, I didn't say it was offensive. I said it was completely out of character for you. Big difference." He grabbed a baseball cap off the shelf in the hall closet and slapped it on his head. "And two. I look fucking hot sweaty." He winked at her cockily as he held open the door and gestured for her to lead the way outside.

She hated the fact that he was right. He did look hot all sweaty. How that was possible was beyond her. Somehow he had this who gives a fuck cocky air of appearance and she felt like a thief in the night slumping off to the store. It wasn't fair. Bailey huffed out a sigh. "I'm really not ready to talk about everything with Brad yet."

At the elevator door he pushed the button then said, "I don't give a fuck, Bay. How many times did you badger me into talking about shit when we were kids?"

"A few," she mumbled.

"Yeah," he scoffed. "And what did you always tell me?"

"It's not healthy to keep stuff bottled up," she grumbled.

He stepped into the elevator and leaned against the wall so he was facing her. "Right. So talk."

"There's nothing to say. We broke up. What more do you need?"

"Why did you break up? And don't give me that bull-shit about timing being wrong and you realized you weren't right for each other. We both know that's a load of garbage."

They stepped off the elevator and into the vacant lobby. Desperate to avoid the subject, she glanced over at him as they walked out of the building. How long did she have before he started in on her? Knowing Gonzo, it wouldn't be long.

Lord knows she did not want to talk about this. She was humiliated enough already without rehashing things. Just thinking about everything made her feel sick. How could she have been so stupid?

He nudged her with his shoulder. "Come on, Bay, talk to me."

Her breath stuck in her throat, and she pushed it out in a loud, deep sigh. "What am I supposed to say? That the guy I was going to marry was cheating on me with my best friend for months." She angrily wiped her hand across her face. "How could I be so stupid?"

He grabbed her arm to stop her from walking. Step-ping in front of her so they were facing each other, he asked, "How are you stupid? Because you trusted him?"

"I trusted both of them." She sniffed. "I thought she was my friend. I was all excited that she was coming to San Diego as his assistant because I was going to have a girlfriend here to do stuff with. How stupid am I?"

"He cheated on you with his assistant?"

"Yeah, what a cliche, huh?" She shook her head sadly.

"So they decided they wanted to be together here?"

"Now? Maybe, I don't know."

"What do you mean, now? That's not why you broke up?"

"Sort of. I mean, we broke up because he cheated. But that was more my decision than his." Once she'd found out he cheated, there'd been zero chance she was sticking around.

Gonzo's eyes widened. "Hang on. He planned to move here with you and still have his piece on the side?"

"Apparently." The humiliation of the entire thing sat like a weight in her gut. Thank god she'd caught them, otherwise she would have moved with the jerk and blissfully continued to have his little side piece as her freaking maid of honor. She could just imagine what a good laugh they'd both been having at her expense.

Gonzo's jaw clenched. "What the fuck?"

Bailey looked down and pulled at her baggy T-shirt. "Maybe he was right and if I hadn't gotten so disgusting, he wouldn't have been so tempted."

"What?" He yelled so loud the woman walking past them scurried to the edge of the sidewalk to get away from them. "What kind of piece of shit were you planning on marrying? Who says something like that?"

Afraid of the pity she'd see in his eyes if she looked up, Bailey refused to look at him. She just continued to twist her fingers in the hem of her shirt. Gonzo stepped closer to her. "Bay, look at me."

She shook her head, no. He didn't move. She could feel him staring at her, but she refused to look up. He pressed his finger to the underside of her chin and forced her head up.

"Bailey, look at me."

Tears burned in her eyes. Forcing herself to look up made her blink and the damn tears broke free.

Gonzo's face softened in sympathy. "There is absolutely nothing disgusting about you."

"You've never seen me naked," she muttered.

"I don't need to see you naked to know you're beautiful, Bay. He's a fucking idiot and a piece of shit if he blamed you for him cheating."

"He's not wrong about me putting on weight the past year. You even said I'd let myself go."

"Whoa." He reared back and held up his hands. "That is definitely not what I said."

"It's what you meant," she muttered.

"That is absolutely not what I meant." He grabbed the front of her T-shirt and pulled it away from her body. "I meant you were going in public with this freaking pepperoni stain on your shirt. That has nothing to do with the body underneath. Don't put words in my mouth, Bay." He looked her in the eye and didn't look away. "And don't compare me to your piece of shit ex."

"Sorry." She broke their eye contact.

"Him cheating on you says more about what a douche he is than anything about you."

"Maybe."

"No, not maybe. If he wasn't happy, he could have broken up with you. He didn't have to cheat."

"I guess."

"There's no guessing about it, Bay. He's a fucking grown up. He made a choice. It's not like she slipped and fell on his dick. He fucked someone else. That's not on you, that's on him. I don't care if you put on a hundred pounds. That's not a reason to cheat."

She shifted uncomfortably. "He can't help it if he doesn't find me attractive anymore." The way Brad had talked about her body was cruel, but it hurt more because it was what she'd already been thinking about herself. It was like he'd been inside her head and said every mean, hateful thing she'd thought.

"Are you fucking kidding me?" Gonzo's voice rose in annoyance. "If he didn't find you attractive anymore, then he should have broken up with you. Not fucked someone else. He could have talked to you, not fucked around."

"He talked to me about my weight. I just..." Tears welled in her eyes again, the effort to hold them in made the back of her throat burn.

"You just what?"

"I don't know. I guess I just felt shittier about myself and—" she sighed.

"So when you say he talked to you about your weight, what did he say?"

Bailey's cheeks grew hot. God, they were probably bright red. How was she supposed to admit to Gonzo that she hated the woman she'd allowed herself to become when she'd been with Brad? Before him, she never would have allowed a man to speak to her the way he had. Just thinking about it made her feel sick.

"What did that asshole say?" Gonzo growled.

She could practically feel the anger radiating off of Gonzo in her defense.

"I don't know the usual stuff guys say about a woman." She flapped her hand. "How I shouldn't wear something because I can't pull it off, talking about what I ate, that kind of thing."

God, this was so humiliating to admit. She claimed to be an expert about the misogyny of the patriarchy and when push came to shove, she fell victim to it just like everyone else and allowed a man to make her feel like shit about herself for months. "It was more the look on his face and—" She clamped her lips together to keep them from quivering as she fought back this wave of anger and tears. "Lately, he never wanted to touch me because—" She looked up at the sky. "Ugh, do we have to keep doing this? I disgusted him. He cheated. End of story." Pissed off, she angrily rubbed her hands against her face to wipe her eyes.

"I want to fucking kill him," Gonzo muttered.

"What? Why?" Bailey blinked back at him. Why did he sound so angry?

"Are you serious?" He gaped at her. "Bailey, listen to me and I need you to hear this. There is not a god-damn thing wrong with you. You're a fucking knock out. You always have been. A couple pounds doesn't change that."

She chewed her bottom lip and dropped her eyes. He crouched down so they were eye to eye. "Brad is a piece of shit. That's 100% on him, not you. Got it?"

Bailey could feel him staring at her. Knowing Gonzo, he wasn't going to move until she answered. Peeking up, she met his eyes and sucked in a breath at the intensity of his stare. Finally she nodded.

"Good. Now let's go eat."

"Thanks, Gonz."

Bailey began walking and he fell into step beside her. "Anytime, babe," he said and gave her a bump with his hip. "You want a full sit-down breakfast or something fast, like coffee and a bagel?"

"I know it's game day for you and you probably have a full day, so something quick is fine. Then I need to hit the pharmacy. I only had a lone tampon in my purse."

Gonzo cringed. "Kay, I didn't really need to know that."

Bailey glanced over at him with a raised eyebrow. "Are you kidding me? I just spilled my guts about Brad not wanting to have sex with me and somehow talking about tampons is an over-share."

"Come on, tampons? Gross. Sex? Always gonna be a subject I want to talk about."

"There is nothing gross about a tampon." Bailey rolled her eyes. "You're such a guy."

"Guilty as charged." He threw his arm around her shoulder. "You still eat a vat of rocky road when you're cruising the red highway?"

"The red highway? My god you're such a child." She shoved him in the side, and he stumbled. With a laugh, he squeezed her tighter against him and she felt the tension leave her body. How did Gonzo always make her feel so at home? She didn't remember feeling like that with Brad, ever. Maybe that should have told her something.

"So I'll take that as a yes on the vat of ice cream?"

Bailey tensed. Unfortunately, yes. But no more. "If I'm gonna lose any of this weight, I should probably skip it."

"Do you want to lose weight?"

"What kind of question is that? Of course I do."

"What? It's a valid question. If you're happy in your body, who cares what anyone else says?"

"Easy for you to say," she muttered.

"Why's that easy for me to say?"

"Come on, Gonz, look at you. Your biceps are the size of most people's thigh."

"Yeah, because I lift a shit ton of weights."

"It's just different for guys."

"True, but just because I'm a guy doesn't mean people don't say shit about my body. They do." He absently ran a hand across his abdomen. "People love to talk shit. It doesn't mean you have to listen."

Memories of her parting fight with Brad instantly swarmed back to her. "Hard not to listen when it's people you care about who say it."

"For sure. But we all get insecure, Bailey. I get it. I can run a little soft, and the locker room can be brutal." He sighed and rubbed his hand over his mouth. "Especially since one of my best friends does fucking underwear ads."

Bailey snorted. "Oh my god, there is nothing soft about you Gonzo." They had very different definitions of soft if he wanted to compare the two.

He shrugged. "In my world, not being cut is soft. I'm one of the strongest guys on my team, but I'm not doing fucking underwear ads. And that's okay because I'll take my batting stats over a sixpack any day of the week. And no one says shit to me anymore." He winked at her.

"Mmm." Easy for him to say. His legs were like muscular tree trunks, while hers were more like table legs.

"For what it's worth, from where I'm standing your body looks fine," he told her.

Bailey snorted. Fine. Now that was what every woman wanted to hear about her body. "I know what I look like, Gonzo."

He raised his eyebrow and looked back at her. "Do you?"

Unfortunately, Brad had made it painfully clear that what she saw and what he saw were the same thing.

"The apartment has a pretty good gym if you want to use it or not. Makes no difference to me," Gonzo said. "You're the one that has to like what you see in the mirror, not me."

Damn, he was coming at her with the straight talk before she'd even had her first cup of coffee. And almost like he could read her mind, Gonzo pivoted. "This place makes the best coffee in the city," he said, pulling open the door to the cafe.

"The best? That's a bold statement." Bailey inhaled the fragrant aroma of coffee. If the smell was anything to go by, it just might be up to the challenge.

"And I stand by that statement." He eased into the line behind a group of women. The blonde in front of them smiled. Gonzo flashed her a quick smile back, then turned to Bailey. "What are you having?"

Bailey chewed her bottom lip as she studied the menu board. When she glanced over at Gonzo, she could swear he'd been staring at her mouth. He cleared his throat. "They make a mean breakfast sandwich if you're into that."

She peered around the girls to look at the display, then looked at him. "Breakfast sandwich sounds good and a non-fat, sugar free vanilla latte."

Gonzo wrinkled his nose. "Why the hell would you want to ruin a beautiful coffee with that fake sugar-free crap?"

Bailey rolled her eyes. "If I'm going to start eating better, it would probably be smart not to drink my daily allotment of calories."

"If you're drinking crap coffee, I get it, but good coffee doesn't need all that other shit."

"Well, I haven't tried the coffee here to know if it's good. How do I know you have good coffee taste buds? I seem to remember you thinking condiment sandwiches were the bomb, so—"

He winced. "Okay, yep, those were kind of gross."

Bailey laughed as she remembered the disgusting mustard, mayo, and ketchup sandwiches on Wonder bread he used to make. He swore the Wonder bread was the secret ingredient that took them to another level and made them gourmet. It wasn't. Not even close. Nothing could have saved those sandwiches.

Gonzo stepped up to the counter and placed their order. Bailey reached into her purse to pull out her wallet and he stopped her. "I got it," he told her.

"You won't let me pay you any rent. The least I can do is pay for your breakfast."

He shrugged. "You can pay next time."

Bailey wrapped her arms around his waist and hugged him tightly. "Thank you. I don't know what I would have done without you."

She tried to ignore how good it felt to have his big arms automatically wrapped around her, even briefly. He'd always given great hugs. But now that he'd been working out so much, it actually felt like he could pick her up with no problem. And she kind of liked it. Not that she would ever admit that out loud.

He gave her a tight squeeze and released her hold. "What are friends for?"

The barista called their order. "Let's eat."

# CHAPTER SIX

When Gonzo left for the game later that afternoon, Bailey stood in the empty apartment and looked around the spacious room.

What would she have done without him? She trailed her hand along the back of the sofa as she walked toward the balcony. As she reached for the door handle, she caught a glimpse of her reflection in the glass. Her hand flew to her head, flattening the hair that stuck up in every direction in the back. She removed her hand and the hair sprung back up. Oh god. Had she really gone out in public like that? She tried to flatten the hair, but it seemed to have a life of its own. Maybe it didn't really look as bad as she was envisioning.

Changing direction, she made her way to the bathroom. The second she rounded the corner and glimpsed herself in the mirror she pulled up short. Yikes, it was so much worse than she'd pictured. Who knew a reflection in the window could be so forgiving? She dropped her gaze to her baggy, stained T-shirt as it clung to her stomach. What the hell was the point of baggy clothes if they were going to stick to your flippin' rolls? That was the whole point of wearing baggy. They were supposed to camouflage, not emphasize the damn things.

Taking a deep breath, she flipped on the bathroom light and winced. Wow, it just kept getting worse. She puffed out a breath and stood squarely in front of the mirror. Bailey fingered her hair in the half-in-half-out messy bun. She'd always loved her hair and been proud of how thick and shiny it was. Women regularly asked her about the color and how she styled it so artfully casual. Those days were clearly long gone.

Stepping closer to the counter, she leaned toward the mirror. She could practically park a car in the bags under her eyes. Everything about the way she looked said she'd given up. And honestly, she had.

Tears burned as they fought to escape. She'd wallowed in being dumped before she moved. She should have moved on already. San Diego was supposed to be a fresh start. A new Bailey. A chance to reinvent herself and instead she'd become this. Gonzo was right, she'd become a person she barely recognized.

Fuck that. Brad had ruined their relationship, but he didn't get to steal her new start from her as well.

Bailey ripped her hair out of the bun and tossed her hair elastic onto the bathroom counter. It was time for a new Bailey. Time to practice what she taught. She couldn't be an empowered woman if she hated what she saw in the mirror. If she wanted to wear stained clothes, she was going to do it by choice, not because she just didn't care what she looked like anymore.

She pulled her phone out of her back pocket and searched for hairdressers in the area. Finding one with a good rating, she pushed the call button. Several minutes later, she leaped at the chance to fill a cancellation the next day.

Her gaze landed on her bare nails and a rush of excitement ran through her. Painting her nails was exactly what she needed to feel powerful and in control. Brad had always hated when she decorated her nails. Told her she made a spectacle of herself by painting them anything other than a plain pale color. Well, screw Brad. He wasn't here anymore, and decorating her nails made her feel beautiful. So fuck him. She'd spent enough time letting that asshole affect her decisions.

Eyeing her toiletries on the bathroom counter, she realized she was missing everything she needed. Well crap, guess she was hitting the storage unit.

Forty minutes later, Bailey let herself back into the apartment with her box of nail supplies. The fact it hadn't made the original list of must haves spoke volumes about her state of mind when she'd grabbed her stuff the day before.

It wasn't that long ago she'd painted her nails every week. Slowly over time, the more Brad commented, the less she'd enjoyed doing it until it got to where she'd just stopped completely. How had she not seen what he was doing even back then? Chipping away at who she was until she'd become almost unrecognizable. Never again.

Bailey set her box on the kitchen island. Grabbing her phone, she scrolled through her library until she found the female empowerment playlist she used for her class. Perfect. She synced her phone with Gonzo's stereo and "I Will Survive" blasted through the speakers. Bailey grinned. Damn, that was a good sound system.

She turned the volume up a little louder and shimmied over to the cupboard in search of olive oil. May as well go all out and hot oil her hair while she did her nails. Bailey pulled it out and poured some into a small bowl and stuck it in the microwave. When it beeped, she grabbed the oil bowl and carried it to the bathroom. Bailey eyed her stained shirt. At least she didn't need to change first. She doused her hair in warm oil, piled it on top of her head, and clipped it in place.

Back in the kitchen, she rooted through her nail supplies. What was she in the mood for?

Spotting the black polish, she grinned. Hawks. That was perfect. Decorating her nails for one of Gonzo's games had been what started her love of nail art. While the other girls were out dating in high school, she'd been elaborately decorating her nails. No one in her family had been safe, not even her dad.

Man, he'd been so annoyed when he found out she'd been painting designs on Gonzo's toenails instead of his fingers like the rest of them. But Gonzo had refused to let her do his fingernails after the guys at school teased him mercilessly after the first time he'd shown up with nail art. He'd said the guys could fuck off if they wanted to make fun of his feet. His logic had made no sense to her, but he'd still been willing to be her guinea pig, so who was she to question it?

Just thinking about it made her smile. They didn't make guys like Gonzo very often. It's not every guy who'd let her paint his nails. Heck, Brad hadn't even liked her to paint her own. There was no chance he'd ever let her paint his.

The more Bailey thought of all the warning signs she'd missed with Brad, the dumber she felt. She'd been so desperate to fall in love and get married like her sisters, that she'd settled for someone who made her feel like shit about herself and then cheated on her, anyway. According to her sister, Deanna, she should just be happy someone wanted to marry her, like she was somehow undeserving of a faithful partner. Screw that.

Bailey hoisted herself up on the stool and spread her supplies across the island.

A big glob of paint fell on her thumbnail. Holy cow, she'd become right dominant over the past few years. Doing her right hand was a lot harder than she remembered.

She bobbed along to the music as she carefully decorated her thumb in a team color design, then added different designs with team colors on her index and ring fingers. She drew a Hawks' logo on her middle fingers, and a baseball on her pinkies. Finally, after a lot of trial and error, she had her fingers decorated just how she wanted. Bailey held her hand out in front of her and wiggled her fingers excitedly.

For the first time in a long time, she felt like herself. She was still admiring her handiwork when her phone rang. Seeing her favorite sister's name on the screen, she swiped to answer it. "Hi Jen," she said as she connected the call.

"Hey how's the new place? You all moved in?"

"Slight change of plans. Just let me grab my earbuds." Bailey hustled down the hall to her bedroom and grabbed her earphones off the bedside table and shoved them in her ears. "Okay."

"What do you mean, you had a slight change of plans?" her sister asked.

"That place was disgusting. No chance I was going to live there." Just thinking about the smell in that room made her stomach churn.

"Then where are you living?"

"I'm living with Gonzo until I find something better." She wandered over to her bedroom window and looked out at the ocean view. It sure as hell didn't get much better than this. Gonzo had said there was no rush to move, and honestly, she didn't want to. The idea of living with Gonzo till she got her feet wet in the city was really appealing.

"I'm sorry, did you just say you're living with Gonzo?" Jen made a whooping sound. "Yes! Please tell me you're finally going to climb that man like a tree."

"Oh my god, we're friends Jennifer. There will be no sex."

"Well, that's a damn shame because I've seen that man and, mmm, if anyone could help you get over Brad, it would be him."

"I was over Brad the second I found him fucking my best friend." She dropped onto the mattress. "Ugh, I'm an idiot. For two years, I let that man chip away at my self-esteem in all these insidious little ways until I became this person I don't even recognize." Tears welled in her eyes. "I saw it and I let it happen. I know better. I teach this for god's sake."

"Just because you have a PhD doesn't mean you're immune to it."

"I know. It's just... I didn't think I'd be here. I got all this education and did years of therapy just to end up here. I feel so stupid."

"You fell in love with the wrong guy. You trusted him with your insecurities, and he used them against you. That doesn't make you stupid, sweetie. It makes him an asshole."

"But did he have to cheat with my best friend?" Her throat burned. "How did I not see it, Jen? How could I not know? She was my best friend." Her eyes burned as tears fought their way to the surface.

"Oh sweetie, no one expects their best friend to do something like that. She's such a bitch," Jen muttered. "That should never happen. You trusted her. Of course it didn't occur to you she'd do something like that. Why would it?"

Well, it would now. Tears streamed down her cheeks, and she brushed them away. Brandy's betrayal almost hurt more than Brad's. "I don't know how the hell I'm supposed to make friends here when I feel like I can't trust anyone."

"You can trust Gonzo."

"Yeah, I can. "

"So trust him until you learn to trust your own judgement again. He's always had a good bullshit meter. Hell, he hated Brad on sight. I always thought it was because he was jealous, but maybe he picked up something about him we missed."

Bailey snorted. "He definitely wasn't jealous."

"I don't know. You guys have always had this weird thing between you."

"It's called friendship."

"Mmm-hmm. Well, I think there's always been something more to it than that. I mean, you practiced kissing your pillow, pretending it was him."

"Oh my god, I was thirteen, let it go already." She laughed.

"I'm just saying the best way to get over someone is by getting under someone else is a thing for a reason. And I can't think of anyone better for you than Gonzo. You know you can trust him. He's anti-relationship, so you know it doesn't mean anything. It's perfect."

There was no way she could have meaningless sex with Gonzo. If they ever had sex, it would mean everything. How could it not? At least for her. "Gonzo would never have sex with me."

"Interesting that you said he'd never have sex with you, not that you don't want to have sex with him."

"Good lord. Can we please stop talking about this? Gonzo and I are friends. End of discussion."

"Fine, but I think you're missing a great opportunity," Jen grumbled. "What'd Mom and Dad say about you living with Gonz?"

"Haven't talked to them yet. So far, you're the only one who knows."

"Oh my god, Deanna's gonna be scandalized." Jen laughed.

Bailey's mouth turned down as she thought about talking to her oldest sister. They hadn't talked since she'd broken up with Brad.

"Have you talked to her since you hung up on her?" Jen asked.

"No." And Bailey sure as hell wasn't going to be the one to call. Her sister had been a bitch and until she said sorry, they had nothing to talk about.

"I'm sure she'll call once she hears you're living with a boy. She won't be able to help herself," Jen said.

"Probably." Bailey could almost hear the lecture that would come out of her bossy siblings' mouth. "I can guarantee she won't be telling me to climb Gonzo like a tree."

Jen snorted. "Probably not, but she should, because that's damn good advice."

"Eh, is it though?"

"Trust me, it is, and you're an idiot if you don't see it," Jen said.

Oh, she saw it all right. She had no doubt sex with Gonzo would be amazing, but that was one line they'd never cross. Nor would he ever want to. Thinking anything along those lines would only lead to her getting hurt, and she'd had more than enough of that to last a lifetime.

"So what's Gonzo's place like?" Jen asked.

"Swanky." Bailey wandered into the living room and snapped a photo of the room that also showed the ocean view and sent it to her sister.

"Holy shit. I know you and you'll be thinking about how you need to find your own place as quickly as possible and all that, but damn, if Gonzo had let me stay there, he'd have to forcibly remove me from his apartment. I'd be claiming squatters right and I'd hunker down for the long haul. That place looks amazing."

"Yeah, it is. Gonzo's been super cool about everything. He said he's barely here during the season, so no rush on finding my own place. I think I'm going to take my time and make sure I find the right apartment."

"Gonzo has always been one of the good ones," her sister agreed. "I'm gonna let you go. I love you. I'm here if you need to talk anytime, you know that."

"I do yeah. I love you too."

"Give Gonzo a big wet kiss from me," Jen teased.

Bailey snickered. "Bye loser."

"Later," Jen sang, then disconnected the call.

Damn her sister and the stupid climb Gonzo like a tree crap. Now that was all she could think about. She ripped her earbuds out of her ear. Nope, that line of thinking was just stupid. And contrary to her relationship with Brad, she wasn't an idiot.

# CHAPTER SEVEN

Gonzo walked into the locker room later that afternoon, nodded to Pete and dropped his bag on the bench beside his friend.

"So how did it go with Bailey yesterday? Did you get her all moved in?" Pete asked.

"Sort of. I mean, her shit's all in storage." He grabbed the hem of his shirt and yanked it over his head.

"What do you mean her shit's in storage?" Pete asked.

Gonzo pulled his jersey off the hook in his locker and replaced it with the shirt he'd been wearing. "The place was a shithole, so she moved in with me."

"Wha..." Pete shook his head in confusion. "What do you mean, she moved in with you?"

He pushed his pants off and hung them on the hook in his locker. With his ball pants in hand, he turned back to Pete. "The place was fucking disgusting. There's no way I was letting her move in there."

Pete tilted his head and banged on the side of it like he was trying to knock something loose. "Sorry, I think I must have something in my ears because there's no way I'm hearing you let your childhood 'female' friend move in with you."

"Haha, funny man." Gonzo rolled his eyes as Pete pulled on his earlobe and continued to shake his head.

"So she's staying for a couple days?" Pete asked.

Gonzo stepped into his pants and pulled them up. "Not sure. We'll see how it goes."

"What the fuck?" Pete asked. "Seriously?"

"What?"

"Come on, man, you can't have a woman living with you," Pete said.

"Why not? You do. And Kendall hasn't killed you yet."

"Yeah, but she loves me so..." Pete shrugged. "Besides. I'm not bringing strange girl's home."

"It's fine. Bailey's cool."

Pete snorted. "Yeah right."

"What? She is."

"Sure man." Pete's eyes danced with amusement. "Wait till the guys hear about this one." Pete reached into his bag and pulled out his cellphone.

"What are you doing?" Gonzo asked.

"Texting Kendall to tell her that I'll be late cuz we're going for a beer after the game."

Gonzo raised his eyebrow in question. "Why? You guys never want to grab a beer anymore."

Pete made a face. "Yeah, but come on, man. You're moving in with a girl, that's huge. This calls for a guys' night."

"I'm not fucking moving in with a girl. It's Bailey. Jesus."

"Yo, Smitty, Ry, beer after the game," Pete yelled across the locker room.

"Not sure I can," Smitty called back.

"Trust me, you want to be there," Pete snickered.

"Jesus," Gonzo muttered as he looked at the shit-eating grin that encompassed Pete's entire face. "Knock that shit off. You look like the fucking Joker."

Pete rubbed his hands together. "This is going to be so good."

"Holy fuck, man. She's a friend who needed a place to crash. That's all. Stop acting like a fucking girl."

"Whatever you say, man." Pete sat down and slid his foot into his sock, then glanced over his shoulder. "So how's she look? Is she hot?"

Now there was a loaded question. Was she hot? Yeah, she was definitely hot. Shit, maybe this was a bad idea.

Pete snickered again. "I knew it."

"She's just a friend," Gonzo muttered.

"For now." Pete smacked him on the shoulder and stood up.

"No, not for now," Gonzo grumbled. "Forever. She's just a friend. It's not like that."

"Sure man. Whatever you say." Pete laughed. "Now hurry up and get your shit on so we can warm up."

Gonzo shoved his foot into his shoe and tied the laces. No matter what Pete thought, having Bailey live with him was going to be fine. Nothing was going to happen between them. Hell, they'd slept in her tree fort together all the time as kids. This wasn't going to be any different. Except Bailey's ass hadn't looked like it did now when she was a teenager. And her skin sure as hell hadn't looked so soft. Fuck. What had he been thinking?

He slammed his foot into his other shoe.

"What's the matter?" Pete asked.

"Nothing. I'm getting fucking laid tonight," Gonzo muttered.

"Geez, I didn't think you'd move that fast on the new roomie."

"Fuck you." Gonzo rolled his eyes.

"You can run, but you can't hide," Pete taunted gleefully.

"Just because you all are happily in love doesn't mean everyone wants that. Some of us still like a little variety and there's a fucking smorgasbord of women out there." Gonzo pulled his other shoelace tight.

"True. Until you realize what you've been missing and you never want to eat anything else ever again."

"Yeah, I don't see that happening." It sounded nice in theory, but so far he'd never met a woman he wanted to be with long term. After a few weeks, he got bored. That's probably why he'd been friends with Bailey for so long because they'd never had sex. And they never would.

He stood up from the bench. "Let's win this fucking game."

The sound of a woman giggling woke Bailey.

Good lord, the way that woman was screaming was ridiculous.

A screeched, "Yes, Gonzo, yes," ripped through the walls.

Bailey eyed the direction of Gonzo's bedroom. Did he bring home a porn star? Holy shit. Who the hell screamed and moaned like that? The woman was going to burst her vocal cords if she kept that up for much longer.

The bed banged against the wall and her throat tightened. *God, why did she feel so jealous?* She covered her face with her pillow. It was just because she couldn't remember the last time she'd had good sex. Except when the woman screamed Gonzo's name again it felt like a whole lot more than that.

Shit.

Bailey threw back the covers. There was no way she was getting any sleep with that racket going on. She padded her way into the kitchen and started digging out ingredients for cookies. If she couldn't sleep, she may as well do something she enjoyed. No reason Gonzo should be the only one getting some enjoyment tonight. Although he sure as hell sounded like he was having a lot more fun than she was.

Bailey rooted around in the cupboards, looking for chocolate chips. At the bottom of the pantry drawer, she unearthed a bag of butterscotch chips. Good enough. After a quick scan of the expiration date, she tossed the bag on the counter with the rest of her dry ingredients.

She pulled out a large copper mixing bowl. Good lord, he had some nice stuff. His kitchen was like something on one of those cooking shows. Definitely different from the dented metal bowls she was used to using.

She popped a stick of butter in the microwave to soften while she lined up the rest of her ingredients on the quartz island. As she cracked the first egg into the bowl, she hummed quietly to herself. By the time she was mixing the wet ingredients all together, she was singing quietly and moving her hips to the beat.

Bailey scooped up big balls of dough and dropped them onto the cookie sheet. She eyed the stereo remote. If she'd been alone, she would have been listening to it full blast. Little different when Gonzo was home with a guest but given how loud the woman was, maybe he wouldn't even notice.

She clicked the remote and turned it on low. Gonzo's guest's moans grew louder, and she could barely even tell that the stereo was on. She clicked the music higher. The woman screamed. Click, click. She upped the volume a little more. When she heard what hopefully was the woman orgasm, Bailey turned the music down slightly. Hopefully, they wouldn't be able to hear it. The last thing she wanted was one of them coming out to tell her to turn it down. Bailey tapped along to the beat, then shimmied her way over to the stove to check on her cookies. Mmm, perfect golden brown. She inhaled deeply. Cookies were like crack to her system. Her mouth watered just looking at them. She pulled out the cookie sheet with one hand and stuck a second tray in the oven to bake.

As she turned with the cookies, she caught movement out of the corner of her eye and bobbled the tray, barely managing to hit the island instead of dropping the whole thing on the floor. She slapped her hand over her racing heart. "Oh my god, you scared me."

"What are you doing up?" Gonzo asked.

"Really? Who the hell could sleep through that performance?" Bailey leaned her hip against the island and eyed Gonzo. "Please tell me you weren't buying that show."

"What can I say? I'm good in bed."

"No one's that good." Bailey snorted. "That was ridiculous."

He picked up a cookie, broke it in half and shoved the broken piece in his mouth. He moaned. "Damn that's good."

She pointed a finger at him. "See that right there? That's what a normal person sounds like when something hits just right." She flicked her thumb toward his room. "Not whatever that was."

"Believe me, Bay, I hit her just right too." He waggled his eyebrows and grinned.

"Pretty sure she wouldn't have been going all overboard with the moaning if you were actually hitting her right, buddy."

"Trust me, she wasn't faking." He scooped up two more cookies in his hand.

"Whatever you need to tell yourself." Bailey leaned her hip against the counter and broke a cookie in half and popped it in her mouth. The warm melted butterscotch chip hit her tongue and she closed her eyes in bliss.

Gonzo cleared his throat. "So um..." He cleared his throat again. "Did you watch the game?"

"I did. Sorry you lost. That sucks." She nodded toward the bedroom. "Guess you found a way to drown your sorrows."

He mumbled some kind of incoherent sound, then took another bite of cookie.

"At least you played well." The timer on the oven buzzed. Bailey slid the oven mitts onto her hands and pulled open the oven door. The smell of hot cookies blasted her face as she leaned over to pull the tray out of the oven. She slid the sheet onto the cooktop. "My dad said to tell your coach, Hernandez's playing too far off the bag for his speed."

Gonzo snorted. "I'll be sure to tell him. So you talked to your folks tonight?"

"You know my dad, he likes to do the play-by-play of the game."

"I didn't know you guys still did that."

"Mmm, we don't do it after every game, but at least once a week he calls during the seventh inning stretch to make sure I'm paying attention." Some weeks it was hard to catch all the games, especially since Brad hated baseball and complained whenever she wanted to watch Gonzo play. Her unwillingness to give up watching had caused more than a couple of fights in their relationship.

"And are you?"

"Of course. I'd never hear the end of it from him if I wasn't." And if he didn't call her, she always called him for their weekly baseball gab session.

"I'm surprised you kept that up."

"Why?"

"I don't know. We haven't talked much in the past couple of years, not like we used to. I just figured you wouldn't be watching as often anymore."

"Just because we weren't talking as much doesn't mean I stopped supporting you, Gonz." She scooped up a ball of cookie dough and dropped it onto the sheet. "Besides, there's no way my dad or yours would let me stop watching."

"My dad?"

"Mmm. He's worse than mine."

"What do you mean?"

She grabbed her phone off the counter and pulled up her text thread with Juan and pushed the phone across the island toward Gonzo.

He picked up the phone. "Holy shit, this is all my dad?"

"Mmm-hmm." Every time Gonzo was mentioned on TV, or anywhere online, Juan sent her a link to make sure she hadn't missed it. The man must have a Google alert set for every possible name combo, so he didn't miss something.

"Uh...wow..." Gonzo rubbed a hand across his mouth. "I had no idea he kept track like that."

"He's very proud."

He was quiet for several seconds before finally speaking. "Yeah. I just..." He shook his head. "Sorry he blows up your phone with it."

"Nothing to be sorry about. As you can see, I send him stuff back."

Gonzo snorted out a laugh. "Where the hell did you find that meme?"

She stood on tiptoe to glance at the phone screen over the island and grinned at the picture of Gonzo dressed like the easter bunny shaking his ass. "I might have made it."

"Of course you did." He chuckled. "Judging by the two full rows of laughing/crying face my dad enjoyed the effort."

"He does enjoy my creative ventures." Bailey looked up to find Gonzo staring at her with some weird look on his face. Unable to look away from the intensity of his stare, he held her gaze captive.

"Gonzo," a whiney woman's voice called, breaking the hold he had on her.

Bailey glanced over at a petite blonde standing at the edge of the kitchen in a man's button-up shirt with all the buttons undone. Damn, Bailey wasn't into girls, but even she could admit the look was sexy. If she thought there was a hope in hell she could have pulled it off herself, she'd be tempted to try it the next time she was with a man.

"Oh hey, did we wake you up?" Gonzo asked.

"Who's she?" the woman demanded.

"Hi." Bailey raised her hand. "I'm Bailey. Don't worry I'm not the girlfriend or anything."

"Obviously, look at you." The blonde looked at Bailey and smirked.

"Wow, okay." Apparently mean girls stayed mean girls into adulthood. Bailey glanced at Gonzo. "I'm just gonna." She flicked her thumb toward her bedroom.

When she tried to slip past Gonzo to get out of the kitchen, he grabbed her arm. "No. Stay," Gonzo ordered. He continued to hold her arm so she couldn't escape. Turning to the blonde, he said, "Now that you're awake, you can go."

"Pardon?" Blondie's eyes widened in shock.

"You need to leave."

"You can't be serious," she snapped.

"Very serious. And leave the shirt."

The woman pushed open the shirt and dropped it on the floor. "Are you sure you want me to leave?"

Holy confidence, Batman. Bailey couldn't believe someone would be that self-assured to just stand there in only her panties and all but challenge someone to send her away.

Gonzo sighed and shook his head. "Yeah, you need to go. Now."

"Ugh," Blondie huffed and turned on her heel and stormed toward the bedroom.

"Gonzo, seriously?" Bailey said.

"Bay, there's no way I'm letting someone come in here and insult you. Fuck that."

When a loud noise came from the bedroom, Gonzo dropped her arm. "I better make sure she isn't trashing my bedroom."

"Yeah." Bailey sagged against the kitchen counter. What just happened? She couldn't believe Gonzo had sent away a gorgeous, willing woman. She couldn't remember the last time someone had defended her like that. No, that was a lie. She could remember. The last time had been in high school and once again it had been Gonzo defending her.

A moment later, the woman stormed out of Gonzo's room. "You can have him," the woman yelled as she slammed the front door.

"That went well," Gonzo muttered.

"Sorry."

"What do you have to be sorry about?" he asked. "You weren't the one who was rude."

"Still." Bailey shrugged. She was the one who'd made it so that he wasn't going to get more sex tonight.

"You tired or you want to watch something?" Gonzo asked as he picked up the remote from the end table.

"What'd you have in mind?" She dropped onto the sofa beside him.

Gonzo grabbed the blanket from the back of the couch and handed it to her. He flicked through the listings. "Trash TV?" He raised an eyebrow as he looked at her.

"Oh absolutely," Bailey replied as she covered herself in half of the blanket and dropped the other half on Gonzo's lap so he could snuggle up as well.

He spread the blanket around himself and settled onto the couch. "All right, but just a couple episodes because I have to get some sleep."

"Deal."

# CHAPTER EIGHT

That was two nights in a row they'd played like shit. Thank fuck they'd managed to pull out the win. Gonzo leaned against the wall of the elevator and eyed his teammates. From what he knew, Brandon was okay. The jury was still out on Charles. All he knew was they better not suck as hard at video games as they did on the field tonight. Fuck, he missed when his friends were single. Now he was forced to make new friends and he was too old for this shit.

"How long you lived here?" Brandon asked.

"Almost five years. Bought it just after I signed."

"You like it?"

"Yeah, got everything I need. No point in having a big house with a yard and shit when it's just me."

The elevator dinged at his floor, and he led the way down the hall to his place. The music pumping inside his apartment practically shook the door as he walked up. *Jesus, Bay.* He rolled his eyes at his friends. "Roommate."

"You have a roommate?" Charles asked. "Why?"

He pushed open the front door and headed toward the living room so he could hit the stereo. Gonzo rounded the corner and immediately saw Bailey, dressed in a skimpy pair of green shorts and matching tank top, like those sexy little things women liked to sleep in. Damn, her curves were insane. Oblivious to them, she threw her head back with her eyes closed as she moved to the music. Her hips gyrated back and forth, and his mind instantly thought of sex. Jesus. Who knew Bailey could move like that?

"Ah, now I see why you have a roommate," Charles said. His mouth curved up in a sleazy kind of smile that Gonzo wanted to smack off his face.

There was no fucking way he wanted his teammate looking at her like that.

Bailey shimmied to the beat. She spun, spotted them, screamed, and dropped to the floor, then scrambled behind the island.

Suddenly, her hand whipped up, and the sweatshirt hanging on the back of the chair disappeared. What the hell?

Grabbing the stereo remote, he clicked the button to turn the music down. After several clicks, he finally managed to hear himself think. "Hi Bailey," he called out.

"Hey, how's it going?" her muffled voice replied.

He chuckled. What was she doing down there? "You all good?"

"Yep, of course." A moment later, she stood up, clad in his sweatshirt. The hood curled up around her head, looking all cozy, and his heart did a weird little stutter step. As she stepped out from behind the island, his gaze landed on her legs, peeking out beneath his oversized hoodie. His dick sprung to life in a little 'hi how are ya' twitch. Why the hell did she look so freaking sexy in his shirt?

"Sorry, I thought you'd be going out with your team-mates after the game." She pulled the edge of his hoodie down further on her thighs and flashed a little embar-rassed wave. "Hi, I'm Bailey."

"This is Brandon and Charles." Gonzo pointed at his two teammates.

Bailey's forehead crinkled and she eyed him curious-ly. "Brandon and Charles?"

He nodded. Yeah, the names were foreign to her. He'd never mentioned them because he'd never hung out with them before. She turned her attention to the other men and smiled. "Nice to meet you." She flicked her thumb over her shoulder. "I'll get out of your way."

Charles rounded the island and walked toward her. "No need, the more the merrier." He wrapped his arm around Bailey's shoulder and guided her toward the living room.

Gonzo's jaw tightened. Brandon made a little snorting sound beside him, then smirked and followed Charles and Bailey into the living room.

He rubbed a hand across his sternum. Why did he care if his teammate homed in on Bailey? She was a beautiful woman. Of course his teammates would notice. So why did he feel jealous? That made no fucking sense. It was Bailey.

Shaking it off, he pulled open the fridge door. "You want a beer, Bay?"

"No thanks, I've got water."

"That bubbly shit?" he asked. How she could drink that flavored crap was beyond him.

"We've discussed this, Gonz. Why drink flat when you can have bubbles?" Bailey picked up her can of sparkling water and took a sip. "Mmm."

When he cringed in disgust, she giggled. Gonzo pulled three beers out of the fridge and handed one off to each of his teammates. He pushed the power button on the gaming console and grabbed the basket of controllers, then sat down on the sofa on the other side of Bailey.

"Do you play?" Brandon asked Bailey.

"Depends on what game it is. If it's like football or something, then no, I suck. If it's shooting things, then absolutely."

"You like shooter games?" Brandon leaned forward in his chair and angled his body toward Bailey.

What the actual fuck. They were seriously both going to flirt with her? And why the hell did he care?

"I don't like girls who play video games," Charles mumbled.

"I'm sorry, what? You don't like girls who play video games?" Bailey's eyes goggled as she looked at him.

"No, there are some things that girls just shouldn't do."

Bailey held up her hand like a stop sign. "Oh my god, please tell me you did not just say that."

"What? I know what I like and I want my woman to sit and watch me play video games, not play them," he scoffed.

"Cuz the little lady's brain can't handle something as complex as a children's video game?" Bailey drawled.

Damn, she was good at that lowbrow accent.

"I didn't say her brain couldn't handle it. I just said I didn't like it."

"Should she be feeding you grapes and sitting in lingerie while she watches you be all manly playing video games there, Chuck?" The annoyance in Bailey's tone was palpable. Gonzo sat back. He fucking loved when she tore into some guy spewing chauvinistic shit. This was the Bailey he knew and loved. Not the meek woman who'd first shown up in town.

"It's Charles."

"Mmm-hmm."

Somehow she'd put a world of meaning into one little word.

Brandon sputtered out a laugh that he tried to cover like it was a cough. "How long have you been roommates?" Brandon asked. The attempt to change the subject made Gonzo chuckle. The guy didn't even know Bailey and he could tell she was about to go on a tear if Charles kept talking.

Bailey took one last look at Charles and shook her head, then turned to Brandon. "I just moved in on Thursday. My apartment fell through and Gonzo was nice enough to let me crash here till I figure things out."

"You just moved here a couple of days ago?" Brandon asked.

"I did."

"That's cool. So are you two..." Brandon pointed his fingers back and forth between them.

"God no." Bailey laughed.

"Cool, well if you need a tour guide let me know," Brandon said.

"Thanks." Bailey smiled.

Gonzo's shoulders tensed. He wasn't loving the way his teammates were looking at Bailey. His gaze landed on her legs, her very naked legs. He made a rough sound in his throat.

Bailey glanced over at him, then down at her legs.

She winced and a blush ran up her cheeks. "I'm just gonna go throw a pair of pants on." She hopped up and dashed out of the room.

Gonzo pinned his teammate with a glare. "What the hell, man? What are you doing?"

"What do you mean what am I doing?"

"You don't date girls like Bailey." Gonzo challenged.

"Nope." Brandon shrugged.

Nope? What the fuck did that mean? Was he interested in Bailey or not? Before he could ask, Bailey walked back into the room. Shit, how much had she heard?

She was going to be pissed if she thought he was blocking her from getting dates again, but he couldn't stand the idea of her dating one of his teammates. Gonzo held his breath as Bailey sat down beside him. What was she going to say?

"Do you guys hang out a lot?" Bailey asked Brandon and Charles. Gonzo breathed a sigh of relief that she hadn't heard him talking to Brandon about asking her out.

"No, not really," Brandon replied.

Charles looked at Gonzo and smirked, then turned and leered at Bailey. "So, how do you two know each other?"

Was the idiot seriously going to flirt with Bailey when he'd just made it clear to Brandon he didn't want that shit happening?

"We were next-door neighbors growing up," Bailey replied.

"Oh yeah? That mean you played doctor?" Charles waggled his eyebrows at her.

Bailey's mouth twisted in disgust. "Seriously?"

"What?" Charles snickered. "Please tell me you weren't like fucking childhood sweethearts who stayed friends or some shit."

"We weren't, but what would be wrong with that if we were?" Bailey pressed.

"Because my opinion of Gonzo would go down a lot if you were."

Gonzo sat up straight and leaned forward. Where the fuck was he going with this? "Oh yeah? Why's that?"

"I've seen the kind of ladies you pull."

"And?" Gonzo's shoulders tensed. It wouldn't be pretty if he said anything to insult Bailey.

Charles shrugged. "Just thought you'd be better in bed, that's all."

Gonzo reared back. "What the fuck?"

"Just saying man." Charles picked up his beer and took a sip. *Bastard throws out an insult and then acts like he doesn't have a care in the world.*

Bailey placed her hand on his arm and instantly some of the tension in his shoulders disappeared. "What is it you're saying exactly?" Bailey asked.

"If you stay friends after fucking, then the sex sucked. You can't be just friends with someone you had good sex with."

Brandon burst out laughing. "What?"

Charles leaned back in his seat and crossed his foot over his knee. "It's true. It's like a scientific fact. If you had great sex, you're always going to want to fuck them. You can't be friends with someone you want to fuck."

"Dude." Brandon shook his head and chuckled like he couldn't quite believe what Charles said.

"Hang on. Are you saying men and women can't be friends?" Bailey asked.

"No, I'm saying men can't be friends with a woman they find attractive, especially if they've had killer sex. Clearly, you two either didn't have sex or it sucked."

"Wow." Bailey ran her hand over her mouth and pinched her bottom lip between her fingers.

"We've never had sex," Gonzo growled.

Charles looked over at Bailey, his leer scanned down her body, then he glanced at Gonzo. "Yeah, that makes sense."

Bailey's body went ramrod straight beside him. "On that note, if you'll excuse me, I'm kind of tired. I think I'm gonna head to bed." She pushed up from the sofa. "It was nice meeting you, Brandon." She glanced at Charles, the disgust she felt for him clear on her face. She rolled her eyes, then looked at Gonzo. "Night, Gonz."

He watched Bailey walk out of the room. Everything in him wanted to kick the guys out and follow her. Unfortunately, he wasn't sure if he wanted to follow her as Bailey the friend, or Bailey the woman he couldn't stop thinking about. He was so fucking confused. So he did nothing. The moment he heard her bedroom door snick shut he turned to Charles and smacked him on the chest.

Charles rubbed his hand against his sternum. "Ow, why'd you do that?"

"Have you never talked to a woman before? Jesus."

"What? What'd I say?" The dumb fuck looked like he didn't have a clue.

"You're a fucking idiot," Gonzo muttered. And there wasn't enough time in the world to explain it to him. Gonzo chucked the gaming remote at him. "Just shut up and play the fucking game."

As the game loaded up on screen, he glanced toward the hallway. It wasn't like Bailey to back down from a fight. Especially not with someone like Charles. He itched to go check on her. And do what?

Shit. The woman had his mind all fucked up.

So instead of checking on her, he settled for destroying Charles at video games. What guy in his right mind would want a woman to sit around and watch him suck that hard at something? Now he was kind of disappointed Bailey hadn't stuck around to watch him kick good ol' Chuck's ass.

Looked like his attempt to find new guys to hang out with had been a flop, at least as far as Charles was concerned.

# CHAPTER NINE

B ailey stood at the top of the stairs and looked down at the stadium seats below her. She took a deep breath, then slowly made her way down the steps to her seat. She stopped at the end of the third row. Her eyes landed on a little boy in a Smith jersey. That must be Max. Having a child in the group instantly made her relax. How bad could it be when you had a little kid jumping up every five minutes?

She moved her way down the row, pausing at a man with his legs shoved out in front of him. The guy looked up at her, rolled his eyes, and tried to shift himself to the side slightly. Bailey eyed him and the narrow space he'd created for her to squeeze through. The guy beside him stood up, creating more space. She smiled at the standing man, then stepped forward to squeeze past the one who hadn't bothered to get out of his seat. He muttered something under his breath and shifted his legs slightly. Bailey smiled apologetically as she pushed past, her thigh pressed against the man's leg to create space.

Would it have been so hard to just stand up so she could get through? She smiled at the standing man as she slipped past him. "Thanks," she mumbled.

"No problem."

She stepped into the space for her empty seat and smiled at the woman beside her. The little boy leaned forward. "Are you Bailey?" he asked.

"I sure am." She sat down and turned to the boy. "You must be Max."

"Yep." Max thrust a package of red licorice at her. "Want a piece?"

Bailey eyed the package of candy. "Absolutely." She reached over and grabbed a piece of the red rope and took a bite. "Mmm, thank you."

"Are you Gonzo's girlfriend?" Max asked.

"No, just his friend."

Max shoved a piece of licorice in his mouth. "Me too," he said as he chewed.

"I know. I've heard all about you."

"You have?" Max's eyes widened. "What'd you hear?"

Bailey grinned at the woman sitting beside her, who she assumed was Max's mom, Kia. "I heard that you're a Mario Kart fiend."

"I am." Max nodded.

Bailey leaned in a little closer and dropped her voice. "Gonzo told me he gives you the bad controller, so he has a chance of winning and you still beat him every time."

"He gives me the bad controller?" he squealed.

"Yep, but don't tell him I told you. So next time, make him switch controllers with you." She winked at the little boy.

Max shoved another bite of licorice into his mouth. "I will."

The brunette woman smiled. "Hi Bailey, I'm Kia."

"Nice to meet you."

The two women on the other side of Max, who'd been staring at her openly, grinned back at her. The blonde flashed a wave. "Hi, I'm Peyton and this is Kendall."

The woman at the end of their group waved. "Hi, it's nice to meet you," Kendall said.

"You too." Good lord, could these women be any more attractive? She'd expected them to be gorgeous. They were dating professional athletes after all, but she'd had a picture in her mind of what they'd look like and these women were not it. They were much more natural than she'd been expecting, which just made how pretty they were all the more startling.

She pulled her Gonzalez jersey away from her body, instantly aware of exactly how much larger she was than these women. It made sense they'd all be tiny. She'd seen the women Gonzo brought home and the women he'd been photographed with. Not a double digit in the mix.

Thank god, she wasn't trying to date in this world because she sure as hell wouldn't fit in.

"That's a great jersey. Is it a special edition one?" Peyton asked.

Bailey eyed her shirt. "No, this is old. It's from Gonzo's first season."

"That's sweet that you've been supporting him throughout his entire career."

The second the jerseys were on the market, Gonzo had mailed her entire family jerseys. Her family had gone over to the Gonzalez house for the first game with everyone wearing their matching jerseys. Her parents still watched opening day with Gonzo's parents every season. It was sweet how into Gonzo's career her dad was. He bought a new jersey every season. Somehow he'd convinced himself that those jersey sales landed directly in Gonzo's pocket. Like that one jersey was going to make all the difference in the next contract negotiation.

"Gonzo said you two grew up together," Kia said.

"We did. We've been neighbors our entire lives."

"That's so cool. So, were you always friends?"

Bailey nodded her head slowly as memories of growing up next door to the Gonzalez family swarmed her brain. "Yep, you didn't mess with the Gonzalez-Reynolds kids. We were like a little gang." She laughed.

"How many of you are there?" Kia asked.

"I'm one of four and Gonzo is one of six, so we were quite the crew on the block."

"Holy crap, ten kids between two houses. I can barely handle the one I have." Kia eyed Max. "That's impressive."

"Yeah, our moms just tag teamed us. If you mouthed off at either house, you paid for it at that house. My mom washed out Gonzo's mouth with soap on more than one occasion."

Kendall laughed. "He still has a mouth like a trucker, so I don't think he learned his lesson."

Bailey snorted. "Not the quickest study on that one. By the time he was a teenager, my mom switched it to doing errands for her. I don't think either mom had to run to the grocery store for forgotten ingredients all through high school because Gonz was always owing someone a payment for his language. It got so bad we had a Gonzo chore list on our fridge."

"Oh my god, I can totally see that," Kendall snickered. "Your mom called him Gonzo too?"

"Yeah, everybody did. It started back in t-ball. Our coach called him Gonzo, then everybody started, including his mom. I think she realized pretty quickly that having six kids all with first names that started with R was good in theory, but not quite as convenient as she'd hoped."

"They all have R names?" Peyton asked.

"Yep, when one of them was in trouble, she'd run through the list. Gonz was the only one spared since he went by something different." Bailey chuckled at the memory of Gonzo's mom, Rose, yelling across the fence at her kids.

She glanced over at Kia, who was watching her intently. "Did you and Gonz ever date?" Kia asked.

"God, no."

"Why do you say it like that?" Kia asked.

"We just didn't have that kind of relationship." How could they when Gonzo was the star athlete in the school, captain of every team and she'd been the slightly heavy, artsy sidekick? There was no way women who looked like these three would understand what it was like to be a plus sized woman in a Victoria's Secret world.

Sure, she'd had a crush on Gonzo in high school, every girl had. But he'd never once looked at her like that. It had broken her teenage heart, but she'd gotten over it and now she was glad they'd never crossed that line because realistically they probably wouldn't have remained friends. "Nah, when you've had food poisoning together at fifteen..." She shuddered. "Some things you can't unsee."

"Ew." Peyton cringed. "I can only imagine."

Bailey laughed. "Yeah, it wasn't good. For either of us."

Max jumped up from his seat. "There's Dad." He bounced up and down, waving his arms toward the field.

Bailey looked down to the field where Gonzo stood with Pete Saunders and Jeff Smith as the three men did some kind of elaborate handshake, dance combo that made Max squeal. The little boy took off his cap and smacked it against his palm, then thigh in an elaborate combo before he spun around in a circle and slapped the hat back on his head. The three men on the field threw their hands up in a cheer that made Max giggle.

Kia rubbed the top of Max's head, then blew a kiss down to the field.

God, that was cute. Bailey's chest tightened. He hadn't changed a bit. Gonzo was still the same guy he'd always been. The guy who'd make a fool of himself in public for a loved one.

Living with Gonzo for the past couple of days, she'd seen a different side to him than she'd ever seen before. He was more polished, more bougie, than the boy she'd known. A part of her wondered if that boy was still in there. This proved he was. He might be a big-time athlete with a personal shopper, but he was still Gonzo.

As the guys started warming up on the field, Kendall leaned forward. "So, how are you liking San Diego?"

"It's good. Definitely different from KC."

"I'll bet." Kendall smiled. "So Gonzo said you're a university professor."

"I am. Sociology."

"I took a couple of sociology classes when I did my degree," Peyton said. "They were interesting. What's your area?"

"Gender studies predominantly." At the open expression on Peyton's face, she continued. "I teach a misogyny in the media class."

"So, would you focus on a particular area of the media for the course?" Peyton asked.

"Yes, for this semester we'll be looking at the way women are portrayed in cartoon and comics."

"That's very cool," Kia said. "I've never really given much thought to that kind of thing."

"And I've probably given it way more thought than anyone ever should." Bailey laughed. "So we probably balance each other out."

"Ooh, the beer guy." Kendall threw her arm up in the air to grab the attention of the man in the aisle with the beer strapped to his chest. "First round's on me. What do you want?"

Bailey eyed the options of cans strapped to the man's chest. "Blue Moon I guess."

"Four Blue Moon," Kendall yelled at the vendor as she handed her money to Peyton to pass down the line.

Once the beer and money were exchanged and passed down the line, Bailey cracked the top and took a sip of the icy cold beverage. It had been a couple years since she'd been to a ball game, and she'd never seen Gonzo play in his home stadium. Seeing all the Gonzalez jerseys in the crowd brought a smile to her face.

How many times had they lain in the tree fort in her yard talking about when they made it big? And Gonzo had done it. Everything on his list could be checked off, while hers was decidedly empty.

The air crackled while the announcer talked about the upcoming game. The crowd roared when they called out the home team players' names. Max's little body vibrated as he stood up, cheering for his dad. Lord, he was cute.

Bailey looked down at third base. Gonzo tipped his hat up to them with a huge smile on his face and she couldn't help but grin back. She rubbed her hands together in excitement.

"Let's go, Hawks," she yelled, then turned to Max and held her hand up. He smacked her hand with all the exuberance of a six-year-old.

"All right, buddy, have a seat," Kia told her son.

Max plopped into his chair. "Dad's gonna hit a homer today," he announced decidedly.

"We've talked about this." Kia turned in her seat to face him. "As much as your dad would like to always hit home runs, he can't do that every game."

"Yeah, but he should still try. Isn't that what you always say to just try your best?"

Kia sighed. "Yes, of course he will try his best, but like we've talked about, just because he doesn't hit one doesn't mean he didn't try his hardest."

"Bunting isn't trying his hardest," Max grumbled.

"But sometimes bunting is what's best for the team," Kia said.

"A home run is better than a bunt."

Kia pinched the bridge of her nose. "Fair enough. But a win's a win and that's what we're going for today. Right?"

"Right." Max jumped out of his seat. "Strike out this bum, Ryan," Max yelled.

"Max." Kia's voice instantly turned into that stern mother tone that every kid knew well, and Bailey bit back a chuckle when Max winced and sat down in his seat.

"Sorry, Mom."

Kia shook her head. "Language." She turned to Bailey. "I swear he's going to be banned from hanging out with Jeff and his friends. Every time they do a boys' night, I have to spend the next week retraining him on what he's allowed to say.

"I guess Gonz isn't allowed to babysit then," Bailey stated.

"Oh no, he babysits all the time. It's cute how hard he tries to clean up his language. One-on-one, they're all good. It's when they get together and start trash talking each other or watching sports on TV that the potty mouths come out."

"So Gonzo babysits?"

"Yeah, all the time. He's Max's first choice."

Why did the idea of that make her tummy feel all weird? Of course, he would babysit for his friends. Gonzo loved kids. She was just being sentimental because there was no way Brad would have ever volunteered to look after anyone. How many times had he talked about how he was going to have a nanny when he had kids of his own? It was one of the things they'd argued over when they talked about what their life would be like. Just one more reason she should have seen the writing on the wall that Brad was not the right person for her.

As Carmichael for Seattle walked up to the plate, Bailey shifted in her seat. His 302 batting average flashed on the screen. The Hawks' pitcher, Ryan, threw the first pitch and Carmichael cracked a foul ball down the first baseline and into the stands.

Bailey's eyes were drawn to Gonzo as he shifted his weight on his feet. The second pitch soared over the plate and Carmichael swung. The ball cracked off the bat and a line drive rifled down the third base line. With lightning-fast movement, Gonzo's arm snapped out and snagged the ball. Bailey swore she could hear the ball hitting the leather mitt from her seat. What an amazing catch. She leaped from her seat. "Yeah, Gonzo, wooooo," she screamed.

She grinned over at Max as she dropped back into her seat and held up her hand to high-five. "That's how it's done, baby."

Max slapped her hand. "Yeah, baby," he yelled back.

Bailey winced and glanced over at Kia. "Sorry," she mouthed.

Kia laughed. "It's all good."

The next two batters didn't make it on base either. Great start to the game.

Several innings later, the score was still zero-zero. Pete Saunders hit a nice little dinger in the bottom of the fifth and jogged to first base. The game had seen lots of action for the fielders, but so far neither team had scored a run. Gonzo had been stranded on second his last time at bat. As he took to the plate, Bailey leaned forward in her chair. She didn't know how the players handled the pressure. She was just watching and her entire body coiled tight with anticipation.

Gonzo said something to the catcher and grinned. A friendly joke? Trash talk? With him, it could be either.

He rolled his shoulders and lined up at the plate. As the first pitch soared across the plate, he swung. The bat connected with a crack and the ball soared toward the fence at center field. Bailey held her breath. The center fielder jumped but couldn't reach the ball as it soared over the fence just out of his reach.

Their entire row leaped to their feet. Fireworks displayed on the jumbotron as Gonzo made his way around the bases. His home run put the Hawks' up two-nothing.

Bailey's heart raced from the excitement of watching her friend hit a home run, and the energy of the crowd buzzing around her. Okay, she took it back. She could entirely see why a person would put themselves through the stress of batting if the adrenaline rush they got when they succeeded was anything close to what it felt like as a fan. That feeling would be addictive as hell.

The remainder of the game was very non-eventful and the Hawks pulled out the two-nothing win over Seattle. As the fans started filing out of their seats, Kendall leaned forward. "You're coming out for a drink with us after the game, right?"

"That's the plan."

"Perfect. It's hard to chat properly here, so it'll be nice to get a chance to really talk."

Kia leaned over and in a stage whisper said, "Prepare to be grilled."

"Shut up, I'm not that bad." Kendall scrunched up her face as she looked at Kia.

Peyton snorted. "Umm yeah, you are. Be glad you aren't dating Gonzo, Bailey, otherwise she would be relentless."

Kendall shouldered Peyton, then looked at Bailey. "I promise I am not that bad. I might go a little overboard when you're dating one of my people, but that's only because I care. But you've known Gonzo forever, so you're good." She waved her hand nonchalantly.

"You're getting off easy," Kia mumbled.

"I hope you have other things planned for discussion because I'm honestly not that exciting."

"Oh, I'm sure Kendall can find something to grill you about," Peyton teased.

"That's true." Kendall nodded in agreement. "I'm crazy nosey, so you've been warned."

"Great." Bailey smiled tightly. Was it too late to back out of this?

Kia looked around the stadium and glanced at her watch. "All right, should we head down?"

"Sure." Bailey gestured for the other women to lead the way.

They took the stairs down and Bailey followed the women down a hallway toward a security guard.

"Hey Carl," Peyton said. "This is Bailey, she's with Gonzo."

"Really?" Carl's eyes widened as he looked her up and down. Bailey's jaw clenched. Yes, she didn't look like these women, but seriously, did he have to look so shocked that she was with Gonzo?

She muttered, "Go figure," when what she'd wanted to say was asshole.

And with one absent comment from some random guy, all of her excitement about the day instantly vanished. Damn it, she hated that something so simple affected her so strongly. So much for all the therapy she'd done over the years. Brad had broken her worse than she'd thought.

Needing a minute to compose herself, she turned to Peyton. "Is there a bathroom nearby?"

"Yeah, there's one just up on the right."

"Great, thanks." Bailey picked up the pace and quickly turned into the washroom. She stood in front of the sink and looked at herself in the mirror. Sure, she might not be a size two like Peyton, but she was comfortable with the way she looked. Her face had always been pretty and with her new haircut she was feeling more like her old self. Overall she looked pretty good.

It had taken a lot of work to get to the point where she could say that. And then she'd let Brad take it all away. "Fucking Brad," she muttered. Before all the shit with him, she was feeling comfortable about her body. She'd done years of therapy. Hell, she'd spent her entire career discussing the perception of women in a patriarchal society. She had a freaking doctorate in the subject, so why the hell was she allowing some man's perception of her to make her feel small? She gripped the edge of the counter and took a deep breath.

No.

Then another breath.

No.

And another.

No.

Not happening. She exhaled audibly. She was a strong, confident woman. She looked in the mirror and pinned herself with a stare. "I am beautiful exactly as I am," she whispered to her reflection. "I will not let anyone else's perception of me change how I feel about myself."

She took another deep breath. Feeling more calm and centered, she looked at herself one last time.

The therapy had certainly helped, but it hadn't curbed that instant feeling of self-doubt that jumped to the front of the line the second she felt someone judge her appearance. Guess she needed to find a therapist here in town because clearly she had some shit to work through still. This healing business was hard.

Bailey took one last look at herself in the mirror and squared her shoulders. The words of her therapist bounced in her head. No one could make her feel anything she didn't allow.

Feeling more in control, she turned on her heel and marched back out into the hallway to join the others.

"You okay?" Peyton asked.

"I'm good."

"Good." Peyton smiled. "I love your nails. Where'd you get them done?"

Bailey glanced down at her hand. "No where, I just did them at home."

"Seriously? You do this yourself?" Peyton snatched up her hand. "Kendall, look at these." She tilted Bailey's hand toward the other woman.

Kendall grabbed her hand and ran her finger along Bailey's index nail. "Wow, where'd you learn to do this?"

"YouTube."

Kia snorted. "You did not learn to do nails like that from YouTube."

"Honestly, that's how I learned."

"No." Kia shook her head. "I mean sure you might have learned some ideas from YouTube, but you did not get that kind of skill from watching a couple of videos. You have a freakin' Hawks jersey on your nails. That's insane."

Bailey glanced at her nails. "What can I say? I have time on my hands at the moment."

"No, girl, that's wild. From one artist to another. Those are cool."

"Can you do mine?" Kendall asked.

"Umm, I guess, I mean I've never really painted anybody else's nails besides my family." Well, besides Gonzo's, but she didn't think he'd appreciate her telling them that.

"You seriously learned that from just painting your own nails?"

"Well, with the amount I messed up playing around, I wouldn't put anyone else through that unless they loved me." Bailey laughed.

"I am more than happy to be a guinea pig to the cause." Kendall wiggled her perfectly manicured hands in front of Bailey.

Bailey wrinkled her nose. "You clearly get those done professionally. I don't know..."

"I do. I want Pete's jersey on my nails." A slow smile spread across her face. "Mmm. Yep, I definitely need those."

"Oh, my god, you just got sex face." Peyton snickered beside her.

"What is sex face?" Kendall asked.

"That face you make when you're picturing having some kind of kinky sex with Pete."

"It's not always kinky." Kendall winked. "But yeah, I was totally picturing his reaction to me having his jersey on my nails."

"I knew it," Peyton said. "I want you to do Ryan's jersey on mine."

"I kind of want to high-five you because I know what you're talking about, but ew that's my brother, so I'm not going to." Kendall wrinkled her nose.

"That's fair because, yep, I'm totally talking about that," Peyton agreed.

Bailey looked down at her hands with Gonzo's jersey all over them. He'd certainly never reacted to having his jersey on her nails. What would it feel like to have it affect him the same way the other women thought it would affect their men? And why did she care? They were friends. Friends weren't supposed to want their friends to get all primal about them. A little zip raced through her belly. So why did she kind of hope he would?

The locker room door pushed open and players began wandering into the hallway. Bailey instantly scanned for Gonzo. He wasn't in the first group of players to exit. Max spotted his dad and raced toward him. Jeff scooped him up and hitched him on his hip. He stopped at Kia, wrapped his arm around her waist and pulled her against him. He kissed her, and Max groaned. "Gross."

"Well buddy, you wanted to be up here and you know I always want to kiss your mom, so you've got no one but yourself to blame."

Bailey giggled as Max rolled his eyes.

"Hey, you must be Bailey," Jeff said as he untangled himself from Kia and stuck out his hand to shake.

"I am. It's nice to meet you. You've got the best baseball fan ever right there." She nodded toward Max. The little boy beamed back at her.

"I know it." Jeff ruffled the top of Max's head, then turned to Peyton. "Ryan is getting iced, so he'll be a couple of minutes."

"Getting iced?" Bailey asked.

"Yeah, his wing is a little tender, so they have him icing it down."

"Oh, gotcha."

"You ready?" he said to Kia.

"Yep." Kia turned to Bailey. "It was really nice meeting you."

"You aren't coming for a drink?"

"No, we gotta get this one home to bed." She pointed at Max. "You want to grab coffee one day this week?"

"I would love that."

"Give me your phone and I'll put my number in." Kia held out her hand and Bailey dropped her phone into it. Kia quickly typed in her number, then handed it back to Bailey. "I texted myself too, so I've got yours. Let me look at my schedule and I'll text you later."

"Sounds good." Bailey turned to Max, sitting on his dad's hip. "Thanks for watching the game with me, Max. I had fun."

"Yeah, good thing they won," the little boy replied.

"Good thing," Bailey agreed.

"All right, let's get out of here," Jeff said. "You all have a good night."

"Bye girls," Kia said. "Bailey, I'll text you."

"Great."

The locker room door pushed open and another wave of players exited. When Bailey saw Gonzo, she sucked in a breath. Damn, he looked good. She had to admit there was something about a man fresh from a win that just really worked. She scanned the men on either side of him. They all looked good. Confidently strutting toward their adoring fans to celebrate their victory.

Gonzo walked up and wrapped his arms around her. Bailey let out a little squeal as her feet left the ground.

"So what'd you think?" Gonzo asked as he set her back down on the ground.

"Eh, you played all right. I've seen better."

"Better? I hit a home run and nearly pulled my groin, making that snag to take out Carmichael. That's some fucking ESPN shit and you say all right," he grumbled.

"ESPN shit," she mumbled. "I'm pretty sure your ego doesn't need me to boost it any further."

"That hurts, Bay." He slapped his hand on his chest. "The first time you've seen me play live in a couple years and I go all out to impress you, and this is what I get."

"Yeah, it was all about impressing me." Bailey snorted.

"Of course it was. Well, you and ESPN." He waggled his eyebrows. "Catch of the day, baby."

Bailey pushed him in the chest. "You haven't changed a bit."

He wrapped his arm around her shoulder and pulled her against his side. "Why would I?"

"No idea." She wrapped her arm around his waist and tilted her head against his chest. She hadn't realized until this moment just how much she'd missed him. Missed watching him play ball, missed his exuberance after the game, missed the way he hugged her when he was riding the high of winning. "I've missed watching you play," she admitted.

"I've missed having you watch." He kissed the top of her head. "It's nice having you here."

At the feel of his arms tightening around her, Bailey's stomach flipped. God, what was wrong with her? This was Gonzo. It was just nostalgia, not desire. But when he squeezed her hip and his hand lingered in a way that made her breath hitch, it sure felt like desire.

"All right, you guys ready to get out of here?" Gonzo asked.

"Absolutely," Pete replied. "Let's do it."

# CHAPTER TEN

G onzo placed his hand against Bailey's back and guided her into the bar. He scanned the room, looking for his teammates.

The place was wall to wall people like it was after every game. The owner was an ex-player, so he usually set aside a couple of tables for players. He paused as a server handed out shots to a group of twenty-something guys. With the shots delivered, she dropped her tray to her side and turned. "Oh hey, Gonz, Pete's already here. They grabbed a table around the corner."

"Thanks, Jenna," He smiled at the server, then tried to guide Bailey forward only to be stopped by the group in front of him.

"Gon-za-lez," shot-taker number one sang out his name.

People around them snapped to attention the way they always did when they realized a player was nearby.

Gonzo raised his arm and smacked the guy's extended hand. The smack connected exactly right, making that perfect high-five sound he loved. Normally when he made the attempt, the other person shifted their hand

and what resulted was an awkward bobble that was just embarrassing.

"Nice game," the guy said.

"Thanks."

"Let me buy you a shot."

"Thanks, but I gotta go easy. We've got to head to LA for a game tomorrow."

"Cool, yeah, of course." The kid's head bobbed up and down in agreement, then he turned to Bailey. "You want a shot?"

"No, I'm good, thanks."

"Your boyfriend is fucking awesome."

Bailey's eyes widened. "He's not my—"

There really was no point in Bailey getting into who she was or wasn't with some random fan, so he nudged her back to encourage her to move forward. Gonzo turned to the guy. "You have a great night."

"Yeah, you too."

"Did you see that? I just fucking talked to Gonzalez." The guy's voice carried from behind him, quickly followed by the sounds of hands slapping. Gonzo inwardly winced as several of the slaps made that sad little sound of an awkward connection. Guess the one he had with the guy was just a fluke.

Bailey glanced over her shoulder and smirked at him.

"Shut up," he muttered. Pressing his fingers against her lower back, he guided her toward the pool table area where Jenna had said Pete would be.

After several more pit stops for congratulations, they finally made it to the table. "Holy shit, it's busy in here already," he said as he pushed a couple of stools away from the pub-style table. Bailey climbed onto one stool and he slid onto the second.

"I already ordered a pitcher," Pete said before he turned to Bailey. "So, Bailey, I'm trying to figure out why you've been friends with this guy for so long. He's a bit of a —" Pete scrunched up his face.

"Haha, asshole," Gonzo mumbled.

"What can I say? I felt sorry for him and then he just kind of stuck."

He shifted in his seat and faced Bailey. "You felt sorry for me? Come on now." He flicked his finger against his shoulder like he was brushing it off. "I was king of that town. Homecoming King, to be exact."

Bailey shook her head and smiled sadly. "Pity votes, all of them."

Pete snickered from across the table. "I knew I was going to like you."

"Glad one of us does," Gonzo grumbled.

"Oh, don't pout," Bailey teased. "You know I love ya.'"

The server set down two pitchers of beer and a bunch of glasses. "Thanks, Danny," Pete said.

"You good with beer or did you want something else?" Gonzo asked Bailey.

"Beer's good."

Kendall grabbed the stack of glasses and was pulling it toward herself when Peyton and Ryan walked up. "Keep pouring, Ken," Ryan said as he pulled out a chair for Peyton, then pushed her up to the table before he sat down in his own seat.

Peyton squeezed Bailey's arm. "I'm glad you came."

"Yeah, now we can properly grill you." Kendall rubbed her hands together gleefully.

"Oh, goodie." Bailey's fake smile made him chuckle.

Growing up, she hated being the center of attention and as far as he could tell, she still did, so her career choice always struck him as a little odd. Standing up in front of hundreds of people giving a lecture ensured she was the center of attention every day. Somehow she felt it was different, which he never understood.

"How are you liking San Diego so far?" Pete asked.

"I haven't really seen too much of it yet, but I've got lots of time to explore."

"Gonzo said you're a sociology professor."

"I am, yes."

"Cool. Gotta admit that is not my wheelhouse," Pete said. "I'm more of a hands-on kind of guy."

Bailey smiled. "I won't hold it against you."

"There're classes happening now?" Ryan asked.

"There are, but not ones I'm teaching. My classes don't start until September, so I have some time to get to know the city before I start work."

"Oh, that'll be nice," Peyton said.

"Why'd you move so early if you don't start teaching till September?" Kendall asked.

"Umm...my lease was up." Bailey glanced over at him. Her eyes widened in a 'help me' plea.

"How's living with Gonz?" Ryan asked.

"It's fucking awesome, of course," Gonzo said. He took a sip of his beer, then smacked his hands together. "Who wants to play darts?"

The tension on Bailey's face instantly disappeared. "I will."

"Cool. Any other takers?"

"I'll play." Kendall pushed her chair back from the table.

"I humiliated myself enough the last time we were here." Peyton shook her head. "Hard pass."

"If we do guys against girls so I can kick my sister's ass, I'll play," Ryan chimed in.

"Done." Kendall stood up. "You any good, Bailey?"

"Not really, no." Bailey grimaced.

"Well, crap." Kendall laughed.

The owner of the bar walked up just as he was standing. "Hey Mark, good to see you." Gonzo stuck out his hand and shook his ex-teammate's hand.

"You too. Great game tonight."

"Have a seat." Pete gestured to the vacated seats around the table.

"You sure?" Mark asked.

Gonzo stepped away from his chair. "Yeah, take mine. We're just going to play darts."

At the board, he grabbed the darts off the shelf. "What's the bet?"

"We're betting?" Bailey squeaked.

"Bay." Gonzo glanced at his friend. How long had she known him? Of course, this was a competition. And winning meant there should be a prize.

"I think if the girls lose, Kendall has to cook dinner for all of us."

"You've seen me cook," Kendall said to her brother.

"Yep, that's why it would be funny."

"Seeing me fall on my face would be funny?"

Ryan's head bounced up and down. "Absolutely. Oh, and you have to pay for the takeout if it needs to be ordered."

"Haha, asshole." Kendall smacked her brother on the chest. She squared her shoulders and stuck out her hand. "Deal."

"Umm, hold on," Bailey interrupted. "That hardly seems fair. If we lose, it will be because I suck. Kendall shouldn't have to cook some elaborate spread because of me."

"We aren't gonna lose," Kendall declared confidently.

Bailey winced. "I'm pretty sure we will with me on your team."

Kendall wrapped her arm around Bailey's shoulder. "It'll be fine."

"So dinner for eight on Ken when the girls lose?" Gonzo said.

"Whoa, whoa." Kendall held up her hand. "We aren't going to lose. What do we get when we win?"

"You're not gonna win," Ryan said.

"You don't know that. I used to kick your ass all the time when we were kids."

"Gonzo's a fantastic cook. How about he cooks dinner for everyone if we win?" Bailey chimed in.

"You can cook?" Kendall asked.

"Of course I can cook." Gonzo rolled his eyes. How the hell did she think he ate?

"Well, I mean like cook, cook, like properly cook," Kendall continued.

"Yes, Kendall, I can properly cook."

"He's really good," Bailey gushed.

Kendall's gaze darted back and forth between him and Bailey. "Interesting."

"What's interesting about it?" he asked.

Kendall's raised shoulders matched her eyebrows as she smirked back at him. "It's just interesting that you've cooked for her, and we didn't even know you could cook."

"I knew he could cook," Ryan interjected.

"See." Gonzo looked at Kendall. "I just haven't cooked for you."

Kendall's forehead wrinkled. "Well, that's just rude."

He snickered. "Then maybe you should be nice."

"I'm always nice," she squawked.

"Eh," Ryan replied.

Bailey stepped closer to him. "I really like your friends."

He set his arm around her shoulder as he watched the siblings squabble over how they were going to decide who got which colored darts. "Yeah, I like them too."

"Ha, I won." Kendall threw her arms up in victory. "Pass over the gold ones." Kendall held out her palm and wiggled her fingers until Ryan set the gold darts in her hand. She stepped toward Bailey and handed her their darts. "You go first."

Bailey accepted the darts and exhaled a deep breath.

"Hey, Bay?"

"Yeah?"

Why did she look so nervous? It was darts. No one was going to be throwing them at her. This was supposed to be fun. "I'm not going to let you win like I did when we were kids."

"Let me win? Oh my god, like you've ever let anyone win anything," she scoffed. "You're going down."

Bailey walked up to the little tape line on the floor. She set the tip of her left shoe on the line, then wiggled her back leg until she was in position. He crossed his arms and leaned against the table as he watched her get set up.

Kendall set her beer down on the table beside him and turned to watch Bailey. "I like her."

"That's good," he replied absently, not taking his eyes off Bailey as she threw the first dart. It hit the wall above the board and bounced to the floor. "Ooh," he winced.

Bailey bolted over and grabbed the dart off the floor and faced the group. "That was just a practice throw."

"Sure." Gonzo bit back a laugh at the serious look on her face. "But you only get one."

"I'll only need one." She pushed her shoulders back and marched to the line like she was going into battle.

"She's really cute," Kendall said.

"Mmm," he grunted.

"Don't you think?" Kendall pressed.

"Yeah, sure," he mumbled noncommittally. There was no way he was getting into a discussion with Kendall about Bailey. The woman was relentless once she got an idea.

"I like her for you."

He flicked a glance at Kendall. "We're just friends."

Bailey squealed, drawing his attention back to her. His eyes instantly latched onto the way her ass shook as she did some kind of weird little wiggle dance.

"Just friends, huh?" Kendall nudged him and he pulled his gaze off Bailey's ass. "I don't stare at my friends' asses like that," Kendall continued.

"Shut up," he muttered.

"Just saying." Kendall eyed him knowingly.

Well shit.

"Did you see that?" Bailey asked.

He flicked a glance at the dartboard. Bailey's gold dart lay perfectly in the middle of the bullseye. "Nice."

Bailey wiggled her hips again. "Bullseye, baby. Told ya you were going down for me this time."

Ryan sputtered his beer, then banged his chest as he coughed.

"What?" Bailey asked in confusion.

"Nothing. I just thought you guys were just friends."

"Huh?" Bailey wrinkled her nose. "Going down?"

And instantly Gonzo pictured Bailey sprawled out on the bed with him between her legs. Now that was a bet he could get behind. Whoa, where had that thought come from? This was Bailey.

Her eyes widened, and she slapped her hand over her mouth. "Oh my god, that is not what I meant." Or at least that's what he thought she said. It was kind of hard to tell since her voice was all muffled behind her hand.

Ryan barked out another laugh. "O-kay."

"I didn't." Amusement danced in her blue eyes when they connected with his. He could swear there was a little flash of heat as they held, but maybe that was just wishful thinking considering the path his thoughts had taken.

"I liked the celebration dance," Hernandez said as he walked up with Sims at his side. The first baseman slowly scanned Bailey like she was an all you can eat buffet and he was trying to decide where to start.

Gonzo's jaw clenched. Not happening. "Hernandez," he said, drawing his teammate's attention from Bailey.

That lasted all of ten seconds before the guy was looking at her again. "I've never seen you before."

"Hi, I'm Bailey." She gave a little wave.

Gonzo sighed. "Bailey, this is Lourdes Hernandez." He flicked his hand toward her. "Hernandez, this is Bailey."

"Nice snag in the third," Bailey said.

"Thanks." Hernandez puffed out his chest at the compliment.

Brandon Sims stood off to the side with his hands buried in his jeans pocket and a slightly annoyed look on his face. Win or lose, Sims always looked like he wasn't sure he wanted to be out at the bar with the team. "And you've already met this grumpy bastard," Gonzo told Bailey.

"I'm not grumpy. I'm just not a fucking golden retriever like you."

"I'm not a golden retriever," Gonzo scoffed. "If you're gonna compare me to a dog, at least compare me to something badass."

"What's wrong with golden retrievers?" Bailey asked.

Was she serious? Who the hell wanted to be called that? "There's nothing sexy about being a golden retriever."

Bailey smirked at him. "Got to be honest with you, Gonz. There's nothing sexy about any dog, so I don't think you need to worry about that."

"Haha." He scowled. "You know what I mean. No guy wants to be compared to a golden retriever."

"Right, because what woman would like a loving, sweet, fun guy that's always there for her, no matter what?" Bailey shook her head. "That sounds awful. Who'd want to date that? Blech." She glanced over at him. Their eyes held and he felt that same little blip in the pit of his stomach.

Brandon cleared his throat and he tore his eyes off her. Whatever this was, he needed to rein it in ASAP. He wasn't going to fuck up his friendship with Bailey just because his dick had decided it wanted a starring role in their relationship.

"So who's winning?" Brandon asked.

"We're just getting started," Ryan said as he walked up to the tape line.

Bailey glanced over at him. Her eyes dancing with amusement and said, "But apparently we established Gonzo's in the mood to go down."

Ryan sputtered out a laugh. Kendall threw her arm around Bailey's shoulder. "Oh my god, I love you."

And Gonzo's dick twitched against his zipper. So much for getting his dick on board with the whole just friends thing. Because yeah, the more he thought about it, the more he realized Bailey was right. That was exactly what he wanted to do. Shit.

He picked up his beer and downed the rest of the glass.

"You okay, dude?" Brandon asked.

"What? Yeah, of course."

Bailey walked over and picked up her drink while Ryan lined up for his shot.

"How long have you two been together?" Hernandez asked.

"We're not together," Gonzo replied.

"Obviously." Bailey snorted. "Can you imagine?"

Why did she make it sound like the idea of dating him was so ridiculous? Women all over the place would love the chance to date him. What the hell was her problem? "Why'd you say it like that?"

Bailey glanced over at him, then her brow wrinkled in confusion. "Look at the women around here." She waved her hand to encompass the bar. "And look at me." Her left eyebrow rose as she scrunched her face into a look that said, duh.

"Wha—?" he grunted. At the same time Hernandez said, "Huh?" Good to know he wasn't the only one that didn't have a clue what she was talking about.

Bailey rolled her eyes, then smirked. "Case in point." She nodded her head toward the two women in Hawks' jerseys coming toward them like a heat-seeking missile.

The women stopped in front of them. The blonde stepped up so close she was practically touching him. "Hi." She batted her heavily made-up blue eyes at him. "You guys were great today."

"Thanks. Were you at the game?"

"No, but we heard you won." She leaned back, drawing his attention to her exposed, tanned stomach.

He flicked a glance at Bailey. Her lip popped out slightly, like she was biting the inside of her cheek the way she always did when she was hurt but didn't want anyone to know. Damn. He didn't know what was going on with her, but he planned to find out.

"Excuse me, ladies, it's my turn." He pointed at the dartboard.

"You want to buy me a drink?" the blonde asked.

On any given night, he would have said yes. She was exactly the kind of woman he usually took home from the bar after a game, but tonight he had Bailey with him, so as tempting as the gorgeous blonde was, it was going to be a big no. He eyed the number on her jersey and rolled his eyes. "You've got the wrong player," he said, pointing to the number on her jersey.

"What?" the woman blinked back at him.

"I'm Gonzalez." He pointed toward his teammate. "That one's Hernandez."

The blonde looked over at his teammate, then back at him in confusion. "So?"

"So, you're wearing the wrong player's jersey."

She stepped in closer to him and pressed herself against his body. "I won't be wearing anything when we get back to your place, so does it really matter?"

Normally, not a bit. But tonight? Yeah, it mattered.

He smiled to soften the blow. "Sorry. I'm up." He pointed at the dartboard, then walked away.

As he glanced at the scoreboard, he winced. Was that really the score? He threw a look at Ryan. How were they losing that badly already? "What the hell? Bailey missed the board on her first throw?"

"Yeah, but Kendall didn't," Ryan grumbled.

He hadn't been paying attention, but from the looks of the scoreboard, Kendall had hit trips every time. They had some ground to make up. Gonzo stepped up to the line and threw his first dart. Triple twenty. Nice. His second dart hit the metal at the edge of the bullseye, bumping it back onto the twenty.

"See, it's not that easy," Ryan said.

"Don't choke, Gonz," Kendall taunted.

He glanced over at Bailey, who stood slightly off to the side, not saying a word. He lined up and threw his third dart. Triple twenty again. He turned to Kendall. "Ha, suck it."

"I don't think Pete would like that," she mocked.

"Haha." He bumped her with his hip. "You're up, Bay."

Bailey pushed off the table and took her place at the line. The blonde from earlier stepped up beside him. "You're really good."

"Thanks," he said absently, not taking his eyes off Bailey as she lined up to take her shot. If he hadn't been watching her so closely, he wouldn't have noticed the way her shoulders slumped when she flicked a look his way before she lined up her shot. The dart hit the wall above the board and stuck. Bailey's chest heaved as she took a deep breath and lined up again.

Geez, she was a terrible dart player, but he had to give her credit for still taking the shots.

The blonde trailed her finger down his arm. The touch drew his attention from Bailey, making him miss her last throw. It pissed him off that he'd missed it. Doing his best to still be polite, he gave the blonde a tight smile. "If you'll excuse me."

He walked up to Bailey and bumped his shoulder against hers. "I don't remember you being this bad at throwing."

"Throwing and darts are two different things." She picked up her beer and took a sip. "Why aren't you over there?" She gestured to the blonde who was watching them.

"Why would I be?"

"Umm, because she's clearly interested in you."

"I'm not interested."

Bailey snorted. "You'd have to be dead not to be interested in that."

He looked over at the blonde. "Yeah, she's hot, but I'm here with you. That's not what tonight's about."

"Gonzo, honestly, it's fine. If you want to hook up with someone, I totally get it, especially when she looks like that."

"What'd you mean earlier when you said it was obvious we wouldn't be dating?"

"Are you kidding me?" Bailey's eyebrows nearly hit her hairline as she gaped at him. "With that woman over there? Are you serious?"

"Yes, I'm serious. Why did the idea of us dating seem so ridiculous?" Sure, he was a baller, but he wasn't an idiot. Maybe intellectually he wasn't in the same league as a professor or lawyer like Brad, but he'd graduated from university on his own steam, which had been fucking hard with his baseball schedule.

"Gonzo, the women you date look like that."

"So?"

"Please don't make me say it," she whispered.

If she wanted to insult him, she was damn well going to say it out loud. He stared down at her without speaking, waiting her out. Finally, Bailey huffed out a breath. "I'm very well aware of how I look."

"What the fuck does how you look have to do with anything?" His mind raced to catch up.

"Umm, everything. You don't date fat girls."

"You aren't fat," he growled. He hated how women always did that. Put themselves down for having a different kind of body. His mom and his sisters did it all the time, and it pissed him off.

"I'm not skinny."

"There's nothing wrong with the way you look."

"I didn't say there was. It's just not the kind of body guys like you go for."

"Guys like me?" Wow. The little jab hit like a knife in his sternum.

"Oh, don't be all offended, you know what I mean."

"Yeah, unfortunately I do." Is that really how she saw him? As some kind of dick who thought a woman was only beautiful if she was a size 2? He pushed off the table. "We should join the group."

Bailey grabbed his arm. "What's the matter? Why do you seem all hurt?"

"Really?" He stared at his childhood friend. "You just told me you think I'm a shallow piece of shit and I'm not supposed to be offended."

"That's not what I said."

"It kind of is." He pushed his hand through his hair. "I think I liked it better when I thought you meant I was too stupid to date."

Bailey's head snapped back. "You thought I was insulting you when I laughed about us not dating?"

"Yeah. You're gorgeous, Bailey, you always have been. Just because we've never dated doesn't mean I'm not fully aware of how attractive you are. What else was I supposed to think?"

"You think I'm attractive?" she asked.

That's what she latched onto? "Yes. Lots of guys like curvy girls, Bailey."

"I know. I just don't see athletes with any."

"How many athletes do you know?"

"What?"

"How many do you know? Besides me, how many do you know?"

She scanned the bar. "Umm, your friends."

"Okay, so like four people? Pretty small sample size for that kind of bold statement."

"I watch TV as well."

"Ah gotcha, the ol' media barometer. Then it must be true. Not a single athlete is married to a curvy girl."

She smacked him on the chest. "Shut up."

"I'm just going to throw it out there, Bay, your assumption says more about you than it does about me and the women I sleep with."

Bailey sucked in a breath like his words had hit the mark.

Good, let her stew on that for a bit. "I'm up." He walked back to the dartboard and threw three bullseyes in a row.

"And that's how it's done," Ryan cheered.

Gonzo glanced at the scoreboard. His last turn had secured the win for the boys.

"Damn it," Kendall grumbled. "I want a rematch. You guys were already warmed up. We were cold."

"What? How were we warmed up?" Ryan scoffed.

"You'd just played baseball. We'd been sitting in the stands. You had an unfair advantage."

Gonzo flicked a glance at Bailey while the siblings bickered over Kendall having to cook. Bailey walked over to him and rested her head on his shoulder. "You're right. I'm sorry."

He wrapped his arm around her and pulled her against his side. "It's all good."

"Ever since Brad, I've been a little—" She flicked her wrist.

Gonzo's jaw clenched. He hated that she'd allowed some asshole to question how amazing she was. "Any guy would be lucky to have you, Bay."

She glanced up at him through her lashes. A sudden urge to kiss her instantly hit him. He clenched his fingers together to stop himself from threading his hand through her thick red hair and pulling her toward him.

A throat cleared beside him, and he pulled his attention off Bailey. Ryan stood to his left with a big smirk on his face. "We're gonna head back to the table. You guys sticking around or—?" Ryan asked.

What the hell was wrong with him? This was Bailey. He needed to knock it off. "Yeah, of course we're staying." He eyed Bailey's empty beer glass. "Let's get you another drink."

Ryan glanced at him and raised his eyebrow in question. Gonzo shoved him to get his friend to move back toward their table. Whatever that moment was between him and Bailey, it was done now and not up for discussion.

As they approached the table, he eyed the newcomers sitting with Peyton and Pete. "Holy shit, Aiden." Gonzo turned to his teammate's wife and gave her a hug. "Good to see you, Sloane. You guys never come out after games."

"We got a sitter so I could come to the game and I'm taking full advantage of it," Sloane said.

"You have a sitter and you guys came here?" Gonzo asked.

"We aren't staying long," Aiden said as he eyed his wife.

"We'll see," Sloane replied. "Aiden still gets to do this when you're on the road, but since we had Madison, I don't anymore, and I miss it."

"And we miss seeing you," Kendall said.

Gonzo pulled Bailey closer to him. "Bailey, this is Aiden Patel and his wife Sloane. Guys, this is my oldest friend, Bailey."

"Friend?" Sloane raised an eyebrow.

Why did everyone do that? "Yes, friend," he grumbled. He gestured for Bailey to take the vacant seat next to Sloane at the end of the table. Kendall hopped into the vacant seat beside Pete. Since there were no more chairs at the table, Ryan picked up Peyton, slid himself onto her seat, and placed her on his lap. She giggled and wrapped her arms around Ryan's neck.

Gonzo's chest tugged as he watched his friends cuddle at the table. He glanced at Bailey and felt an odd pull in his chest that he kind of wanted to do the same to her. Geez, he'd been spending too much time around couples lately, if that's where his head went.

"So Sloane, how's the daredevil business?" he asked.

Sloane rolled her eyes. "It's good, busy, which I love."

Bailey raised an eyebrow and looked at him, then turned to Sloane. "Daredevil business?"

"I run a skydiving company with my brother," Sloane said.

"Wow." Bailey's eyes widened. "I don't think I've even met someone who jumped out of a plane before, let alone someone who did that for a living. How did you get into that?"

Sloane chuckled. "I was upset after I got dumped and needed something to kick my ass into making some changes. I thought skydiving would do that. Little did I know what felt like a terrible decision after a crappy breakup turned out to be the best decision I could have made for myself."

"So you went skydiving for the first time after getting dumped?"

Gonzo shifted so he could see Bailey's face. Was she seriously thinking about jumping out of a plane because of Brad? "You aren't thinking about doing that are you?" he asked.

"What?" Bailey flicked a look at him. "No, no, I like my feet firmly on the ground."

"Well, if you change your mind, I've found nothing puts things in perspective quite like taking a leap." Sloane dug into her purse and handed Bailey a business card.

"How come you've never tried to get me to jump?" Gonzo asked.

"Well, one because if your contract is anything like Aiden's, skydiving is a no-no activity, and two, I think you'd be too scared to jump."

"Ack, how dare you say I'd be scared?" He pretended to be offended by the suggestion, then chuckled. "But there's zero chance I'd jump out of a plane even if it wasn't in my contract. I don't need to prove anything to anyone." Honestly, he thought it was insane to jump out of a plane, not that he'd say that to his teammate's wife.

Sloane rolled her eyes. "It's not about proving anything to anyone. Sometimes it's about proving something to yourself, or at least it was to me." Sloane glanced at Bailey as she spoke. Bailey flicked the business card between her fingers and nodded. "I'll keep it in mind." She stuck the card in a little pocket in her purse.

The TV screen above their table caught his eye and he shifted to watch the highlights from the league.

"Oh-ho, Gonz," Pete called when a clip of Gonzo hitting a home run flashed on the screen. They posted his stats so far for the season and the feeling of pride he felt made him smile. The TV cut to the highlights for New York and he glanced away from the screen to find Pete and Kendall watching him with amused looks on their faces. What was that about?

Suddenly he noticed that he'd been absently playing with Bailey's hair as he'd watched the TV. He pulled his fingers away from her hair and stuck his hands in his pockets. Bailey glanced over her shoulder at him.

"Sorry," he mumbled.

"For what?" she asked.

Had she not realized he'd been playing with her hair? He sure as hell wasn't going to admit to it if she hadn't known. It was kind of embarrassing. "Nothing, don't worry about it," he told her.

When he glanced back across the table, Pete raised an eyebrow at him. Gonzo pulled his hand out of his pocket and subtly flashed his friend the middle finger. Like the cocky bastard he was, Pete just smirked back at him. Gonzo grabbed his beer and took a sip. Despite what Pete thought, it didn't mean anything. Bailey was just his friend. Except his fingers itched to play with her hair again. Now that he knew how soft it felt against his skin, he couldn't help but wonder what it would feel like elsewhere. Fuck. "Anyone want to play pool?"

"I will," Aiden said.

"Cool." He turned to Bailey. "You good here?"

"Absolutely."

Thank god. He needed some space. Being around all these couples had clouded his brain for a minute, that's all. "Great, let's go, Aid," he said, pushing away from the table.

# CHAPTER ELEVEN

The next morning, Bailey stood outside Ananda Yoga & Wellness Center. Hopefully Peyton didn't oversell how amazing this studio was.

She pushed open the door, the bright crisp smell of some magical aromatherapy mixture instantly hit her nose. Oranges and something else. Whatever it was smelled amazing. She kicked off her flip-flops and set them on the shoe rack at the door, then wandered over to the check-in counter.

"Welcome," the woman behind the counter said as she flipped her braid behind her shoulder. "I'm Shyla. How can I help you?"

"Hi there, umm, I have an appointment with Rayne at 10:30 but wanted to drop in on the 9 o'clock hot yoga class. Rayne had said drop in was fine."

"Absolutely drop in is more than fine. Have you ever taken a hot yoga class before?"

"Once and if I'm honest, it wasn't my favorite thing, but Rayne suggested it might be good to try before my session with her." She shrugged. "I'm willing to give it a shot."

"Jeremy's classes are fantastic. I think you'll really like it."

"It's a man teaching?"

"Yes." Jenna studied her for a couple of seconds, then smiled. "He's amazing. You have nothing to worry about. I think you'll really like it if you give it a chance."

Well, that was embarrassing. Now she looked like some judgmental idiot. "Of course. I've just never had a male yoga teacher, so it surprised me." She held up her hand and reassured Shyla. "Pleasantly surprised me. I'm a sociologist, so I just—"

"Bailey?" a male voice said her name.

She turned toward the man. "Brandon? Hi. What are you doing here?" Gonzo's gigantic teammate was the last person she'd expected to see at the yoga studio.

His full lips turned up slightly as he smirked back at her. "Taking yoga."

"Right, of course." She chuckled. "Sorry, I just didn't picture you as a yoga guy."

"No? How did you picture me?" His gaze skimmed down her body.

What was happening here? Why did it seem like he was flirting?

"No, I haven't, I just, umm, what I meant was I assumed you worked out more like Gonzo, with the running and weights and all that. Not this." She flapped her hand to encompass the studio.

"I do all that as well. But Kia convinced me to do a session with Rayne and now this is part of the routine."

"Yeah, I'm trying out a class before an energy healing thing with Rayne that Peyton convinced me I needed to try. She got Rayne on the phone last night and organized everything before I had a chance to change my mind."

The corner of Brandon's eyes crinkled in amusement as his lip curved ever so slightly, almost like smiling wasn't something that came naturally to him. "Guess you'll be becoming a regular like me."

Bailey wrinkled her nose. "I'm not sure. As you can tell, I'm not really one to workout much."

Brandon's gaze swept down her body. "Once Rayne's gotten at you, you'll be a lifer like the rest of us."

"She's that good?"

"Yeah." He paused for several seconds. "So, what class are you here for?"

"Hot yoga?" Her voice hitched as she said it.

"You're not sure?" He chuckled.

"No, I'm sure. I—" She sighed. "I'm just not sure I'm gonna like the class."

"I hear ya. I didn't think I'd like it either." He hitched his yoga mat strap up his broad shoulder, drawing Bailey's attention to his size. The man was huge. "You ready?" he asked.

Bailey took a deep breath. "As I'll ever be." She followed Brandon down the hall to their studio. The sign on the wall said Fire studio. Geez, that sounded ominous.

Bailey stopped at the back of the class and set up her mat. Brandon laid his down beside her.

"You don't have to hide back here with me," she said.

"Nah, I always set up in the back. I don't want to block anyone's view of Jeremy."

"How tall are you?"

"6'5."

She'd never seen a man as muscular as him in any of the yoga classes she'd ever taken. Usually guys with muscles like him and Gonzo thought stretching was a waste of time.

"I can't imagine Gonzo coming to a yoga class."

"I tried to get him to come with me, but it's not his thing." He sat down on his black yoga mat. "Wasn't my thing before either. But my range of motion used to suck, so this helps. Having better movement helps my swing so my batting average is better."

"Really? I'm surprised Gonzo didn't want to try it then."

"He doesn't really need the help with his batting like the rest of us."

"Yeah, he's having a pretty great season."

"What's the deal with you two?" Brandon asked.

Bailey looked over to find him watching her intently. "We're friends, have been forever."

"Just friends?"

"Can you imagine Gonzo dating someone like me?"

He tilted his head to the side thoughtfully. "I don't know, but then I don't really know him that well."

"Well, trust me. I'm not his type."

A slim man walked into the classroom. "Welcome everyone, please take your mat."

Bailey stood at the top of her mat as the door to the studio shut. Instantly, it felt like the room warmed several degrees. What had she been thinking? She was going to melt in here.

Ethereal music played through the speakers, while Jeremy led them through some light flows to begin class.

Bailey bit back a groan as she eased into her first down dog of the class. She heard a little snicker from beside her, and she scowled over at Brandon. "Shut it," she whispered.

His chuckle grew louder. "Didn't say anything. I'm just not used to hearing f-bombs in here."

She whipped her head to the side. "Did I swear?"

"Yep." Brandon's eyes sparkled with amusement.

"No talking, please," Jeremy admonished.

Bailey scrunched up her face at Brandon. He flashed her a wink and continued to follow Jeremy's instructions.

Forty minutes later, Bailey had a paddling pool worth of sweat lingering on her mat. She'd moved past feeling like she wanted to puke from the heat and slid into some kind of weird floating feeling that she never wanted to end. Her body moved and stretched in ways she didn't know it could.

Jeremy stopped at her mat. "Press your hips out slightly." He stepped toward her. "Is it okay if I touch you to show you?"

"Of course," she replied.

He placed his hand on her lower back. "Breathe into your sacrum."

She took a deep breath and exhaled.

He tapped his hand where he wanted her to breathe. "Bring your breath here."

How the hell was she supposed to breathe into that area? It was nowhere near her lungs.

"Picture your breath moving through your body and into your sacrum," Jeremy said.

Whatever, buddy. Bailey took a breath and visualized the breath moving down her body and into the space beneath Jeremy's hand. Suddenly, the muscles in her lower back released and a wave of emotion swept through her, making her suck in a breath.

"That's it," Jeremy said. "And again, deep breath in and send the breath."

Bailey took another deep breath and felt it move through her body. She exhaled audibly.

"Beautiful." Jeremy released his hand on her back and continued walking around the room. "Now let's breathe into the root chakra," he said.

She flowed through the last several movements of class, listening to the sound of Jeremy's instructions. As she lay in shavasana for the final pose of class, dripping in more sweat than she'd ever imagined was humanly possible, her body felt better than she could ever remember.

"You can stay here for a couple more minutes or if you're ready, roll to your side for a moment and come into a seated position."

Bailey rolled to her side and sat up crossed legged on her mat.

"Hands to prayer. Deep breath in and out. And bow," Jeremy said. "Namaste."

"Namaste." Bailey raised her head and sighed.

"Well?" Brandon said from beside her.

Bailey glanced over at him and smiled. Why was it that men looked so good all sweaty and she was sure she looked like she'd been dragged in from the rain?

When she didn't speak, Brandon chuckled. "What time's your appointment with Rayne?"

"10:30." Her head felt all light and floaty, and yet she was weirdly exhilarated.

Brandon shifted on his mat beside her. "You all good?"

"I think so," she mumbled. She stood up and instantly the world spun around her.

Brandon's arm clamped around hers as he held her up from falling.

"Whoa." She laughed nervously. "Got a little dizzy there."

"What'd you eat today?" Brandon asked.

"Umm nothing, I don't like to eat before I workout."

"Are you kidding me?" He shook his head. "All right, let's go," he ordered.

"What? Where?" Feeling a little more stable on her feet, she blinked up at the giant beside her.

"We're getting you a smoothie before your appointment with Rayne."

"I don't need a smoothie. I just stood up too fast."

"It wasn't really up for discussion, Bailey."

She placed her hands on her hips and glared up at the big man. "You realize I'm a grownup, right?"

He glared back at her. "Then how about you act like it and put some fucking food in your belly before you pass out."

The lightheadedness continued to make her vision waiver. "Fine. But just for the record, there's a nice way to look after someone and there's whatever the hell that was." Bailey attempted to storm away and stumbled slightly as her legs buckled.

Brandon's arm clamped around her elbow. "Duly noted." He held her steady while she got her feet back under her.

Jeremy came jogging over. "Oh my gosh, are you okay?"

"Fine. Just stood up too fast," she mumbled.

"And didn't eat or drink anything today," Brandon added.

"Narc." She scowled at him, then turned to Jeremy. "Sorry, I don't know what's wrong with me. I was completely fine all during the class." She smiled, hoping to reassure him it was nothing he had done wrong with the class.

"It can happen like that sometimes after you work out too hard without enough fuel." Brandon leaned down and grabbed her sweaty mat and quickly rolled it up and shoved it into her bag. He grabbed his bag off the floor and slung both bags over his shoulder. "All right, let's get you a smoothie and some fresh air."

"Good idea." Jeremy's head bobbed in agreement. "I hope you enjoyed the class but promise me you'll eat first next time. It's important you fuel your body properly before strenuous exercise."

"I know, that was my bad. I was just thinking it's yoga." She waved her hand. "It didn't occur to me it would be a problem."

"Hot yoga is a bit different because you sweat so much. It's easy to get dehydrated."

"Lesson learned." Bailey smiled. "I did really enjoy the class a lot. Thank you."

"My pleasure. Now go get something in your body. Drink lots of liquids today."

"Got it."

Brandon gestured toward the door. "Let's go."

"You really are bossy, you know?"

"So I've been told."

Once in the lobby, she followed Brandon over to a side entrance that led into the vegan cafe next door. She looked up at the menu and wrinkled her nose. Who named these things? *Ananda Sunrise. Soul Good. Ananda Bandha.* Sheesh. Although she had to admit the Ananda Sunrise sounded pretty good. Coconut water, peaches, strawberries, banana, and OJ? Yes, please!

"What'll it be?" Brandon asked.

"Can I get the Ananda Sunrise, please?"

"And can I get the Green Machine and we'll both have protein in there too please," Brandon ordered.

"Of course," the woman behind the counter said.

Brandon pulled out his credit card and tapped the machine before she could even pull out her wallet from her bag.

"Thank you," Bailey said.

"No problem. I'd never hear the end of it if I let you pass out."

"I wasn't going to pass out." Although she could admit to herself at least that it had been close. "But thank you, I really appreciate it."

The woman set their smoothies on the counter in front of them. Brandon grabbed them both, then handed her the pink one. She eyed the green concoction in his hand. "That looks disgusting."

He put the straw up to his mouth and took a big sip without saying a word. Brandon glanced at his watch. "Let's get you some fresh air before your appointment while you pound your drink."

As they made their way into the parking lot, Brandon veered toward a black sports car. The trunk lifted as they approached. He threw his yoga mat inside and slammed it shut so quickly Bailey barely even had to slow her pace. At Gonzo's SUV, she pushed the button to raise the trunk.

"Is this Gonzo's?" Brandon asked as he threw her yoga mat inside.

"It is. I had to get rid of my car before I moved, so he's letting me use his." And thank god for that. After getting stuck with half of the non-refundable wedding deposits, her bank account was a little slim. Fortunately, Gonzo had two vehicles so he didn't even miss this one.

"You sure there isn't something going on with you two?"

"I'm sure."

"He must really trust you. I don't let anyone drive my ride."

"Not even your family?"

"Fuck no," he muttered.

Bailey eyed Brandon. As much as she wanted to say more, his body language made it very clear the subject was off limits.

"So, you've been here a couple of seasons now. How do you like San Diego?"

"It's good." Brandon turned left and started walking down the block. "How'd you know I've been here for a couple of years?"

"Because I'm a Hawks fan, so I know who our players are."

"Oh yeah?" His eyebrow hitched up like he didn't quite believe her.

"Yeah, ask me something."

"Okay, who was the winning pitcher when we won the World Series?"

Bailey rolled her eyes. "Ryan Graves."

"Okay, that was too easy." Brandon narrowed his eyes thoughtfully. "Who owns the team?"

"I think it's a group of people actually, but the face is Matthias Hoffman."

"Damn, I'm impressed."

"Told ya," Bailey said.

Brandon took a long sip of his gross looking green drink. "How about you? What brought you here?"

"A job." There was no way she was getting into the whole thing with her ex, with some guy she barely knew.

"What do you do?"

"I'm a sociology professor."

"No shit?"

"Nope."

"Very cool." Brandon glanced at his watch. "You better pound that thing, Rayne will be waiting for you."

She took a big sip, then another as they walked back toward the studio.

"How you feeling? Any better?" he asked.

Embarrassed, she took another sip before answering. "I'm fine, thank you."

"No problem." Back at the studio parking lot, Brandon held out his hand. "Give me your phone."

"Why?"

"So you can call me if you want to take another class."

"I think I can just organize coming back through Rayne."

Brandon chuckled. "Yeah, I was thinking more like having someone beside you to catch you when you pass out."

"Haha, smart ass," she said.

Brandon flicked his fingers for her to give him her phone. "Brandon, I'm not really interested in being anyone's pity date."

His head snapped up. "What?"

"I heard you and Gonzo the other night when he said you didn't date women like me. And I appreciate you being so nice, but I don't really want to be anyone's pity date."

"What are you talking about? Gonzo didn't say that because he thought it was a pity date, he was making it known you're a good girl. And I don't date good girls."

Good girl? What the hell was that? She'd had a one-night stand before. "I'm not a good girl."

Brandon snorted. "Ugh, yeah you are."

She planted her hands on her hips. He couldn't tell that just by looking at her. That was rude.

Brandon chuckled and held up his hands. "Easy Tiger, it wasn't an insult. I respect the hell out of it. I'm just not a relationship guy. Besides, I'd have to be an idiot not to see what's happening with you and Gonzo." He flicked his finger for her to give him the phone again. "Give me your phone. I could use a yoga buddy."

"What do you mean? There's nothing going on between us."

"Not yet maybe. But I'm gonna have fun bugging the shit out of both of you till you admit it."

Yeah, right, if only that was true. But she'd given up on that childhood dream back in high school. She handed him her phone. "Gonzo's not really a relationship guy either."

"I don't know. Eventually we all meet that person we can't walk away from, and I think you might be his." Brandon typed in his number, then handed her phone back. "Now you better hurry up, Rayne will be waiting."

"Good luck at your next game," she said as she took her phone back. Was he right? Could there be something between her and Gonzo? Things felt different between them ever since she'd moved in. Sometimes she'd swear he was looking at her like a woman instead of Bailey, the best friend, but she'd written it off as wishful thinking. Could it be more? No. She shook her head. She was just being stupid. If she couldn't hold the attention of Brad, there was no way she'd even get the attention of someone like Gonzo, let alone hold it. It was stupid to even dream otherwise. She should just be thankful they were friends, like they'd always been. Wishing for something more would only make things awkward because it was never going to happen.

Bailey walked back into Ananda. A gorgeous brunette stood behind the counter. Her brown hair shone in the sun.

"Bailey?" the woman asked.

"Yes."

The ethereal goddess smiled. "I'm Rayne."

Of course she was.

Rayne stepped out from behind the counter. Her shirt flowed down her body and hung off her shoulder in that effortless way it did on some women. Bailey had never been able to pull off that kind of look. Probably because she required an industrial strength bra to keep her boobs contained. A wave of envy stabbed Bailey in the gut and she bit it back. Nope, she wasn't going there.

"Come on back," Rayne said.

As they walked down the hall, Rayne glanced back over her shoulder. "Thanks for filling out the forms on-line. It gives me a great starting point."

Starting point? That was the most thorough form she'd ever filled out in her life. It covered everything from when she ate, to her menstrual cycle, to whether she preferred hot or cold liquids to drink.

"Sure, no problem," Bailey replied.

Rayne stepped into a room. There was a massage table on one side of the room and a pair of comfy looking chairs facing each other on the other. Some kind of aroma puffed out from a vaporizer in the corner.

"Have a seat," Rayne said, indicating the chair against the wall.

Bailey sat down and stared in awe as Rayne dropped onto the opposite chair and pulled her legs up under herself like a pretzel. The human body wasn't supposed to move like that.

"Peyton tells me you just moved to San Diego?"

"I did yes."

"How do you like it so far?"

"Good, I guess. It's a bit early to tell."

"You came here for a job?" Rayne asked.

"I suppose." If it hadn't been for Brad getting a transfer, she probably never would have even considered moving. She'd been happy at her job. She'd been on the tenure track, getting recognized in her field. But Brad needed to move for his job and she'd agreed that following him would be the best thing for their relationship.

"What do you mean you suppose?" Rayne pressed.

"Umm." How much did she really want to get into with this woman? She was here for some kind of fancy massage, not therapy.

The other woman smiled kindly. "This is a safe space, Bailey. You don't have to go into anything you don't feel comfortable talking about. Why don't I tell you a bit about what to expect and we can go from there?"

"Okay."

"As you know, I'm a licensed massage therapist, but I also combine massage with various other modalities of body and energy work."

"Okay? What does that mean?"

"If means depending on what your body tells me, I may go in a slightly different direction with a treatment than what we have originally discussed."

"What my body tells you?" Bailey couldn't keep the skepticism out of her tone.

The corner of Rayne's eyes crinkled with a smile. "Energy gets stored in the body for various reasons, and sometimes it gets stuck. It might feel like a heaviness in your chest, sometimes it's a little pinch of a muscle in a certain area. We'll start with some chakra work and then move into moving some energy, then dig deeper into the muscles as needed."

"Moving some energy with my chakras, got it." Wow, who knew Gonzo was friends with someone so new-agey? She couldn't picture him talking about chakras and energy.

"I take it this is a bit different for you."

"You could say that, yes. Honestly, I've only had a couple of massages in my life, period."

"Really? Why's that?"

"I don't know. I don't really love strangers touching my body."

"That's helpful for me to know. Are there any areas that you would like me to work on or anywhere that you aren't comfortable with me touching?"

"Umm, my neck is always tight, but whose isn't, right?" She chuckled.

"Anywhere you're uncomfortable with since you said you don't really like being touched by strangers?"

Pretty much everywhere, she thought. She settled for saying, "My stomach, I guess."

"Okay, is that a hard and fast don't touch or is it something you're willing to explore?"

Bailey shifted in her seat. "Umm I don't know." The muscles in her stomach didn't hurt. The scar from her surgery had healed perfectly. She couldn't imagine energy, or whatever, would guide Rayne to need to touch there.

"The reason I ask is that your stomach is a pretty central part of your body. It stores a lot of energy and it can get pretty blocked and tight."

The idea of someone as physically perfect as Rayne touching her stomach was mortifying. "I'm sure it does, but...it's...it's just my stomach." She puffed out a breath. "You wouldn't understand."

"Why wouldn't I understand?"

Bailey snorted. "Look at you."

"I'm sorry. How does the way I look have anything to do with my ability to be compassionate and sensitive to what's needed?"

"It's not that I don't think you could be compassionate, I just don't think you could ever understand."

If Bailey hadn't been watching, she wouldn't have seen the way Rayne's jaw clenched slightly before she rubbed her lips together on a breath. "Bailey, please don't do to me, what you hate having done to you."

Yikes, was that what she was doing? She sure hoped not. "That's not what I'm doing."

"Isn't it?" Rayne asked.

Shame clenched in her gut, making her even more aware of her body. "Sorry, that wasn't my intention at all. I'm just..." She looked up at the ceiling as she tried to figure out how to explain herself. Screw it. Maybe Rayne was right and she did have a lot of stuck emotion that needed to be moved. She sure as hell had a pit in her stomach at the moment and it seemed to be swirling like a vortex because the more she thought about her body image, the more emotional she felt. "I hate my body. I've never liked it, but after my last relationship I...I don't know, I'm kind of ashamed of it."

Rayne's eyes softened, and she smiled in a way that made Bailey think maybe she understood. Although how that was possible, she didn't know.

"Oh Bailey, I understand that feeling more than you could ever know." Rayne's mouth clicked. After a couple of seconds, she finally spoke. "I had an eating disorder in high school."

"What?" Bailey's eyes widened as she looked at the other woman. Rayne looked like the picture-perfect female body.

"I spent most of 11th grade in treatment. It was pretty bad. So I may look different than you do, but I'm very well aware of body image issues, shame and all the other feelings we can have about who we are or aren't, as the case may be. That's why I do this kind of work and why I'm so confident in saying emotion and energy get stuck and need to be worked through."

"Wow, umm, I don't really know what to say," Bailey said.

"The only reason I shared that with you is because I thought it might help. I get it, Bailey, and I really think I can help you. But I need you to trust me just a little. Can you do that?"

Could she? If it would help her flush through all the damage Brad had caused, she'd be willing to do just about anything. "I can try."

"Good." Rayne stood up. "I'll let you get undressed. Underwear on or off, it's up to you whatever you're most comfortable with. I'll get you to lie on your stomach with your face in the cradle and I'll be back in a few minutes."

Bailey watched as Rayne left the room. The second the door closed, she hopped up and started quickly undressing. She had no idea how long Rayne would give her to undress and the last thing she wanted was for Rayne to open the door when she was standing there in nothing but her panties. It was one thing to be practically naked on the table. It was a whole other thing to be caught trying to awkwardly peel off a sweaty pair of leggings with your bare boobs hanging out.

She quickly folded up her clothes in a neat pile, then jumped onto the table on her belly. She awkwardly shimmied the sheet up to cover as much of her bare back as she could. After a couple of seconds, she shifted to get more comfortable, then shifted again as she tried to relax.

"Grr," she groaned. God, she hated that she'd let Brad change how she felt about herself. Fuck you, Brad. No more. She exhaled all the breath in her lungs and her body let out a little sigh as it melted into the table a bit. A light knock sounded on the door. "Yes," Bailey called out. A second later, the door snicked open.

"I'm just going to put on some music and we'll get started," Rayne told her.

Here goes nothing.

# CHAPTER TWELVE

Gonzo sat down at their gate and pulled his earbuds out of his carry-on bag. As he flipped through his playlist, someone stopped near him. His gaze traveled up to the giant form in front of him. He knew it was Brandon Sims before his eyes even hit the guy's face. Very few people took up as much space as this guy did. Gonzo popped out one earbud. "Hey man, you ready to hit the windy city?"

"You bet. What about you?"

He rolled his shoulders. He'd be a lot better once they were in Chicago. Soaring through the air in a giant tin can wasn't natural. But there was no way in hell he was admitting to his teammate that even after all the flying they did, he still hated to fly. No weakness. "I'm definitely ready to kick Chicago's Ass." He held up his hand and Brandon smacked it as expected.

"So how's Bailey doing?" Brandon asked.

Gonzo leaned back in his chair and crossed his arms over his chest as he looked up at the other man. "She's fine."

"Good, I'm glad she's feeling better."

"What do you mean, feeling better?"

Brandon rocked back on his heels and held up his hands. "Whoa, fuck. I'm just making sure she's okay after this morning."

"When did you see Bailey?"

"Geez dude, for someone who's just friends with the girl, you sure have the whole possessive thing going." Brandon laughed. "Relax man, I'm not after your girl."

"She's not my girl," Gonzo grumbled.

"Could have fooled me," Brandon muttered under his breath.

"Why were you with Bailey this morning?"

"We both were at Rayne's for yoga. Bailey hadn't eaten, so the heat and everything affected her more than normal."

"What do you mean, it affected her?"

"She got dizzy."

Gonzo pushed up from his seat. "What do you mean, she got dizzy?"

"Relax, man, she's fine. I got her a smoothie and some fresh air before her appointment with Rayne. I'm sure she would have said something if she wasn't feeling well when she got home."

Why hadn't Bailey mentioned it to him? "Yeah probably."

"Rayne would have called you if there was a problem." Brandon clapped his hand on Gonzo's shoulder. "Bailey seems really cool."

"She is."

"So you and her?" Brandon raised his eyebrow in question.

"Nah."

"Interesting. So she's single?"

"No."

"No? Huh could have sworn she was."

"Yes, she's single. No, you can't ask her out."

Brandon's head cocked to the side. "Why not exactly?"

"Because I don't want you hitting on my best friend."

If at all possible, Brandon seemed to get even bigger. "Why's that?"

"Bailey is..." How did he describe her? Naïve wasn't the right word. But she lived in a different world than they did. Academia and baseball were light years apart.

"Too good for me?"

"Yeah." Bailey was too good for everyone. He couldn't think of a single person who deserved her.

"Right. Nice to know how you see me." Brandon turned away and then spun back. "For the record, I'm not interested in dating Bailey. She's not my type."

Offended on her behalf, Gonzo squared off with his teammate. "Why the hell not?"

"Are you fucking kidding me? First, I'm not good enough for her and now you're annoyed I agree."

"What do you mean, you agree? You said she wasn't your type."

"Exactly."

"What the hell does that mean?"

"It means I don't chase after women who are in love with someone else."

Gonzo's chest tightened. Who the hell was Bailey in love with?

"My god, you are as fucking stupid as your friend." Brandon pinched the bridge of his nose. "The line between friend and lover isn't that wide, dude. Figure it out." Brandon turned and walked several chairs over and dropped into one, away from the rest of the team. The big man pulled the headphones from his neck up and over his ears.

What was Brandon talking about? Bailey wasn't in love with him. What the hell had they talked about that would give him that impression?

His phone buzzed and Bailey's name flashed across the screen. And a little zip went through his stomach. Fucking Brandon and his bullshit theories.

Gonzo unlocked his phone and clicked on the text. A picture with bottles of bubble bath covered most of his bathroom floor. With the caption.

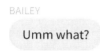

BAILEY

Umm what?

He snorted out a laugh and texted back.

GONZO

'shrugs'

BAILEY

Nope, you aren't getting out of it that easily

GONZO

What? I like bubble baths

BAILEY

There's like and then there's slipping into the problem category. I think we both know where this falls. You have 36 different kinds of bubble bath. Who needs that many?

BAILEY

There's like and then there's slipping into the problem category. I think we both know where this falls. You have 36 different kinds of bubble bath. Who needs that many?

GONZO

Hey judgy. If you weren't snooping you wouldn't find shit.

BAILEY

I wasn't snooping I was familiarizing myself with my new home.

GONZO

In my bathroom?

BAILEY

I figured you'd have bubble bath. But this? WOW!!!!!!!!!!!!!!

GONZO

Well with that attitude I'm not sharing.

BAILEY

Ahh come on. I'm just kidding.

GONZO

Too late. You blew it. And yes there's a lot of bottles but I know what each one is.

BAILEY

Bullshit.

GONZO

I do.

BAILEY

There is zero chance you're using a bubble bath called Winter Wonderland.

He had a bubble bath called that?

GONZO

I am. It's perfect for the holidays.

There was no way she could argue with him about that.

BAILEY

You are so busted. It's pine cone and juniper berry. You HATE all things pine scented. I can't even believe you have this in your cupboard.

Ew, that sounded disgusting. Why did he have that?

GONZO

Okay I guess I could let you have that one.

BAILEY

You're ridiculous and just for that I'm taking one of your four bottles of lavender bubble bath. No one needs four bottles.

Four bottles? Why the hell did he have four bottles? Maybe she was right and he had a problem.

GONZO

Fine but only because I'm a good roommate.

BAILEY

Whatever you need to tell yourself, bubble
boy.

GONZO

Bubble boy? Now that's just rude.

BAILEY

If the bubble bath fits...

GONZO

I was going to offer to let you use my tub
since it's better but now I'm not.

BAILEY

Whoa, I can use your tub?

GONZO

Not anymore you can't.

BAILEY

I'm sorry. If anything you're the bubble man,
not boy.

BAILEY

Now can I use your tub?

BAILEY

Please.

GONZO

I suppose. But that's King of the Bubbles to you.

BAILEY

Got it. Guess I'm going to have to go back to calling you Ram instead of Gonzo.

BAILEY

Gotta go. I've got a steaming tub of bubbles to jump into.

Shit. Now he was picturing Bailey naked in his tub. Not good.

"What's that look for?" Smitty asked as he dropped into the seat beside him.

Gonzo closed the text thread before looking up. "What look?"

"I don't know? That goofy look on your face. Who you texting?"

"No one, just Bailey."

Smitty shifted in his seat. "Bailey, huh? How's that going?"

"So far, so good." Surprisingly good, actually. Sure, it had only been five days, but after two he was ready to kill his siblings when they came to visit.

"Not weird living with a girl?"

"Not yet."

"That'll change once her stuff starts taking over everything. What was once your half will now become your quarter." Smitty shook his head.

"Little different when you're sharing a closet. I'm not too worried about it since we both have our own space.

"Just wait."
"Yeah, not gonna happen."

# CHAPTER THIRTEEN

H e needed to get laid, and fast. Maybe then he could stop thinking about his best friend. What she looked like, what she smelled like, what she'd feel like underneath him.

Damn. Gonzo banged the back of his head against the elevator wall as he waited for it to ascend to his apartment. He was just gonna drop off his bag and head out to meet Sims and Hernandez. No matter how badly he wanted to stay home and hang out with Bailey, he wasn't going to do it. He was meeting the guys, finding a willing woman, and fucking her brains out. Ever since Bailey had moved in, he'd been feeling all weird and confused. Over the past few weeks, it was just getting worse. He kept choosing to hang with her instead of going out like he normally did. It was ridiculous. He'd been acting like they were a couple or something instead of just friends. It was fucking with his head and he didn't like it. Tonight, that stopped. And the best way he could think of to stop thinking about one woman was to fuck another.

He pushed open the door to his apartment. It was quiet. No sign of Bailey in the main living area. His stomach fell. The fact he was that disappointed not to see her solidified how badly he needed to fuck her out of his system. He wandered toward his bedroom. Bailey's bedroom door stood open as he walked past. He glanced inside. Her bed looked like a tangled mess. The sheets were half-on-half-off the bed like she'd been thrashing around in them. Instantly, a wave of jealousy gripped his chest and he clenched his jaw. Was she having sex? The idea of Bailey having sex with anyone but him made him want to hurt someone. That was exactly why he needed to go out tonight and find someone else.

Suddenly, he heard the telltale sound of someone being sick coming from Bailey's bathroom. He dropped his bag on the floor and rushed toward the sound.

At the bathroom door, he paused briefly when he saw Bailey slumped over the toilet, her head resting in her arms like she was too tired to move.

"Ah, Bay," he said. That looked rough.

She lifted her head slightly and cringed. "God, please tell me you aren't seeing me like this."

He stepped further into the bathroom. "Afraid so, babe." Sweat made her hair stick to her head. Her normally pale skin had a grayish green hue. His girl looked rough.

He grabbed a washcloth from the linen cupboard in the corner of the room and ran it under cold water. He placed the cool fabric against the back of her neck and she let out a loud sigh.

"Thank you," she said weakly.

"How long you been sick?"

"Forever."

He chuckled. Been there.

Suddenly, Bailey reared back. "Get out!" she yelled a second before her body convulsed.

There was no way he was going anywhere. He swept her hair back from her face and pulled it into a pony with his hand.

Bailey groaned. After several more convulsions. She finally emptied her stomach and dropped her head against the toilet seat. "Kill me now," she groaned.

He rubbed small circles on her back the way his mom used to when he was sick.

After several minutes, she lifted her head and pushed back from the toilet. "I think I'm done."

He helped her stand up and walked her to the counter, where he liberally added toothpaste to her brush and handed it to her.

He took in her sweat stained T-shirt and blotchy face as she leaned weakly against the counter to brush her teeth.

"Why don't you hop in the shower? Nothing makes me feel better when I'm sick than a nice shower."

"Don't wanna," she grumbled.

He chuckled. "I know, but you'll feel better. While you're doing that, I'll change your sheets."

"Oh god, you don't have to do that." She closed her eyes. "This is mortifying."

"Why? I've seen you puke before."

Bailey raised her head and looked at him, then smiled sadly. "Right." With a sigh, she glanced at herself in the mirror. "Maybe a shower would be good."

Happy to have something he could do to help, he turned the shower on to heat up. "You need help getting in?"

"God no, there's no chance I'm adding to the humiliation of this by having you help me undress."

The idea of seeing Bailey naked even under these conditions made his dick spring to life. Maybe it was better she didn't need help. The last thing she needed when she felt like shit was him leering at her like a perv. "Kay, well call me if you need help."

"Will do." She slouched against the counter and closed her eyes.

"You sure you don't need help?"

"What?" She blinked at him. "No, I'll be fine." She pushed her pajama pants down her legs and stumbled as she tried to step out of them.

"Just let me help you," he said.

Tears filled her eyes when she looked up at him. "Ah, Bailey." He stepped toward her and pulled her into a hug. Her entire body slumped against him as he wrapped her tightly in his arms. The smell of puke drifted to his nose. Yuck, it must be in her hair. He could only imagine how shitty she must be feeling.

"Let me help you. I promise not to look."

"Like you'd want to," she mumbled.

Oh, he definitely wanted to. That was kind of the problem. But what kind of asshole would he be if he took advantage of the opportunity when she was sick.

"Come on. Let's get you cleaned up. If you need me to come in and wash your hair just holler."

"Thanks, Gonz."

"What are friends for?" They were friends, first and foremost, despite what his body had been feeling lately, and he needed to remember that.

"Friends," Bailey replied. Her voice sounded almost sad when she said it. What was that about? Was she having feelings for him as well? He glanced at her puke covered hair and pale face. Even if she was, now was not the time to discuss it.

"All right, let's get you in the shower." He walked her closer to the shower door and pulled it open. A light spray of water misted their skin without the door to block it. Once he had her in place, he closed his eyes and peeled her T-shirt up and off her body. It took everything in him to keep his eyes closed. He'd never wanted to peek at something so bad in his life.

He felt Bailey move away from him and a second later, he heard the shower door click shut.

Forcing himself not to give into temptation and look, he left the bathroom.

Back in the bedroom, he pulled open dresser drawers until he found the one with her pajamas. He grabbed what looked like a comfy pair, then continued to root around until he found her underwear. He grabbed the first pair of panties he saw. Knocking once on the bathroom door, he peeked his head inside. "I'm just gonna leave some clothes on the counter for you."

"Thanks."

Gonzo stared down at the ground as he made his way to the counter. Bailey let out a little groan of satisfaction.

He knew it was just that satisfied feeling that came from hot water hitting sore muscles, but the sound made him think of sex. He needed to get the hell out of here. She was in no place for him to be thinking about her like this. She trusted him as her friend.

He dropped her clothes on the counter and hustled out of the room.

While he waited for her to finish in the shower, he quickly changed the sheets and threw the dirty ones in the wash.

He pulled his phone out of his pocket and typed out a quick text to Brandon to let him know he wouldn't be meeting them after all. May as well get comfy since it looked like he was staying home tonight. He chucked his dirty travel clothes into the laundry basket and pulled on a pair of sweats and a T-shirt then made his way back to Bailey's room to wait for her.

After several minutes, the bathroom door opened and Bailey stepped out. Although still ridiculously pale, she looked a million times better after her shower.

"How you feeling?" He asked.

"Better thanks." She slowly made her way toward the bed. Her movement was slow and painful, like every muscle she had hurt.

He pulled back the sheets and helped her climb into bed.

Once he had her all settled, she looked up at him. "Gonz, I feel like shit. Can you just cuddle me for a bit?"

His chest pounded. Climbing in bed with her was probably a horrible idea, but how could he say no? "Uh yeah, sure." He peeled back the other side of the bed and crawled in beside her. "How do you want to be? You want to lie on my chest or have me spoon you?"

"Spoon please."

He tucked his arm under her head and pulled her against his body. She fit perfectly against him. She sighed and snuggled back, nestling her ass against his crotch. Fuck. The road to hell was paved with snuggling your sick friend, apparently. He racked his brain for things to think about other than how good she felt as he willed his cock to stay down.

"I love you, Gonzo, you're the best," she sighed sleepily.

"Love you too, Bay," he replied like he always did when she said it. For the first time, the words caught in his throat, and he couldn't help but wonder if it was because the meaning of the words were starting to change. Now what was he supposed to do?

Bailey shifted back against the warm, male body behind her. A hard cock pressed up against her ass. "Mmm," she wiggled to get closer. Suddenly, her eyes popped open. Hang on a second. Why was there an aroused man behind her?

She peeled open her eyes and saw a hairy male arm wrapped around her, cupping her breast. Definitely not dreaming. She'd recognize that arm anywhere. Holy shit, Gonzo had her boob in his hand and he was obviously excited. *Oh my god, oh my god, oh my god*. What should she do? She opened her mouth, her tongue stuck to the roof of her mouth like a dry sponge.

Immediately, memories of the night before flashed through her mind. Gonzo holding her hair as she puked, him holding a damp cloth to her head. And the pathetic way she'd begged him to cuddle her after.

Mortified, she scrunched up her face and cringed. He wasn't in her bed because he wanted her. He was here because she was his best friend. And his body was having a very normal reaction to having a boob in his hand and an ass rubbed against his cock while he slept. The moment he realized it was her, he was going to jump out of this bed like the sheets were on fire and she'd really rather not wait for that to happen. It was bad enough she'd practically sleep assaulted him by rubbing herself all over him. The last thing she needed was to see the look on his face when he realized it.

She eased his hand off her breast and slid out from under his arm. She was just shifting her body toward the edge of the mattress when he spoke. "Where you going?" he asked.

"Umm, I need to go brush my teeth," she squeaked. How was it possible his voice sounded even sexier when it was all rough from sleep and hers sounded like one of the chipmunks?

Gonzo scrubbed his hands over his face, like he was waking himself up, then shifted his body on the mattress. His eyes widened and he shot her a look and winced. "Please tell me I didn't harpoon you with my morning wood."

"Nope, you didn't." There was no way she was admitting that to him.

"Thank fuck, the last thing you want when you're feeling like shit is a dick literally stabbing you in the back. If I did, sorry."

Bailey glanced over at him. Why did he look so calm about it? Not even a hint of embarrassment about her knowing he was aroused. Did he wake up like that so often it didn't even phase him?

"How you feeling?" he asked.

"A lot better, thanks. Sorry about last night. When I asked you to cuddle me, I didn't mean you had to stay all night."

"Nah, it's fine. I tried to leave a couple times, but you just kept wrapping around me, mumbling about the best teddy bear ever. With that endorsement, how could I possibly leave?"

Bailey's eyes widened. "Please tell me you're joking."

"Nope." He chuckled. "For my birthday, I kind of want you to get me a human teddy bear T-shirt."

Bailey closed her eyes and willed the bed to open up and swallow her. This just kept getting better and better. "I'm so sorry," she mumbled.

"Nothing to be sorry for, Bay. Not the first time I've seen you puke. I'm sure it won't be the last." He stretched, drawing her attention to the way his T-shirt pulled tight against his biceps. How the hell she'd compared him to a teddy bear when the man was rock hard, she'd never know.

"Besides, you were like my own little blast furnace. I slept like a log." Gonzo looked at her and his forehead wrinkled. "Why are you being all weird?"

"I'm not being weird," she replied, forcing herself not to look at his stomach as he scratched his bare skin. Why couldn't he scratch on top of his clothes like a normal person? Unable to help herself, she flicked a quick glance, then instantly regretted it when her gaze dropped to below his waist.

"Busted." He laughed. "You totally just looked at my dick."

"What? I did not." She shoved off the bed and stood up.

"It's okay, Bay, I stabbed you while I was sleeping and now you want to know if it looks as good as it felt. I can't blame ya, really."

She stormed toward the washroom. "You wish, buddy," she called over her shoulder.

He mumbled something, but she couldn't make out what it was as she closed the bathroom door.

Too embarrassed to go back out, she flipped on the shower. She was just about to step in when Gonzo knocked on the bathroom door. "I'm just grabbing a quick shower as well, Bay. I'll probably be gone when you get out. We're on the road for ten days this time, so I'll see you when we get back."

Ten days. He was going to be gone for ten days. She wrapped a towel around herself and pulled open the door. Gonzo's eyes widened and his nostrils flared as his gaze scanned her body. She glanced down to make sure she was fully covered. She was.

"Thanks for looking after me, Gonz. I really appreciate."

"Anytime. Glad you feel better." He leaned in and pressed a kiss against her forehead. "Take it easy while I'm gone."

He turned to leave. She closed the door and slumped against it. Her hand touched her forehead where he'd kissed just a moment ago. Stupid, Bailey, stupid. She couldn't have feelings for Gonzo. That was never gonna happen. Looked like she had ten days to get over her stupid crush on her best friend.

# CHAPTER FOURTEEN

"So what have you been doing while I've been away? You done all the tourist stuff yet?"

Bailey shrugged. "Not really. I've gone to the pier and the beach a few times."

"You been to Old Town?"

"No, not yet."

"You want to go there for dinner?" he asked.

Bailey's eyes brightened. "Yes. But are you sure you want to do that? It's pretty touristy and I'd imagine that would be a pain for you."

"Nah, it'll be fine. Plus, there's good food. Leave in half an hour?"

"I'll be ready." Bailey hopped up from the couch and hurried down the hall to her room.

It was nice having her here. The apartment didn't feel so empty. The second he'd opened the door, he'd known she was home and he hadn't even seen her yet. The apartment just felt different.

The start of the season had been tough. For the first time in his career, he'd been lonely. Now that his closest teammates were all in committed relationships, he was on his own a lot more. They didn't want to go for beers when they got back to town. They were too eager to get home. He understood it, but it still sucked for him. Until now. Having Bailey here changed that.

He wandered into his bedroom and headed straight into the walk-in closet. The zipper stuck on his beat-up overnight bag. The brown leather bag had been one of his first purchases after he'd signed with the Hawks' farm team. Since then, the old bag had gone everywhere with him. There were a lot of memories in this thing. The zipper snagged again and he cursed. He didn't want to have to get a new one. When he finally got it open, he pulled out his dirty clothes and dumped them in the laundry basket. He peeled off his shirt and tossed it on the top of the pile, his pants quickly followed suit. The moment he got home, the first thing he always did was change out of his travel clothes. Who the hell knew what was in those seats? Planes were like a giant petri dish. He had no intention of turning his apartment into one as well. He grabbed a pair of jeans off the hanger and stepped into them but didn't bother to do them up.

"Um Gonz?" Bailey called.

"Yeah?" He popped his head out of the closet. Bailey looked at him and her eyes widened and, if he wasn't mistaken, lingered on his waist. He looked down at his undone jeans and bit back a grin. "Eyes up, Bay."

Her head snapped up. "What?" She shook her head. Almost as soon as her head stopped moving, her cheeks instantly turned red.

Busted. She'd definitely been looking. "You need something, Bay?"

"Sorry. I just wanted to check what kind of place you wanted to eat at, so I knew what to wear."

"I'm going jeans."

"Um...so I s—see," she stammered.

He couldn't help himself, he had to flex, just a little, and was rewarded with a visible swallow from Bailey. The kind of swallow that says her brain had short-circuited ever so slightly. "I was thinking we'd do Mexican. There are a couple of cool places with outdoor seating and live music. Gotta good casual vibe."

Her eyes dipped to his waist again, then quickly snapped back up. "Right, casual, good." She flashed him a thumbs up.

What the hell? Gonzo barked out a laugh. "You okay?"

"Of course." She sighed. "But my god why are your pants undone? And why does it look like you aren't wearing underwear?"

"Because I'm not."

"Who does that?" she screeched.

"I only have a couple of clean pairs left, and I need them for the next road trip. I'm taking you for dinner. I don't have time to do laundry."

Bailey stepped past him and grabbed hold of the laundry basket and dragged it toward herself.

"What are you doing?" he asked.

"Your laundry. Now put some damn underwear on," she growled. Turning on her heel, she hoisted the basket into her arms and marched out of the bedroom.

"Wouldn't have taken you for a prude, Bay," he called after her.

"I'm not a prude, it's just good hygiene," she yelled back.

Alone in the closet once more, he glanced down at his waistband. Then shrugged and pulled up his zipper and buttoned the jeans. Why bother? The jeans were already on.

He pulled a blue henley off the shelf and slipped it over his head.

Grabbing his shaving kit out of his overnight bag, he wandered into the bathroom to brush his teeth. Gonzo stood in front of the mirror and looked at his reflection. He flicked his hand through his hair to tame the little tuft that seemed to have a mind of its own. The hair instantly popped straight back up. Fantastic. He stuck his hand under the tap and wet his fingers, then slapped his hand onto the unruly tuft. After several more attempts, the thick chunk of dark hair finally surrendered and lay flat.

He quickly brushed his teeth, used the washroom, then grabbed his wallet off the dresser and made his way to the kitchen.

When Bailey walked in several minutes later, he sucked in a breath. "Wow, that's some top," he told her.

Bailey chewed her bottom lip, looked down at herself and flattened her palm down the front of her outfit. "Does it look okay?"

"Looks more than okay." His eyes instantly darted back to her chest, and he forced himself to look away from her breasts. Damn.

She fidgeted with the deep V of the shirt and pulled it up slightly. "I'm not sure I can pull this off."

Gonzo walked over to her and grabbed her hand. "Stop. You look beautiful."

She shifted her shoulders forward like somehow the movement would adjust the neckline.

"Bay, shirts like this were made for a body like yours."

She grimaced. "It's a lot of cleavage."

His eyes instantly darted to the cleavage in question. She wasn't wrong. The sight of her full breasts on display like that practically made his mouth water. He bit back a groan. "Like I said, that shirt looks like it was made for you. So stop fidgeting and own it."

Bailey took a deep breath. "Thank you."

"No problem." Sometimes being a good friend sucked. Bailey might be feeling more confident, but now he was going to have to fight to keep his eyes on her face all night instead of looking at her chest.

Once they arrived in Old Town, they wandered down the street, weaving in and out of the shops before stopping to watch a couple of older women making tortillas in front of a Mexican restaurant. Bailey stood raptly, watching the woman rolling the dough.

Gonzo eyed the large outdoor seating area at the attached restaurant. "You want to just eat here?"

"Sure."

He placed his hand on the small of her back and guided her toward the host stand. "You want me to ask for a seat so you can keep watching?" he teased.

"No, but you gotta admit that was impressive. I thought your mom was good at it, but that lady? She whipped out like ten tortillas in the time I would have been able to maybe do one."

"I'm pretty sure she has a lot more practice at it than you do."

"But still." Bailey glanced over her shoulder at the woman again. "We're buying some of those on our way out."

"Two please," he said to the hostess.

"Inside or out?"

Gonzo looked at Bailey for confirmation. "Out?"

"Yes, please."

The hostess picked up a couple of menus. "Follow me, please."

The woman wove her way through the tables and stopped at a table for two against the railing that enclosed the restaurant. Gonzo smirked at Bailey. "Look at that. You can still watch her." He nodded toward the old woman. "You take this side." He pulled out the chair facing the tortilla stand and gestured for Bailey to sit.

Bailey slid into her seat and he adjusted her chair behind her. He pulled out his own chair and sat down. He gripped the arm of the chair to pull himself closer to the table and his finger sunk into something sticky. Gross. He pulled his hand back and pink bubble gum stuck to his fingers. He held up his hand to the hostess. "Can I maybe get a different chair?"

The woman's eyes widened in horror. "Oh my god, I'm so sorry. Of course. Let me get you a new table."

"Nah, the table's fine. Just a different chair would be awesome." He smiled reassuringly at the hostess, then looked down at his hand and wrinkled his nose. "I'm just gonna go wash my hand while you grab a new chair." He glanced down at Bailey. "Be right back."

Conscious of not wanting to touch anything with his gummy fingers, he held his hand out from his body as he wove his way through the restaurant toward the washrooms at the back of the building. As he was passing by a table, a guy grabbed his arm. Gonzo looked down at the hand still wrapped around his forearm, then raised his eyebrow at the hand's owner.

"You're Ramon Gonzalez right?" the guy asked.

"Yeah, I am."

"You guys sucked against Atlanta."

What the fuck? The dude seriously stopped him for that? "It wasn't our best showing."

"No shit," the guy scoffed. "You guys gonna win this time?"

Gonzo's jaw clenched at the guy's douchebag tone. What he wanted to do was just keep walking, but he'd had the whole PR optics talk drilled into him so many times he knew the importance of at least trying to be nice to the fans. "That's always the plan," he said.

Douchebag snorted. "Yeah, that's working well."

What the hell was wrong with people? Gonzo closed his eyes briefly and sighed. "If you'll excuse me, I need to wash my hands and get back to my table." He flashed a tight smile and stepped away from the table. "Asshole," he muttered to himself.

He'd barely walked past two tables before he was stopped again. "Sorry to bother you," the man at this table said.

"Mmm-hmm." Gonzo pasted on a tight smile.

"Any chance I can get an autograph for my kid?" the man asked.

A little girl who looked like she was about eight years old looked up at him shyly in her Hawks jersey.

He smiled down at her. "I like the shirt."

"Thank you," she said.

"Turn around and show him the back," the dad said.

The little girl spun in her seat. Gonzalez was sprawled across the back of her jersey.

"Nice. You've got good taste."

The dad held up a pen hopefully.

Gonzo looked down at his hand and winced. "Ugh, let me just wash my hand. I stuck it in some gum. I'll sign it for you on my way back."

"Sure, thank you."

He quickly washed his hands. Why the hell would someone stick their gum under the arm of the chair? Under the middle of the table maybe, but the arm of the chair? Gross.

On his way back to his seat, he stopped at the family's table. "Who am I making this out to?"

"Her name is Sadie." The dad looked fondly at his daughter as he said her name.

Gonzo scrawled the little girl's name and his signature on the napkin and handed it to her. "Dream big, Sadie," the little girl read out loud. "Thank you."

"I want one too," her little sister whined.

"You don't even like baseball," Sadie scoffed.

"Do too." The little girl scowled back at her sister.

Gonzo grabbed another cocktail napkin off the table. "What's your name?"

"Jessica." The little girl stuck out her tongue at her sister.

He quickly wrote on the napkin and handed it back to her.

"What's it say?" Jessica asked.

The dad chuckled. "Jessica, Baseball Rules. Ramon Gonzalez." He ruffled his daughter's head, then turned to Gonzo. "Thank you so much, sorry to pull you from your evening. We really appreciate it."

"No problem, have a good night," Gonzo said.

He stepped away from the table and the asshole from earlier held up a pen. "Can I get one too?"

"Are you serious?" Gonzo asked.

"Yeah."

"You literally just said how much I sucked."

"So?"

"So, sorry, man, no. Autographs are just for the kids tonight."

He dimly heard the guy talking to his friend about what a dick he was as he walked past. Talking to fans when he was out and about was one thing. Giving any attention to assholes like that was not worth his time.

As he rounded the corner of the restaurant and glanced toward his table, he pulled up short. What the fuck? There was a guy in his seat. It took him a second to take in the pinched expression on Bailey's face before his brain connected the dots on exactly who the guy was. Brad.

He stalked toward the table. The second Bailey's gaze landed on him, her face lost the deer in headlights look.

Without thinking, he walked up and cupped the back of her head with his palm and brought his mouth down onto hers. The second their lips touched he knew it was a mistake. There was no way he was going to be happy just being friends with her. Not after feeling her lips against his and knowing what it felt like to kiss her. Bailey's lips parted slightly, and he couldn't help himself he needed more. He swept his tongue out and brushed it against hers. Fuck, he wanted to take this deeper.

But now was not the time or the place. Reluctantly he stopped. "Sorry that took so long."

When he pulled back, Bailey had that deer in the headlights look again, but this time instead of panic it was more of a wow, kind of daze. He knew exactly how she was feeling. Steeling his breath, he turned to Bailey's ex. "You're in my seat."

"What the hell's going on here?" Brad demanded.

"You're in my seat," he said again.

"What happened to just friends?" Brad glared at Bailey.

"What happened to being faithful?" Bailey snapped.

"Bay, you done talking with good ol' Brad here?" Gonzo asked.

"I was done before we started."

Gonzo crossed his arms over his chest, making sure to flex as he did, just in case Brad neglected to notice the difference in their sizes. "Like Bailey said, she's done, so I'm gonna ask you again to get out of my seat."

"Fine, I'll let you get back to your pity date," Brad laughed mockingly.

Bailey's eyes flared with anger. "Pity date?"

"Come on Bailey, you can't honestly believe he'd be interested in you."

The spark in Bailey's eye that had been there a moment before vanished, making every protective instinct in Gonzo flare to the surface. "Why wouldn't I be interested in her?" he asked.

Brad snorted. "Because I've seen the pictures of the women you date. Bailey's not even close to being in the same league."

"No, you're right, she's not." He paused, then seeing the brief glimmer of malicious glee in Brad's face, he said, "She's better." No longer caring about public appearances, he allowed his disgust at the other man to show on his face. "You were just too stupid to see it."

Gonzo stepped closer to Bailey and smiled down at her. "Thank god I wasn't," he said. Threading his fingers through her hair, he cupped the back of her head as he leaned in and placed another kiss against her mouth. He kept his hand on the back of her neck when he stood up to face Brad again. "I guess I should be thankful she'd already taken the job here before she found out what an asshole you are, otherwise I wouldn't have gotten my chance."

Brad shoved back from the table, and without saying another word, he stalked back to his own table.

Out of the corner of his eye, Gonzo could see the men at Brad's tables looking over and talking. He bit back a smile at the pissed off look on Brad's face. San Diego was full of Hawks' fans, and it looked like Brad was sitting at a table full of them. Turned out being recognized wasn't all bad.

"What was that?" Bailey whispered.

He pulled his attention off Brad and his friends and back to Bailey. "What was what?"

"That." She flapped her hand. "The whole kiss and — ugh."

"He pissed me off." Why was she getting annoyed with him? Brad had been the one being an asshole.

"Obviously. But why would you pretend we were dating?"

"Where the fuck does he get off saying shit like that? Like you couldn't hold my attention. That's bullshit," he grumbled.

"Gonzo, we both know I couldn't."

His head snapped up. "Fuck that," he growled. "You could hold my attention just fine." More than fine, unfortunately, that was part of the problem. He wasn't supposed to notice how sexy his friend was.

"Right," she mumbled.

Hating the insecurity so clearly obvious in the way her body slumped, he reached across the table and grabbed her hand. "Bay." He paused. "Look at me."

She raised her head. Tears swam in her eyes and it broke his heart.

"Brad's a fucking pussy. He's not man enough to handle a woman like you, and he knows it. That's why he fucking cheated." He stroked her wrist with his thumb, enjoying the way her pulse raced beneath his finger. He'd probably regret saying this, but what the hell. "I am and believe me when I say you've got my attention. You always have."

Bailey snorted. "Yeah right."

"Who was the first person I called after the draft?"

"Me."

"And after my first pro game?"

"Me," she whispered.

"And when I was going to make an offer on my place?"

"Me." She raised her head. Their gaze connected and held. Surely she could feel it too.

"But that's just because we're friends."

"Bailey, you're the first person I want to call when I have good news and the only person I want to have by my side for the bad. That means something."

"Yeah, that we're still best friends." She looked at him, then sighed. "You've never looked at me like that, like a woman, though."

"You don't know how I've looked at you."

"Come on Gonzo, you fucked anything in a skirt when we were in high school."

"Yep, and did I ever get serious about any of them?"

"No."

"Exactly. I've fucked a lot of girls, Bay. Never loved any of them."

"You never wanted to fuck me."

If only that were true. "I never wanted to lose you."

Bailey glanced around the restaurant. "Are we really having this conversation here, of all places? With Brad right over there."

"Seems so." He slid his chair around the side of the table closer to her, so his knees bracketed her thighs.

Bailey sighed. "I appreciate what you're doing, but you can't rewrite history, Gonzo. You never wanted me."

"I never let myself want you. There's a difference."

"What do you mean?"

"I was a fucking kid, determined to make it out of our shitty town. Nothing was going to hold me back from that."

"Okay?"

He looked down at their hands as he dragged his thumb back and forth on her wrist. "Even as a kid, I knew what you could mean to me if I let you."

Bailey leaned closer. "What are you talking about?"

"Us, you and me." He sighed. "Nothing was going to fuck up me reaching my dreams and you could have."

"How?"

"I wasn't in a place to have a relationship with anyone then and I wasn't going to fuck up our friendship just to get you in bed. So I didn't even let myself think of you like that. I couldn't go there with you." He dragged his hand through his hair. "I probably shouldn't now, but here we are."

Bailey glanced over his shoulder. "Is this about Brad?"

"What?"

The server walked up to their table. "Can I get you something to drink?"

This probably wasn't the time or the place. "Yeah." Gonzo shoved his chair back, then looked at Bailey. "You want to do margaritas?"

When she looked up, she had that deer in headlights thing going on again and he cursed himself for getting into this now. It hadn't exactly been his smoothest delivery.

Bailey nodded. "Sure."

"Can we get a couple of margaritas and some chips and guac, please?"

"Of course. Do you need more time with the menu?"

"Haven't even looked at it yet, sorry. We'll be ready to order when you get back."

"Take your time," the girl said.

Once they were alone, he looked over at Bailey who sat watching him, her face the picture of confusion. "Why don't we table this till we get home?"

"But—"

"Bay, if we are going to have a hope in hell of convincing Brad that there's something going on between us, you're going to have to lose the shellshocked look."

"I'm just trying to wrap my head around what you just said."

"Why's it so hard to believe I've always thought you were attractive?"

"Because I look in the mirror every day, Gonzo. I know what I look like."

"Well, clearly you're not seeing what I see." What kind of number had Brad done on her that she didn't see how beautiful she was?

"Gonzo, you don't date girls who look like me."

"That's because there's only ever been one you, Bailey." Finally, something he said seemed to land and an incredibly sexy blush swept across the swell of Bailey's breasts and up her cheeks.

She glanced up and rolled her eyes. "Very smooth, Gonz."

"Simply telling it how it is."

"Mmm-hmm, all right, Casanova, how about you dial it back?"

He barked out a laugh and covered his hand over his heart. "Ouch and that right there is why I love you, Bailey. You sure know how to keep a guy grounded."

"Mmm-hmm, anyway." The corner of her mouth tipped up with amusement. "How was the road trip?"

"You saw the game against Atlanta." He was still pissed off about the shitty call in the bottom of the fifth. There was no way the guy had been safe. He'd tagged him long before Richards touched the bag, but the asshole swore up and down he hadn't connected and the angle of the replay wasn't clear. Next time he'd bruise the fucker he'd tag 'em so hard.

"Sucks you guys lost all three, but you played well every game."

"For all the good it did."

"The curse of the team sport. All you can do is give it your best and hope your teammates do as well." Bailey placed her hand on his thigh and squeezed his leg the way she always did, but it felt different tonight.

He placed his hand on top of hers and linked their fingers. "I don't think some of the guys got the memo. Management needs to make some changes to the line-up. There's no way Knight should be batting lead. He's setting the tone for the entire game and he fucking sucks right now."

Bailey smirked at him. "I see that hasn't changed either."

"What's that?"

"Coach Gonzalez is in the house."

He lifted his hand off her lap slightly and flipped her the bird. Bailey burst out laughing like he knew she would.

"I'm just saying." Bailey clicked her cheeks. "Easy to coach from the sidelines."

"Easy to see when you're batting cleanup and have no one to fucking hit home, too."

"Well, if that's the problem, it sounds like more than just Knight didn't get the job done against Atlanta."

"Yeah, Pete's head was up his ass because Kendall was late."

"I didn't realize she went to your away games."

He chuckled. "Not that kind of late."

"Oh." Bailey's eyes widened. "Is she pregnant?"

"No idea. Guess we'll find out." Now that he thought about it, it was kind of weird that Pete hadn't texted the group chat either way.

"Brad keeps looking over here," Bailey mumbled out of the side of her mouth.

He pulled his chair closer to hers again, bracketing her legs with his. "Well then, let's give him something to look at." He reached out and picked up the pendant of her necklace. "I like this. What is it?" Allowing the back of his hand to rest against the swell of her breast, he ran his index finger along her collarbone as he held the crystal between his other fingers.

"Umm." Her breath hitched. "It's citrine."

"Citrine? Never heard of it."

"Mmm, it's supposed to be good for joy and abundance and balance. Or at least that's what Rayne told me."

"It's pretty. The color reminds me of the sun."

"The sun, huh? Look at you being all poetic."

"What can I say? I'm a deep guy." He allowed the stone to drop against the top of her breasts. His gaze lingered on the stone resting in her cleavage.

"Gonzo?"

He snapped his head up. Bailey stared back at him expectantly. "Sorry what?" he asked.

"Got mesmerized by the sun there, did ya?" she teased.

"Absolutely." He flicked another glance at the yellow stone resting on her breasts. "I'm just gonna be a total pig here and get this out of the way. I remember you having a great rack, but I don't remember it being this great."

She snorted. "The only benefit to the extra pounds I've put on."

"I don't know that it's the only benefit. Your ass looks pretty good, too."

"You don't think it's too big?"

"Too big for what?"

She chewed on her bottom lip and shrugged.

Hating how insecure she seemed to feel about her body, he slid his hands up the side of her thighs and rested them on her hips. Bailey's chest rose and she licked her lips.

What he really wanted to do was grab her ass and make it crystal clear there wasn't a single thing wrong with it, but this wasn't the place for that. Needing to keep it PG, he squeezed her hips with both hands. "Feels perfect to me."

"Brad said, anything more than a handful was a waste."

"I thought we've already established Brad's a fucking idiot."

"We did," she replied.

"So he doesn't deserve any space in this head of yours." He held her stare. "What was that lecture of yours I sat in a couple years back? Kinks through the ages or something like that, right?"

"Yeah?" Her forehead wrinkled as her eyes narrowed in question.

"So explain to me how Brad needing to denigrate a woman to get off means there's something wrong with you."

Bailey's gaze darted toward where Brad was sitting. "What do you mean?"

"Come on, Bay, you teach this shit. Clearly, you can see exactly what kind of guy Brad is."

"Umm." She blinked several times like her brain was trying to play catch-up with his train of thoughts.

"He puts you down, makes you feel like shit about your body to the point you're grateful for any scraps he gives you. Meanwhile, he's doing the whole power play fuck his assistant thing and stringing you both on?" The guy sounded pretty pathetic to him.

"Oh my god, you're right." Bailey gaped at him. "Why did I not see that?"

He raised one shoulder. "Like you said, sometimes it's hard to see when you're in the middle of the game."

A server walked up to their table carrying two plates. He held up his right hand slightly. "Taco platter?"

Bailey raised her hand. The server slid a steaming plate filled with tacos, rice, and beans in front of her.

"That must mean you're the enchiladas divorciadas," the man said as he set a large platter in front of Gonzo. "Can I bring you anything else?"

Gonzo looked over at Bailey, staring raptly at her plate. "I think we're good, man."

"Enjoy."

He leaned down and inhaled his dinner. "Smells good."

"I'm never going to be able to eat all this," Bailey said.

"Feel free to pass over anything you don't want."

Bailey picked up a taco and set it on his plate.

"You haven't even started. How do you know you aren't going to want it?"

"Trust me, I know. There's enough food for two people here." Bailey opened her napkin and draped it over her lap. She eyed his plate. "Everything looks so good."

"Is that your way of saying you're hoping for a bite of mine?"

"No," she scoffed.

He cut off a small section of each enchilada. "Yeah right. Bring your plate over." He laughed.

Bailey grinned and slid her plate toward him. "Thank you. Brad hated sharing his food with me."

"Why?"

She sighed. "I don't know, but then again, he would have taken one look at my platter and immediately said I needed to take half of it home."

"Hold up." Gonzo held up his hand. "Are you seriously telling me he policed what you ate?"

Bailey nodded.

"What the hell, Bailey. Why the fuck did you stay with him so long?" he growled.

"He didn't do it at first and slowly, over time, it started and..." She pursed her lips tightly, then shrugged slightly. "I don't know."

Gonzo glanced over his shoulder at Brad's table. The asshole sat with his buddies like he was holding court. Turning back around, he pinned Bailey with a stare. "All right. From now on, let's agree you're a smart, grown ass woman who can make up her own mind. No more doing shit you don't want to do."

He held out his hand toward her. Bailey raised her hand and placed her palm in his. Gonzo firmly shook her hand. "You want to eat something. You eat it. You want something in the bedroom you say so and you sure as fuck speak up if you don't. Deal?"

"Who says we'll be doing stuff in the bedroom?"

How cute. A slow, confident smile spread across his face. "Oh, there's no doubt we'll be going to the bedroom, Bailey. The only question is when."

# CHAPTER FIFTEEN

Bailey glanced over at Gonzo as he leaned against the wall of the elevator, watching her. Her gaze trailed down his body. The way his hands rested in his pockets drew her attention to his cock. Did he realize how standing like that emphasized the size of it?

She glanced up to see him smirking back at her. Probably. Knowing Gonzo, he was probably very aware of what made a woman think of sex. He'd certainly done a good job with her. Ever since he'd mentioned that he wanted to have sex with her, it was all she could think about.

He'd said if she wanted something, she should ask. "Were you serious about wanting to have sex with me?"

His muscles tensed. "Definitely."

The elevator doors popped open at his floor and she stepped out. She could feel him watching her ass as she walked.

Neither of them spoke as they walked in silence down the hall to his apartment. Gonzo unlocked it and they stepped inside. He locked the door behind them.

Nerves danced down her spine. She'd been feeling bold in the elevator, but the pause in conversation had her questioning herself. If he was interested, wouldn't he have pushed her up against the wall or something the moment they walked inside? Isn't that what people did when they really wanted someone? Maybe he'd just been trying to be nice.

Gonzo stepped toward her. She could feel the heat pouring off his body. The man radiated heat like no one she'd ever met. "You're thinking too much, Bailey," he told her.

She snorted. "Probably."

He tucked a piece of hair behind her ear, and she shivered as his fingers touched the skin of her neck. "You want me to fuck you, Bay?"

God yes, but more than that, she wanted him to make her feel desirable. "Make me feel beautiful, Gonzo."

"Gladly." His hand curved around her neck and into her hair as he pulled her toward him.

Gonzo grabbed her around the waist and hoisted her up. With a squeal, she wrapped her legs around his waist and tightened her hold on his neck.

"That's better." His hands kneaded her ass and he buried his face in her neck. "Fuck, I love your ass."

Warmth spread through her. When he'd first picked her up, she'd been scared he wouldn't be able to hold her, but as he shifted his hips to grind his hard cock against her, any concern she had about that disappeared. She'd never had a man pick her up before. Never dated anyone strong enough to do it. Who knew it would be such a turn-on? She felt safe. Cherished. Desirable.

The next thing she knew, her shirt was whipped over her head. How the heck did he manage to do that without dropping her?

As her shirt hit the ground, Gonzo's lips collided with hers. His tongue pressed into her mouth and she ground her core against him as a wave of longing rushed through her. No question the man could kiss.

Gonzo walked down the hallway with her in his arms. He pushed open the door to his bedroom and stalked toward the bed.

They were really doing this. They were crossing this line.

Gonzo set her on the bed and followed her down. His hard body pressed against hers and she wrapped her legs around his waist, pulling him tightly against her. He rocked his hips back and forth against her core as his tongue tangled with hers. It wasn't enough. Jean on jean just wasn't getting the job done.

"These jeans need to go," Gonzo said, taking the words right out of her mouth.

He leaned back on his knees and looked down at her laying on the bed in her bra and pants. Half of her body was still covered but a wave of nerves zipped through her. She looked nothing like the women he normally slept with. What if he didn't like what he saw? Self-conscious, Bailey tried to shift away from the scrutiny.

"Stay," he commanded. "Let me look at you."

"Wouldn't you rather do this with the lights off?"

"No."

Bailey swallowed past the lump in her throat. Why was it so hard to believe that he could find her attractive like this?

"You sure?" she asked.

He raised his head and looked her in the eye. "Bailey. I'm not your fucking ex. It's just you and me here. I would never hurt you." He continued to hold her stare. "Have I ever lied to you about something that matters?"

"No," she whispered.

"So why do you think I'd lie to you about this?"

"I don't know," she shrugged.

"Bay, you've been driving me crazy for weeks, walking around here in your little pajamas and shit."

"I have?"

"Jesus, Bailey, I wouldn't be crossing this line with you if I had any choice in the matter."

"Of course you have a choice."

"No, I don't. You're in there." He tapped the side of his head. "And I can't get you out." Gonzo's eyes roamed down her body. "There isn't a single thing about you I don't find sexy as fuck."

The sincerity on his face made the knot in her stomach unclench slightly.

"Now we can turn the light off if you need to, but I really want to fucking see you." He trailed his finger along the swell of her breast as he traced the lace cup of her bra. "Because what I'm seeing so far is even better than I imagined."

"It is?"

"Yeah, and what I imagined was pretty fucking good." He ran his knuckle between her breasts and down her stomach toward the snap of her jeans. "Your skin is so soft." He leaned down and ran his tongue along the swell of her breast and up her neck. "And the way you smell." He inhaled deeply.

Bailey shivered.

"You gonna let me leave the light on and look at you?" he asked.

Her nipples tightened as his breath puffed against the sensitive skin by her ear with each word.

"Yes."

"Good girl," he said and nipped her earlobe.

Those two little words were like a lightning bolt to her clit. Holy shit. Maybe she was a good girl after all because she sure enjoyed hearing it out of Gonzo's mouth. Bailey bit back a groan.

"Sit up," he ordered.

Bailey fought the urge to cover her stomach as she felt it roll over the edge of her jeans when she sat. Before she had a chance to follow through on the urge, Gonzo ran his tongue up her neck and whispered, "Stop thinking."

Easier said than done. But when his teeth sunk into the pulse point on her neck, all thought left her mind. What was it about that spot? "Mmm," she moaned.

Gonzo reached behind her and unhooked her bra. He eased the straps down her arms as he peeled the fabric away from her body slowly. Before the bra had even hit the floor, Gonzo pressed her back against the mattress and covered her with his body.

It was like he knew she needed him to ease into being completely naked in front of him. He kissed down her neck to the swell of her breasts. Her back arched off the mattress when his mouth latched onto her nipple and sucked.

Threading her fingers into his hair, she wrapped her legs tighter around his waist, shifting her pelvis to gain the friction she wanted. "Ugh," she groaned in frustration.

Gonzo sat up between her legs and smirked. "Sorry, I said we needed to lose the jeans and I got distracted by your tits."

"I'm definitely not going to complain."

"Well, I'll have to make sure I don't give you any reason to complain about this next part." He looked down at her and winked. "Gotta prove to you that no one fakes it with me."

She smacked his chest. "Oh my god, are you really bringing that up right now?"

He chuckled and shrugged. "You questioned my prowess. I gotta prove myself here."

"You know how you can prove it? By not talking about another woman when I'm half naked in front of you," she grumbled.

"You are the only woman I'm thinking about."

"Mmm-hmm."

"Have you seen your fucking tits?"

She laughed. "Yep, I've seen 'em."

"Clearly you've never really looked at them, or you'd know there's no way in hell I'm thinking of anyone but you."

"Right." She rolled her eyes at him.

"Guess I'll have to prove it to you." He waggled his eyebrows and winked. "I'm gonna make you eat those words, Bailey. You're gonna scream so fucking loud the neighbors will call the cops."

"You can try," she teased. That was one challenge she wouldn't mind losing.

A confident grin kicked up the corner of his mouth and he licked his lips. Bailey swallowed hard. Maybe the woman the other night hadn't been faking. No one would look as cocky as he did if they didn't have the goods to back it up. Damn, she really hoped he had the goods.

Gonzo undid the button on her jeans and kissed her stomach. He ran his tongue along the upper right side of her abdomen. She shivered. No one had ever kissed her scar before. Brad thought it was gross.

"This healed good," he mumbled and ran his tongue along it again. "Jen's lucky to have you." He flicked his tongue against her bellybutton.

"No talking about my sister," she growled.

Gonzo smirked at her. "Right sorry. The only talk you want is dirty. Got it." He slowly peeled her jeans down her legs, his tongue tracing every inch of skin he exposed. He dropped her jeans on the floor beside the bed and sat back on his heels to look at her. His nostrils flared as his gaze traveled slowly down her body.

The way he was staring at her was unlike anything she'd ever experienced. No one had ever looked at her like they were planning all the nasty things they wanted to do to her. If the light was on, Brad always gave her a quick glance, then turned it off. Gonzo acted like he wanted to eat her alive and she loved it.

She'd never felt sexier in her life. Bailey arched her back, loving the way his gaze latched onto her breasts.

He shifted himself in his jeans, then hopped off the bed. "Hang on, these need to go or I'm gonna cut off the circulation to my dick." He shoved his jeans down in one swoop and kicked them off.

No underwear in sight. *Oh, my god.* She was seeing her best friend naked. Very, very naked. And wow. "Geez, you're really packing," she blurted.

Gonzo threw his head back and laughed. "And there she is."

She shrugged. "I'm just saying."

He fisted himself and dragged his hand slowly down his hard cock. Bailey's eyes widened. It should be weird to see her best friend touching himself, but it wasn't. It was really fucking hot.

"What are you saying exactly?" He continued to stroke himself as his gaze slowly trailed down her body.

The way he watched her gave her a confidence she'd never felt before. Bailey arched her back, loving the way his eyes darkened as he stared at her breasts. "I'm just saying maybe you should get over here."

Gonzo grinned. "Gladly." He kneeled at the foot of the bed. She widened her legs to make room for him. He trailed his tongue up her inner thigh.

He brought his face closer to her center and blew his breath against her clit. Goosebumps danced across her skin. She shifted, hoping he would take the hint and put his mouth on her rather than just teasing her.

"You've got a very pretty pussy, Bailey."

Heat rose across her chest and up her cheeks at the compliment. Didn't they all pretty much look the same?

He inhaled, groaned, and closed his eyes.

Apparently not.

He continued to look down at her. Why wasn't he touching her already? She squirmed.

"Stay," he told her.

As she lay naked on the bed with Gonzo's muscular body looming between her legs, a wave of nerves swarmed through her again and she shifted.

Gonzo's hand clamped onto her thigh and held her in place. "I said stay." His stare remained glued between her legs and he licked his lips. "Damn, baby girl. I'm going to fucking devour that pussy," he growled.

His breath danced across her clit a second before his hot, wet mouth touched her. His tongue flicked against her sensitive flesh. Bailey lifted her hips.

Gonzo sucked her clit into his mouth. The jolt of desire running through her body made her arch off the mattress. Holy shit.

A deep masculine chuckle rumbled against her skin. Bailey threaded her fingers in his hair. Damn, he was really good at this.

Gonzo inserted a finger inside her, then sucked her clit again.

"Oh my god," she groaned.

He inserted another finger, fucking her with his hand as his tongue tormented her clit. The pleasure built. She squirmed to get closer, to pull away. She wasn't sure. "I'm close, Gonz."

"Not close enough," he muttered.

Her brain tried to compute what he meant but couldn't. She was going to come any second. How could she not be close enough? "What?"

"Let me hear you scream, Bailey."

He curled his fingers inside her and she gasped. Oh good lord, what was that? Wow! "Gonzo," she moaned.

"That's it, Bay, say my name," he growled. "You're so wet. Your pussy is clamping on my fingers. I can't wait to feel you do that to my cock."

"Me too," she gasped. His lips wrapped around her clit and he pressed his finger against the spot she'd only ever hit with toys before and she saw stars. A loud groan tore from her chest.

She bucked her hips off the bed. He tucked his hands under her ass and held her pussy against his mouth as his tongue swirled and licked against her clit.

She pushed against his head. "I'm done," she gasped.

"No, you're not," he said, then sucked her firmly into his mouth.

"Fu...uck," she moaned. The orgasm that she'd thought had been over rocketed up again and over the edge. All she could do was hang on.

Bailey closed her eyes and gasped to catch her breath. When she felt like she could finally speak, she peeled her eyes open to see a very smug Gonzo kneeling between her legs.

"Okay, I take it back. She clearly wasn't faking."

He grinned. "Told ya."

Bailey allowed herself to look her fill of his body. Her gaze lingered on his hard cock. After that orgasm, she should be done, but she wasn't even close. She crooked her finger toward him. "Get up here and fuck me."

His eyes darkened. "Gladly."

He leaned over and grabbed a condom from the bedside table. She couldn't tear her eyes away from him as he sheathed himself. Gonzo winked at her knowingly, then moved back between her legs. Bailey shifted her hips and closed her eyes when she felt his hard cock against her skin. He positioned himself at her entrance and paused. She opened her eyes to find Gonzo looking down, watching her. Once they crossed this line, there was no going back.

Bailey threaded her hands through his hair and smiled as she pressed her hips against him, drawing him inside. That was all the invitation he needed. Gonzo thrust into her, filling her completely.

"Jesus," he groaned and touched his forehead against hers to give her a second to adjust to his size. "You feel incredible."

"So do you." She closed her eyes and moved her hips, seating him further.

"Fuck," he groaned. "I gotta move."

"Please do," she gasped.

Gonzo pulled back and thrust into her slowly, drawing out the sensation. Bailey wrapped her legs around his waist and moaned when he hit exactly where she needed. "Right there," she told him.

He swiveled his pelvis, and her eyes rolled back in her head. How did he do that? How did he hit her g-spot and her clit at the same time? That wasn't even possible, was it? It sure as hell never had been before. It was like his body was made for hers.

Gonzo's mouth crashed against hers. His tongue thrust into her mouth, matching the movement on his hips.

She curled her hands into his hair and dug her heels into his ass as she held on, matching him stroke for stroke.

Her orgasm built. Holy shit, she'd never come from intercourse before. She hadn't thought it was possible.

Clearly it was. Needing air, she broke their kiss. "Oh my god, Gonzo," she gasped.

"Right there with you, Bay, holy shit," he grunted.

He grabbed her hips and the angle changed slightly. She hadn't thought it could feel any better than it had. "Gonzo," she groaned as an orgasm tore through her.

He continued to thrust several more times before his back tensed and he shuddered against her with his own release.

Gonzo's hands fell from her hips and he dropped onto the mattress beside her. He chucked the condom in the trash can beside the bed, then reached out and pulled her against him.

Bailey curled into him, resting her head against his chest. Her mind raced. A direct contrast to how satiated her body felt. What was she supposed to say after he'd just destroyed any preconceived ideas she'd had about what good sex felt like?

After several seconds, he finally spoke. "Why have we not been doing that before now? Jesus, Bailey."

Thank god, he was feeling what she was. She relaxed into him, snuggling in to get more comfortable. "No kidding. Probably a good thing we didn't know that back in high school or we might not have graduated."

Gonzo snorted. "No shit. I'm not sure I want to leave this bed ever again." He reached down and grabbed her leg and pulled it over his body so she was half on top of him, half beside. "Who knew you were a snuggler after sex?" she teased.

"I'm normally not." He kissed the top of her head. "I think you broke me."

Bailey giggled. "You don't sound too upset about it."

"After that orgasm? No, I'm definitely not upset." He sighed and pulled her tighter. After a couple minutes, his breathing leveled out and she was pretty sure he'd fallen asleep.

Should she stay? Should she go? He hated when women tried to stay over. She knew that, but was it different with her? Bailey chewed her bottom lip as all her old insecurities rushed back.

"Why can I hear you thinking?" Gonzo grumbled.

"Umm, just trying to figure out if I should go back to my bed."

"Don't even think about it," he growled.

"But you—"

He covered her mouth with his hand. "Bay, shut up."

How many times had she heard that from him over the years? That she complicated things that didn't need to be complicated. Was this one of those times? It didn't feel like it. This thing between them felt huge.

Using his strength, he shifted both of their bodies so he was spooning her from behind. "Go to sleep, Bay."

Was he right? Did they not need to talk about it? Just because it felt huge didn't mean it had to be complicated. Right?

Within seconds, Gonzo's breath evened again and he snored lightly in her ear. Apparently, he thought so. Guess they could figure it out tomorrow. All she knew was right now, this felt really, really good.

# CHAPTER SIXTEEN

L ast night with Bailey had been phenomenal. Better than he'd ever imagined. For the first time in his life, he was excited about moving forward with a woman. Not just a woman. Bailey.

He poured the coffee beans in the grinder at the top of his espresso machine and hit the button. He knew exactly how Bailey liked her morning coffee. Besides himself, he'd never really bothered to pay attention to how people took their coffee or if it changed. With Bailey, it did. Her first coffee of the day was always a straight double shot of espresso. Later in the day, she'd switch to fancy creams and flavors. But when she woke up, just give her straight and as strong as possible.

He packed the fresh grounds into the portafilter and connected it to the machine. He'd just pushed the button for the espresso when Bailey walked into the room, freshly showered, looking all prim and proper. It immediately made him want to rumple her back up.

Bailey glanced at him shyly, then looked away like she wasn't sure how to behave.

Fuck that. They weren't gonna have some awkward morning after between them. He stalked toward her, wrapped his arm around her waist, and pulled her against him. Bailey gasped as her body crashed against his. That was better. He threaded his hand through her hair and brought her mouth to his for a searing kiss. "Morning," he mumbled against her lips.

"Umm, morning." She blinked up at him in a daze.

Pleased with himself, he grabbed her coffee off the machine and handed it to her. Bailey eyed the drink, then brought it up to her mouth, closed her eyes and inhaled slowly, like she always did before she took the first sip. Once she'd taken the first drink, she opened her eyes and smiled. "Perfect. Thank you."

"No problem. I know how you get if you don't get your caffeine." Now that she'd showered, he began assembling the ingredients for French toast.

Bailey watched him. "What are you doing?"

"Making you breakfast." He pulled out four slices of brioche and set them on the counter.

"Why are you making me breakfast?"

He flicked a glance over his shoulder. "What do you mean? I always cook for you when I'm home."

Bailey chewed her bottom lip. "I know. I just wasn't sure after last night."

Gonzo stopped what he was doing and faced her. "What do you mean you weren't sure after last night?"

Bailey shrugged. "I don't know. I mean, what are we doing here?"

"I thought that was pretty obvious," he said.

Bailey looked at him and sighed. "Come on Gonzo, you aren't a relationship guy, we both know that."

"True, yeah." But that was before her.

"Gonzo, you hook up with a different girl in every city. I don't see that changing just because we had sex."

His stomach clenched like she'd punched him in the gut. "Whoa, that's not exactly fair. Just because I've slept with a lot of women doesn't mean I can't settle down."

She tilted her head to the side and studied him. "Gonzo, I'm not stupid. I'm very well aware of your reputation."

His reputation. Right. Because how could he possibly be more than that? "Bay, sometimes a reputation's just a glimpse of a man's past. It doesn't determine his future."

Bailey smiled sadly. "Gonzo, when's the last time you dated a woman for longer than a year? Hell longer than a couple of months?"

"Just because I haven't been in a relationship for longer than a year doesn't mean I don't want one. I do. I see what my friends have. Who wouldn't want that?" He pushed his hand through his hair. "But I also look at some of the other guys on the team and how wrecked they've been when their relationships fall apart, and yeah, maybe I've steered clear. The idea of anything fucking up my game, no thanks."

He put his hands on her waist and hoisted her up on the kitchen counter, so they were eye level. "I've never had a woman in my life who made me want to take the risk." He picked up her hand and rubbed his thumb absently against her finger. "But you're different..." He took a deep breath. "Not being with you is fucking up my game already, so what's the difference?"

"How am I fucking up your game?"

"Jesus, Bay, you're all I think about. You're in my head whether I want you there or not. When I'm out with the guys, I want to be at home with you. Someone tells a joke and I immediately want to tell it to you just so I can see that little smile you get when you think something is ridiculous, but you can't help but laugh."

She dipped her head.

"I'm fucking gone over you, Bay." He nudged her knees apart and moved his body closer so he was standing between her legs. "You make me want to risk it."

"Really?"

"Jesus, Bay, I wouldn't have slept with you if I didn't want to give us a shot. I wouldn't risk our friendship over one night. I told you that last night."

"I know, but what if we don't work out? "

"What if we do?"

Bailey chewed her bottom lip as her eyes searched his face. "I don't want to lose you over sex."

He sighed. "Pretty sure we should have had that discussion before we ended up in bed. We can't exactly put the cat back in the bag, so I figure we see where this goes."

"You really want to date me? Take me out with your friends and to parties? Have me wear your jersey at games?"

"Don't we already do that?"

Bailey huffed out a breath. "It's different if I'm your girlfriend and not just your friend."

He slid closer to her and wrapped his arms around her waist. "I know. If you're my girlfriend, I'll get to put my hands on you instead of just wanting to."

She smacked him on the arm. "Gonzo, I'm being serious."

"So am I. What's this about, Bailey?" Holy shit, maybe she didn't want to date him. "You don't want to date me?"

"What? No. God, that's not it at all. Just what will people say when they see us together?"

"Who gives a fuck?"

"Gonzo come on."

"Bay, the people who matter already know I'm crazy about you. The ones who don't will quickly realize it and can get on board or they can fuck off."

"And when some sexy girl, who looks like the women you normally go home with, hits on you in a bar?"

Annoyed at the implication, he clenched his jaw. "Then I'll tell her I'm taken."

She raised an eyebrow at him, and the annoyance became anger. "What are you implying, Bailey?"

"I don't know, I just—"

"Bay, am I the type of asshole who would cheat on a woman? Is that really who you think I am?"

"No," she admitted.

"I wouldn't have crossed this line with you if I wasn't serious about us," he growled. How could she even suggest he'd be the type of asshole who would purposefully hurt her?

"I know that."

"So then, what's the problem? Will I get hit on? Probably. But how's it any different from Pete or Smitty or whomever getting hit on?"

She ducked her head again and shrugged.

He tucked his finger under her chin and forced her to look at him. "Bay, I'm crazy about you, always have been. I'm not looking at other girls anymore."

Bailey smiled sadly. "I want to be the girl you see."

"You are. You just need to believe it when you look at her, too." Where did she get these ideas that she wasn't everything he wanted? It sure as hell wasn't coming from him. "Come here." He grabbed her hand and pulled her to the mirror in the front entryway. He placed her in front of the mirror and stepped up behind her. "Tell me what you see."

She shifted uncomfortably from one foot to the other, then adjusted the hem of her shirt.

"Umm, I see me."

He sighed. "You want to know what I see?"

She chewed the inside of her cheek, then finally nodded.

"I see my best friend. The most selfless person I know. Someone who'd be there for me no matter what." He bit back a smirk when she frowned a little because he wasn't saying anything about what she actually looked like. He ran his hand down her side. "I also see a woman with a beautiful face." He kissed the side of her neck. "Tits that I could spend all day worshipping." He kissed just below her ear. "And the sexiest curves I've ever felt."

Bailey tensed at the mention of her curves. "But Bay, until you love yourself it doesn't matter what I say because the only voice you're gonna hear is that negative one telling you that you're not good enough. I don't know how to compete with that." He squeezed her hip reassuringly. "What happened to the fierce girl I grew up with who said fuck 'em all?"

"I don't know. But I want to find her," she whispered.

"Well, let's find her together."

Bailey's eyes met his in the mirror and she nodded.

"And until then, we both know I've got enough confidence for both of us." He winked at her and she snorted like he knew she would.

Bailey held his stare for several seconds. Her chest rose as she took a deep breath. "I want to see where this can go," she admitted.

"Good, me too."

"I'm just scared. I don't want to lose you."

"Fuck, me neither. This scares the shit outta me, too. But I'm in. Are you?"

She licked her lips, squared her shoulders, and nodded. "I'm in."

With a whoop, he grabbed her and hoisted her over his shoulder, firefighter style. Bailey squealed. "What are you doing?"

"We're getting dressed and I'm taking you out for breakfast." He carried her down the hall toward the bedrooms.

"But you were going to make me French toast."

"Nope, we're going out. We're not hiding, Bailey, so get on board."

"You're ridiculous," she complained.

"Yep, but that's one of the things you love about me. Don't even try to pretend it isn't."

"You caught me. That's what I love about you," she teased back.

His chest caught at the word love slipping from her mouth. Sure she'd said it before but it felt different now that they'd had sex. It shocked him how much he liked it. It was way too soon for that shit. Shaking it off, he set her on the ground outside her bedroom. Pressed a kiss against her mouth and said, "We leave in fifteen."

Bailey cupped the side of his face and smiled. "I'll be ready."

"I'm counting on it."

# CHAPTER SEVENTEEN

Bailey shifted her body and moved her legs slightly further apart as she stood at the mirror doing her hair the following morning. Her body protested the movement. She was sore in the best possible way. Yesterday, after their breakfast out, they'd rushed back to the apartment and barely left the bedroom for the rest of the day. She'd never had this much sex in her life. Now she knew how the women in her smutty books felt. Bloody amazing!

"Bay," Gonzo called from her bedroom.

"In here, I'm just about ready."

Gonzo wandered into the bathroom. His gaze slid slowly down her body, then back up.

Bailey paused mid-curl. "Uh-uh, mister, stop looking at me like that."

He stalked closer to her. "Like what?"

"You know what. Don't even think about it." She held out her curling iron and pointed it at him. "I have to get you to the airport. We don't have time for that, and I'm way too sore for what you're thinking."

He pulled up short and winced. "Did I hurt you?"

Bailey rolled her eyes. "You didn't hurt me. I'm just a little tender, that's all."

Gonzo grinned. "Want me to kiss it better?"

Bailey laughed. "No. What I want you to do is let me finish getting ready so I don't make you late."

"You don't have to take me to the airport, Bay."

"I want to." When Gonzo had mentioned he'd never had a woman drive him to the airport before, she'd immediately offered. It surprised her how much she wanted to take him. She didn't just want to be the first woman to take him, she wanted to be the only woman.

He grinned. "Good." Gonzo leaned against the wall and crossed one foot over the other like he was settling in.

"What are you doing?" she asked.

He shrugged. "I don't know, watching you get ready."

"Don't you have better things to do than watch me curl my hair and do my makeup?"

"Nope. I'm a seasoned traveler. I'm all set."

"You're so weird." She picked up the curling iron and grabbed a chunk of hair. Why did she feel nervous? She'd curled her hair a million times. This was nothing new. Except she'd never had a man watch her before. Suddenly, something so mundane felt intimate in a way she'd never expected. She glanced over at him as she twisted the curling iron. Gonzo watched her intently. The way his nostrils flared reminded her of what he looked like during sex, and suddenly her nipples tightened. Good lord, the man was potent. How could one little nothing look have that effect on her?

"I like your hair like that." He pushed off the wall and walked toward her.

Bailey's breath hitched. What was he doing?

Gonzo picked up a curl and twisted it around his finger. Their eyes met in the mirror. He groaned, dropped her hair, and stepped back. "Yeah, I'm gonna fuck you if I stay in here any longer. I'll wait for you out there." He flicked his thumb toward the door.

Bailey swallowed past the lump of lust she was feeling. Unable to speak, she nodded.

Alone, she slumped against the counter. How was it possible to still want him this badly? As sore as she was, if he'd asked, she wouldn't have said no. She couldn't. Need coursed through her. This wasn't normal, was it? To want someone this badly?

It was probably a good thing that he was going on the road for a few days. It would give her a chance to get her emotions back under control because this was ridiculous.

Shaking it off, she picked up her curling iron and curled the last two pieces of hair. She fluffed it out, then began her makeup.

Fifteen minutes later, Bailey walked into the living room. Gonzo's eyes flared when he saw her and she bit back a grin. It had definitely been worth it to take the extra five minutes on her face.

"Jesus, you look hot," Gonzo muttered as he stepped toward her. His gaze dragged down her body, then back up to linger on her face. "All that just to drive me to the airport?"

"Well, you know." She flicked her hair over her shoulder. "Gotta look good to drop off my man."

Gonzo wrapped his arms around her waist. "Your man, huh?" His mouth curled up in a cocky grin. "I like it."

Bailey smoothed her hand down his chest. "Me too."

His brown eyes narrowed as he looked at her mouth. "You put that lipstick on just so I wouldn't fuck up your makeup, didn't you?"

Bailey laughed. "I put it on because I like it." Honestly, the idea of him wanting her so badly she needed a barrier in place to hold him off had never occurred to her. It was a heady feeling, knowing he wanted her that much. No one had ever made her feel as desirable as Gonzo did. A little surge of feminine power swept through her, and she liked it.

"Oh no, I've created a monster." Gonzo chuckled.

She smacked him on the chest. "Shut up."

He grabbed her hand and placed a kiss against her palm. "I appreciate you going to all this effort for me, Bay. It means a lot."

"Of course."

Gonzo stepped back. "All right, let's get out of here, so I don't catch shit for being late."

They rode the elevator to the basement parking garage. At Gonzo's SUV, Bailey paused. "Do you want to drive?"

"Heck no. If my girl's driving me to the airport, then she's driving." He threw his bags in the trunk, then walked to the passenger side and climbed in.

Bailey slid behind the driver's seat. It was a little strange driving Gonzo's vehicle with him in it. Normally, when they went anywhere together, he drove. She hit program two on the door panel and the mirrors and seat slid into her programmed position. After checking to make sure everything was in place, she glanced over at Gonzo. He sat there watching her with an amused smile on his face.

"What?" she asked.

"Nothing. It's just kind of nice having you chauffeur me."

"Chauffeur?" She pretended to be offended.

Gonzo chuckled. "Just saying you look good behind the wheel."

"Mmm-hmm." She turned the car on and backed out of the parking space.

Gonzo leaned forward and was just about to punch a button on the stereo when he paused. "I'm guessing you don't want to listen to the sports channel."

"Not even a little bit." She flicked the blinker and changed lanes.

Gonzo pushed a button and classic rock pumped through the speakers. He adjusted the volume to a level that was conducive to having a conversation, then turned to her. "So, what are your plans this week while I'm away?"

"I need to start planning out my classes for September. I haven't taught first year since I was in grad school, so I need to update a few things."

"I thought you were teaching your gender-based stuff."

"I am, but in order to be full time, I had to pick up an extra class and that was all that was available." She glanced in the rearview mirror. "I'm hoping next year to be exclusively upper-level classes, more in line with my specialty once they've seen for themselves what I can do."

"I have no doubt you'll knock 'em on their ass."

She glanced at him. He'd always had so much faith in her. Even when she hadn't had it in herself. "Thanks, Gonz."

"For what?"

"Believing in me."

"Always." He winked at her.

She flicked on her blinker and followed the signs for airport departures.

"Just park in the drop off area," Gonzo told her. "Not much point in coming inside since I've got my ticket. I just need to dump my stuff and head to security."

"You sure?"

"Yep."

She pulled the car up to the curb behind the line of other cars dropping off.

He leaned over and kissed her. "Just cuz I said you didn't have to come inside doesn't mean you don't have to get out of the car," Gonzo told her. He pushed open the passenger door.

Bailey hopped out of the car and met him on the sidewalk.

Gonzo set his bag down, then wrapped his arms around her waist and pulled her against him. "That's better," he said. His hands trailed down her sides until he cupped her ass. "Mmm, couldn't do that in the car."

"I had to get out of the car so you could grab my ass?" She laughed.

"Absolutely." He squeezed her ass again. The way he touched her made her feel like there wasn't a damn thing wrong with the size of her butt. Quite the opposite, in fact.

"Well, well, what do we have here?" a male voice said.

Gonzo glanced toward the newcomer. "Sims," he said, but didn't unwrap himself from Bailey.

Bailey looked over at the amused look on Brandon's face. "Hi, Brandon."

"Hey Bailey. Looks like you two finally figured your shit out," Brandon mumbled. "See you inside, Gonz. I'll let you get back to it."

Bailey buried her face in Gonzo's chest and giggled.

"What's so funny?" Gonzo asked.

"You didn't let go of my ass the entire time he stood there." Even now, his fingers clamped around her butt cheeks.

"Yeah, so?" He kissed the side of her neck. "I'm not going to see you for a couple of days. I gotta fill up the bank."

"Oh my god, you're filling up the spank bank here?" she screeched.

Gonzo snorted. "Bailey I'm appalled. I was talking about getting my fill of touching you." He sounded scandalized, but the amusement twinkling in his eyes gave him away.

"Haha," she mumbled.

"But yeah, filling the spank bank works, too." He chuckled and squeezed her ass again. "Okay, I think I'm good."

"You're a pervert," she told him.

"Yep." He pressed a kiss against her lips. "Do you want to cop a feel before I go? Don't want to leave your spank bank empty." He waggled his eyebrows at her.

Bailey snickered. "I'm good, thanks."

"Your loss," he joked. He threaded his fingers through her hair and cupped the back of her head. "Thanks for driving me."

"Anytime," she mumbled as she waited anxiously for him to kiss her. His lips touched hers, softly at first, then he deepened the kiss. Bailey moaned and wrapped her arms around him tightly as she fell into the kiss. When they finally broke apart, they were both breathing hard.

"That'll have to hold me over," he said, then pressed one more firm peck against her mouth. "Gotta go." He dropped his arms from around her and stepped back. "See you in a few days."

"Good luck," she told him.

"Thanks, I'll call you later." Gonzo grabbed his bag and slung it over his shoulder. With the other hand, he grabbed his suitcase and wheeled it behind him.

A feeling of ease settled over her as she watched him walk toward the entrance. For the first time in longer than she cared to admit, she felt happy. Truly happy. She tossed the car keys up in the air and caught them. Today was going to be a good day.

# CHAPTER EIGHTEEN

The travel schedule had never bothered him before this season. In fact, it was always something he really enjoyed. But as he made his way back to his empty hotel room after losing the game against St Louis, he found he just wished he was in his own bed, preferably with Bailey wrapped around him. Outside of the bedroom, she wasn't much of a toucher. She'd always said she thought PDA was stupid. He was working on changing her opinion on that one. So the fact that she wrapped around him like a vine while she slept had been a surprise. An incredibly sexy surprise.

He tapped his room card against the panel and waited for the little click to show it was unlocked before pushing against the door. He kicked off his shoes and plodded through the empty hotel room.

He pulled his phone out of his pocket and hit the Facetime app. Bailey's name sat at the top of the list.

Gonzo pressed her number and waited impatiently for it to connect.

Finally, she picked up. The second Bailey's face filled the screen, he breathed a sigh of relief.

"Hey." She smiled into the screen. "Tough loss tonight."

"If we keep playing like this, we might not even make the playoffs."

"You will. You've got time. How's the leg?"

He pulled up his pant leg and angled the camera to show her the bruising that was already visible on his calf.

"I can't believe they didn't eject Caldwell for that," she snarled. "Any idiot could see that he went into that slide spikes up."

"He says it was an accident."

"Well then, he's a liar. All they had to do was pull up the replay." Anger flared in Bailey's eyes.

Gonzo bit back a grin at how offended she was on his behalf. He enjoyed knowing she felt protective of him.

"It's all good. It didn't break the skin." He flexed his foot and his calf cramped. Broken skin or not, the fucking charlie horse it had left behind hurt like a bitch.

"What was that little wince for?" Bailey asked.

Shoot, he hadn't meant for her to see that. "Nothing," he mumbled.

"How sore is it? Truthfully."

He flexed his foot again and the bruise made itself known. "It doesn't feel great."

"Well, it's not bubble bath, but I put a dead sea mineral bath salt in your bag."

"You did what?"

She looked down instead of into the camera. "I didn't want to pack a liquid in your bag, but I thought you might miss taking your nice baths when you were on the road."

The embarrassment on her face was so fucking cute. "Bailey, look at me."

She raised her head and looked at the screen.

"Thank you."

She shrugged. "I know it's not the same as your fancy bath stuff here or your hot tub, but I figured it was better than nothing. It's just a couple of packages of bath salts. It's in the front zipper pouch of your case."

He hopped off the bed and went over to his suitcase. He unzipped the pocket and pulled out two packages. Gonzo looked at the first one. Dead sea mineral bath. Nice. The second package said it was a juniper muscle soak. Fuck, that sounded like heaven. "Thanks, Bay. I don't usually have a bath at the hotel, but I'm gonna tonight since I'm on my own. Ryan and Pete are meeting up with a buddy from high school and who knows what Kia and Smitty are up to."

"Mmm, right, Ryan and Pete have that dinner and Kia and Smitty are doing their kid-free weekend."

"Yeah, not sure how much alone time they'll get between the tattoo convention and games, but hey, at least I can have a bath."

"When I packed the salts, I just assumed some of those hotels had great baths."

"Yeah, they do, I never take one." There was no way he was letting his teammates know how much he loved a good bubble bath. He'd never hear the end of it. Soaking in the tub with a woman the guys would understand, but enjoying a good soak by yourself, the more bubbles the better, probably not. Although if the fuckers actually tried it, they'd probably like it. A steamy bubble bath after a game felt a hell of a lot nicer than the ice baths the team trainers often had them do. Even if the ice was better for him.

"You gonna have a bath with me?" he asked.

"Kind of hard to do when I'm here and you're all the way across the country." Bailey's cheeks turned red and she looked away from the screen.

"Why you blushing, Bay?"

"Nothing." She batted her eyes at him innocently.

"You're a terrible liar. What'd you do?"

"I might have watched the game from your tub."

"You watched me play while lying naked in my tub?" His dick fired to attention.

"I did." She licked her lips. "Might be my new favorite way to watch you play."

"Please tell me you touched yourself while in there."

"Maybe." She smiled coyly.

"Fuck." He stuck his hands down the front of his pants and shifted his hard cock before it got strangled by his boxers. "You want to crawl in there and do it again while I watch?"

Bailey giggled. "Nope, sorry, I'm all good."

"Come on, you can handle more than one little orgasm in an evening."

"Who said it was one little orgasm?"

"Greedy girl, you had more than one?" His cock pulsed.

"There are a lot of innings in a ballgame, Gonzo."

His dick was like a fucking sledgehammer it was so hard. "Please tell me you used your toys."

"Of course I did." Her teeth dug into her bottom lip as they looked at each other through the screen.

What a difference a couple of weeks made. He couldn't imagine the woman who'd shown up in San Diego a couple of months ago being confident enough in her body to tease him about masturbating. Hell, she'd practically melted into the floor out of embarrassment when he'd found her vibrator. The change in Bailey was sexy as fuck.

"You sure you don't want to show me?"

She blushed again. "I'm not masturbating via Facetime, Gonzo. I'd feel like I was making a porno."

"A porno?" he teased.

"Shut up," she giggled, like she was embarrassed. "You know what I mean."

"Yeah, I do. Would it feel the same to do it in person?"

Bailey chewed on her bottom lip. "I don't know."

The look on her face said she wasn't opposed to the idea which was progress. "I think it'd be fucking hot to see you playing with your toys in front of me."

"You do?"

"Fuck yeah."

"Why?"

Why? Why the fuck not? Everything about Bailey turned him on. Seeing her taking what she wanted, fucking herself with a toy, showing him exactly how she like it. Having that visual. Damn.

"Because I think it would be hot to just sit back and really watch you and how beautiful you look. Normally I'm watching, but I'm also selfishly focused on making sure I'm getting you where you need to go rather than just sitting back and looking at you."

Now that was all he could think about. Damn. "I've watched you gain confidence over the past few weeks, and I think it would be sexy as fuck to watch you take control of your own orgasm. Forget about anyone else, and just take and take until you're so wrung out you could barely move. Fuck yourself so hard you couldn't possibly think about having another orgasm. That's what it sounds like you did tonight and I really wish I'd seen it."

"Oh."

"Do you have any idea how hot you look when you come? The way your nipples get all tight and flushed just begging me to suck on them." He could picture it perfectly. "Then you get that little hitch in your breath that makes you bite your bottom lip." She shifted like she was imagining it, too. "Your body tells me exactly what you want as your blush works its way up your chest and onto your cheeks, and your eyes go from their normal blue to this inky color that's like looking into the depth of the ocean."

He paused and looked at her face. That flush he was talking about was clear on her face right now. His girl liked him talking about this.

"My eyes don't ever look like the ocean," she said.

"Yeah, they do. When you're turned on, like really turned on, they—I don't really know how to describe it. You know when you're on a boat and you look into the deep sea for too long and everything in you wants to just jump in and see where it takes you?"

Bailey's breath hitched, and she nodded.

"It's like that." He licked his lips.

"Wow," she whispered.

"Yeah."

"Okay."

"Okay what?" He leaned forward on the bed.

"I'll show you when you get home."

"Seriously?" His dick twitched, then twitched again like the fucking thing was clapping it was so excited. He knew the feeling.

"Mmm-hmm."

Her cheeks flushed and he could tell even through the screen how badly she wanted to look away, but she didn't. His girl had gotten so brave. "Fuck, I wish we didn't have two more games before we came home," he groaned. "Any chance you want to be on my bed waiting for me when I get home?"

Bailey lowered her head shyly and nodded.

"Any chance you want to give me a little preview now?" he practically begged.

"I told you I'm not going to do that." She rolled her eyes.

"Can't blame a guy for trying." He shifted his hips to ease the restriction on his dick.

"The anticipation will be good for you," Bailey teased.

"Or kill me." He shifted again.

"I can confidently say no one has ever died from masturbatory anticipation."

Masturbatory anticipation? "Fuck, I love when you sound all academic and shit."

Bailey rolled her eyes. "How was that academic?"

"I don't know. It just sounded smart." He pushed the pillow behind his head to get more comfortable. "So that was a hard no?"

"Yes. You're a big boy, you'll be fine. Or I guess you could tug one out in the tub as well."

"Yeah? You want to watch?"

"Uh...uh..."

He burst out laughing at the way Bailey's mouth gaped like a fish at the very idea. "Just kidding, Bay."

His calf cramped and he winced. He really needed to do something about this or it was going to fuck with his game tomorrow. "But I am going to go jump in the tub and use those bath salts you packed for me."

"Good."

"Do me a favor?"

"Of course."

"Sleep in my bed till I get home."

Bailey's forehead wrinkled with confusion. "Why?"

"I just want you to."

"Gonzo?" Bailey pressed.

He sat up and rubbed the back of his neck. "I don't know, Bay, I can't be there with you, but I just like the idea of you sleeping in my bed even when I'm not there."

"Okay."

"Yeah?"

"Yeah."

"Cool." He bobbed his head up and down. "Night, Bay. I'll call you tomorrow after the game."

"I'll be here. Now go take care of yourself."

He snickered at the double entendre. "I'll take care of myself all right." He filled his voice with all the innuendo he could muster.

Bailey sighed. "Oh god, that wasn't what I meant and you know it. Look after your calf, you perv."

"I'm a good multi-tasker," he teased.

The corner of her mouth tilted up as she bit back a smirk. "Goodnight, Gonzo."

"Night, Bay."

He disconnected the call and dropped his arm over his eyes. *Sleep in my bed?* Where the hell had that come from? The idea had come out of nowhere, but the second it popped into his head, he knew he wanted it. Not just while he was away, but always. Fuck, he was gone over her. Was this how his friends felt when they'd met their women?

He pushed off the mattress. Whatever the hell it was, he wouldn't figure it out tonight.

# CHAPTER NINETEEN

The music pumped through the speakers in the living room as she loaded the dishwasher. Her watch buzzed, letting her know she had an incoming call. Howard Marx's name flashed on the screen of her watch and she scrambled to grab the stereo remote and her phone before her new boss hung up.

Bailey swiped the screen to answer the phone. "Hello."

"Could I speak to Bailey, please?"

"This is."

"Bailey, this is Howard Marx.

"Hi Howard. How are you?"

"I'm doing well. Listen, I know you aren't supposed to start work until September, but I was wondering if you'd be able to come in and discuss a speaking opportunity."

Speaking opportunity? "You want me to guest lecture?"

"I'd like to discuss a couple of opportunities. Do you have time today or tomorrow to meet?"

"I'm available either day."

"Wonderful. How is today at 3:00? I can get you setup in your new office at the same time."

"3:00 works great."

"See you then."

Bailey hung up the phone. A couple of opportunities. What could that possibly be about?

At 2:30 pm, Bailey strolled around the University bookstore, familiarizing herself with the books they carried for the sociology department. She'd wandered around the campus a couple of times since she'd been in town but hadn't really spent much time here yet. When the school year started in September, it would become her home away from home. No point in spending too much time there already. She hadn't planned on getting her office set until July or August. It was barely June.

She glanced at her watch and slowly made her way toward the sociology building.

A few students sat scattered across the lawn, studying. The scene would look completely different come September when classes were fully in session.

Bailey pulled open the door to the Social Sciences building.

She wandered down the hall in search of Howard's office. She checked her watch one more time. 2:55 pm. Perfect. Better early than late. Bailey knocked on the door.

Howard stood as she entered the room and shook her hand. "Bailey, good to see you. Thank you for meeting me on such short notice."

"Of course."

Howard gestured for her to take a seat, and he sat back down at his desk. "How are you enjoying San Diego so far? Are you getting settled in?"

"I am yes."

"Wonderful. You're probably wondering why I've asked you in today."

She shifted in her seat. "I am."

"Two reasons, actually. First. Would you be interested in teaching a summer session?"

"This summer?"

"Yes. Daphne was supposed to teach a class in July, but she's had something come up and needs a leave. We'd rather not cancel the class, so I'm hoping you'd like to teach it."

"What's the course?"

"Social perspectives in a social media age."

"With what focus?"

"Daphne's specialty is social change, but we are open to narrowing it down to something in your area, since the course description is deliberately vague at the moment."

July wasn't that far away. Not a lot of time to plan a course, depending on the subject matter. "Although I've taught lessons on social media, I haven't taught an entire class on the subject. I'm not sure I'd be ready."

"Daphne has left all of her course material and lessons for whoever takes over the class. I'm confident you will be able to pull it together. We've had an overwhelming response to your upcoming class this fall. It seems the students here are extremely interested in your expertise. We believe they'd also be interested in something similar in a class about social media."

Could she get a course together by then and do it well? Yes, it would certainly mean a change to her current routine, but she was finding herself a little bored when Gonzo was out of town, anyway. "I'd be happy to teach the course as long as in my evaluation you take into account the short notice."

Howard smirked. "Of course."

She wasn't stupid. In this land of publish or perish, she was only too aware of the fact that she had no tenure. A stream of bad reviews could be the difference between teaching next year and unemployment. In her experience, institutes of higher learning were not tolerant of their teachers needing a learning curve. "Given the short timeframe, I will predominantly need to use Daphne's course material."

Howard handed her a USB stick and pointed to a file box beside his desk. "Everything is in there."

"Perfect." Bailey itched to dig into the box and see exactly what she'd just signed on for. "I haven't been given my office yet."

"I'll take you over as soon as we're done here." Howard leaned back in his seat and watched her. "Are you familiar with the GWE Gender and Equality conference that's being held in New York this year?"

"Of course." It was the biggest conference on women's issues in the country.

"They reached out to us about having you speak."

"I'm sorry? You want me to speak?" Wow, she hadn't expected the University to choose her to represent them or even that they would be represented, for that matter.

The University was more known for international issues rather than gender.

"No, they were having trouble reaching you, so they contacted us to get ahold of you. Apparently, you come highly recommended, and they wanted to ensure the University would support you attending. Which I assured them we would."

"They want me to speak?" Did he really just say that they wanted her to speak, not someone like her, but her? She clamped her hands in her lap to stop herself from doing the little jig her body wanted to do.

"Yes, they specifically wanted you to do a seminar on misogyny in the media." Howard tapped his fingers on the desk. "I thought their request tied in nicely to the summer class."

Ahh, now it made more sense why he was so open to her changing the existing syllabus. Being asked to speak at this conference was not only a big deal for her, but it was also a big deal for the University. People came from all over the world for this conference. And they wanted her. Holy shit. They wanted her. She couldn't wait to tell Gonzo.

Howard passed over a piece of paper. "This is the number for Colette Beringer. She is the conference committee chair. As I told Colette, it goes without saying the University would like you to speak at the conference. I assured her you would be more than happy to present. We will organize any coverage necessary for your classes."

Bailey looked at the contact information on the sheet. Her body practically vibrated with excitement. How had the committee even heard of her? This was the kind of opportunity everyone in her profession dreamed of and never believed would happen. Her foot bounced anxiously on the floor in front of her and she fought to keep it still. "I will give Colette a call this afternoon."

"Please do." Howard stood. "Now let me show you to your office so you can get started."

Bailey grabbed the box with all of Daphne's course info and followed him.

"You never mentioned you knew Anisa Behman," Howard said as they walked up a flight of stairs.

Anisa? Where did that come from? "Anisa's research was instrumental in my master's thesis. We spent a lot of time together while I worked on both my master's and PhD."

"Didn't you work under Jeffrey Long for your PhD?"

"I did, yes, but I spent about 6 months with Anisa, doing research on gender violence as part of my master's."

"Mmm, I must have missed that. I was more focused on your PhD when you applied for this position. From what Colette said, Anisa spoke very highly of you and they are eager to hear you speak."

Bailey bit back a smile. Thank you, Anisa. Even with her colleague's endorsement, she still couldn't believe she was getting asked to speak at this conference.

Howard continued up the next flight of stairs to the fourth floor. At the end of the hallway, he pulled out a key and unlocked the door. She stepped into the office and scanned the room. A smile immediately spread across her face.

"Wow, I have a window." Bailey wandered over and looked outside. The view wasn't great. Mostly just a parking lot, but it was still a window. Her last office had been in the basement and wasn't much bigger than a closet. This office was darn near palatial. Empty bookcases lined one wall and a filing cabinet sat alone in the opposite corner. The scarred desk looked like it had seen better days but would get the job done. Definitely an improvement from her last office.

"I hope this will be satisfactory," Howard said.

She spun around to face him. "This is fantastic, thank you."

Howard held out the key. "Be sure to call Colette. And let me know once you've confirmed the speaking engagement and we will put it up on the website and in your bio."

"Will do." If she'd had any doubt about why she'd been called in today, this certainly solidified it. No mention of the upcoming summer class, just the advertising the conference would give the University. Not that she blamed them at all. Alumni loved stuff like this. And the school depended on donor dollars.

Once Howard left, she grabbed her phone out of her pocket, took a deep steadying breath, and dialed Colette's phone number.

"Hello?"

"May I speak to Colette Beringer, please?"

"Ms. Beringer is not in. May I take a message?" the woman on the other end asked.

"Yes, this is Bailey Reynolds."

"And what is this regarding?"

"She was trying to reach me about speaking at the upcoming conference in New York." It took everything in her to remain professional when she said that. Every fiber in her being wanted to squeal and jump around with excitement.

"What's the best number to reach you at?"

Bailey relayed her number to the receptionist and hung up. Giddy, she dropped into her chair and spun in a circle. She kept spinning until she was facing the window. Holy shit, she was going to speak at the GWE convention.

She grabbed her phone back off her desk and pulled up Gonzo's number. She was just getting ready to leave a message when he picked up.

"Hey, Bay, what's up?"

"Oh, I didn't think you'd answer."

He chuckled. "Then why'd you call?"

"I don't know. I was excited and you were the first person I wanted to call."

"I like the sound of that. What are you excited about?" Gonzo asked.

She could hear voices in the background. "Where are you?"

"Just in the locker room, about to head onto the field. So what's up?"

Shoot, she knew how important it was for him to focus before a game. He had this whole routine he always followed and didn't like when anything made him veer off course. "Sorry, we can talk after the game."

"Bay, I wouldn't have answered if I didn't want to talk to you. So spill."

"You sure?"

"Bailey, talk."

"Umm, turns out I'm going to be teaching a class this summer now as well, so I just got my new office."

"Cool. So why do you sound like you're about to jump out of your skin?"

How was it he knew her so well? "Umm, apparently they want me to speak at the GWE convention."

"What's that?"

"Global Women's Equality." She couldn't contain the giggle that burst out of her. "I can't believe it."

"That's awesome, Bailey. I take it being asked is a pretty big deal."

"Yeah, you could say that. It's kind of like the World Series for gender sociologists."

"Holy shit, that's incredible. I'm so proud of you."

Even over the phone, she could feel how happy he was for her. This was exactly why she'd called him. If anyone would understand what it felt like to realize your dreams, it was him. "Thanks," she whispered.

"Gonzo, get your ass in gear," a male voice yelled in the background.

"Sorry, Bay, I gotta go, but I'm really fucking happy for you. When I get home, we'll go out to celebrate and you can tell me all about it."

"Sounds perfect. Good luck at your game."

"Thanks. Send me a picture of your new office. Congrats, babe. I'm really proud of you."

Before she could even say anything else, he hung up. She stared down at the phone. Times like this his travel schedule sucked, but at least he'd picked up the phone.

She snapped a photo of her empty office and sent it off to him. By the time he got home, she'd have a decorated office and, hopefully, officially be listed as a speaker at the conference. She covered her face with her hands and squealed as she pounded her feet on the ground. Best day ever. Time to go shopping.

# CHAPTER TWENTY

The door snicked shut behind him and he set his keys in the bowl by the front door. Fuck, he was tired. Their plane was supposed to get in at 9:00 pm, but because of some kind of mechanical error, it was now a little after 1:00 am. Thank god they were only flying to Texas this week and not back to the east coast.

A light illuminated the kitchen. Was Bailey still up? He veered toward the kitchen. No sign of Bailey. His chest tightened. She'd clearly left the light on for him, so he didn't come home to a dark house. He'd never had that before. Even when he lived with roommates, it was every man for himself. No one ever left the light on for the last guy who came home.

He flicked off the light and padded down the hallway in his sock feet toward the bedroom. At the bedroom door, he pulled up short when he saw the outline of a person in his bed. The fist around his chest tightened almost to the point of pain. Fuck, everything about seeing her in his bed, waiting for him, felt right.

Although he'd asked her to sleep in his bed, he hadn't really thought she would, especially when he'd messaged her earlier to say how late they were going to be getting in. Some animalistic piece of him wanted to tear the covers off her and stake his claim on the woman in his bed, to leave no doubt in her mind that she belonged to him.

Needing a minute to get his emotions under control, he went into the bathroom and brushed his teeth. When he finally felt like he had control of himself, he clicked off the bathroom light. As his eyes adjusted to the darkness of the room, he could hear Bailey's body shift against the sheets. Instantly, his body was back on alert. The exhaustion he'd felt a few minutes ago was nowhere to be seen.

"Gonzo?" Bailey's voice was husky with sleep.

"Yeah, it's me. Sorry I woke you."

"No, that's okay. I'm glad you're home. You must be exhausted." Bailey shifted and the sheet slipped down her body, exposing her breast. Her very naked breast and his cock instantly awoke.

"I was. I'm kind of awake now." The second he saw her in his bed, any thoughts of sleep had instantly vanished. "I like seeing you in my bed."

"Good. I'm glad."

"How tired are you?" he asked.

"I'm awake now." Her voice filled with amusement as she spoke.

"Good." He stepped closer to the mattress. "Then lose the sheet."

"What?"

"Lose the sheet, Bailey. It's been a long road trip and I'm tired of seeing you only in my imagination. I need to look at you."

Her foot wrapped around the sheet and she slowly slid it further down, exposing her naked body, inch by delectable inch. The moonlight shining in through the window hit her skin, making it shine like alabaster.

Normally he wanted the lights on completely when he was with Bailey, but tonight he appreciated the romance of the moonlight. He picked up the remote for the blinds and opened them further.

"What are you doing?" she asked.

"Just enjoying the way your body looks in the moon-light."

"Oh."

"Fuck, Bailey, if you could see the way you look right now," he muttered.

"What do I look like?"

For once, he was at a loss for words. Talking dirty was easy. But saying the romantic shit that was floating around in his mind out loud, that was way out of his comfort zone. How could he possibly explain that she looked like a sexy Grecian goddess and the comfort of home all wrapped up in one incredibly sexy package?

He wasn't the kind of guy who was going to tell a woman her skin looked like alabaster even if he thought it. So instead of saying any of those things, he simply went with what she would expect him to say. "You look like a fucking wet dream. Jesus, Bay, when I said I wanted to come home and find you in my bed, I didn't have a fucking clue it would feel like this."

"What does it feel like?"

"Everything."

"Gonzo," she whispered, and her hand pressed against her chest.

He kicked off his boxers and fisted his cock, loving the way Bailey's eyes followed the movement of his hand as he tightly moved his palm down the shaft. "I'm more an action speak louder than words kind of guy. Why don't I show you?"

"Mmm, why don't you?" Bailey arched her back and pulled up one knee. The pose was so confident he couldn't help but grin. Fuck, yeah, he loved seeing her like this. Every time they were together, she became more and more comfortable in her skin. A few weeks ago, she never would have been confident enough to pose on the bed.

He walked to the foot of the bed and pressed his knee against the mattress. "Spread your legs," he ordered.

Bailey's knee dropped open slightly, giving him a teasing view of her pussy. It wasn't enough. He grabbed her ankle and moved her foot out wider, exposing her completely to his view. "Beautiful," he murmured then picked up her foot and placed a kiss on her ankle bone. "So, did you use your toys and think of me again while I was away?"

"Mmm." She shifted on the mattress.

He slowly kissed his way up her calf. "You gonna show me?"

"That would be me showing you, not you showing me, wouldn't it?" she teased.

Well, she had him there. He chuckled. "Technically yes, but..." Gonzo ran his tongue along the tender skin at the inside of her knee. "I'll make it worth your while." He blew gently on her inner thigh and Bailey shifted her hips against the mattress. "You know you want to show me how fucking hot you look when you masturbate."

"I'm pretty sure that fantasy is yours, not mine."

"It's definitely my fantasy. I haven't thought about anything else all week."

"Really?"

"God, yes," he groaned. It was like he was back in fucking high school with the amount he beat off this week. "Please."

Bailey's head snapped up. "Did you really just say please?"

"Yeah."

"You never ask nicely in the bedroom, you're more the order me around type," she teased. "You must really want this."

He sat back on his heels and stared down at her. His eyes narrowed as she smirked back at him in amusement. "Get your toy," he ordered.

The smirk on Bailey's face vanished. "What?"

"You heard me. Get your toy and show me how you make yourself come."

Bailey sucked in a breath. "What happened to please?"

"I think you made it pretty clear me asking nicely didn't turn you on."

"It wasn't that it didn't turn me on, it just surprised me."

He could see the way her chest rose and fell as she watched him. She might not admit it, but his girl liked being bossed around in the bedroom.

"I want to see you fuck yourself with a toy, Bailey. I'll even be nice and let you pick which one."

"Oh you will, will you?" She raised one eyebrow in amusement.

"Mmm-hmm, but you better grab it quick, otherwise I'm picking."

"You don't know which one works best."

"So pick."

"Fine, but you're so bossy," she muttered and rolled to her side. She pulled open the drawer of his bedside table.

"Holy fuck, you have your sex toys in my bedside table?"

She paused and turned around. "You told me to sleep in here."

"I'm not complaining. That's fucking hot." How many toys did she have in there? "Show me."

"You are so weird." She rolled her eyes at him.

Reaching into his bedside table, she pulled out a red toy that looked like a rosebud. What the hell was that thing? He'd been expecting some kind of giant dildo or something, not a little red rose.

Bailey turned around with the toy in her hand and eyed him nervously. "This one works really good."

If she honestly didn't want to do this, he wouldn't push, but the cues her body were giving said she did. Her nipples had instantly become little rocks when he'd suggested it. He crawled forward and placed a kiss against her lips. "You good with this?"

"Yes, I just hope you won't be disappointed."

"There's nothing you could do that would disappoint me, Bailey." He gently kissed her again, and her body melted against him. "Now show me how that thing works."

Chuckling, she shook her head at him. "I still think it's weird you want this so badly."

He looked at her until she made eye contact with him. "You telling me you don't think it's hot when I touch myself?"

"Umm."

He fisted his palm around his cock and Bailey's eyes widened and stayed glued to the movement of his hand. Even in the moonlight, he could see the way her nostrils flared as she watched. "This doesn't turn you on, just a little?" he pressed.

Bailey's hand fluttered against her collarbone. "No, no, it definitely does." She licked her lips.

"Exactly." He squeezed his cock harder and Bailey gasped. "See how the way I touch myself is different from how you touch me?"

Bailey's teeth bit into her bottom lip as she nodded.

"I want to see how you look. What you do to yourself that I'm maybe not doing. I want to be 100% focused on what you look like when you come."

Bailey lay back on the mattress and the little red rose buzzed to life. She trailed the toy over her nipple and down her stomach. Her hips shifted on the mattress, and she widened her legs as she touched the rose against her pussy. She moved the toy around slightly, then gasped.

"What just happened?" he asked.

"It's a..." Her head arched back and she closed her eyes. "It kind of sucks on my clit."

He moved down the mattress so he could see better. Bailey's hips bucked and she began panting. Damn, that thing was impressive. "It works that fast?"

"Mmm-hmm," she moaned.

His dick throbbed as it tried to demand he let it join the party. It took all his self-control to keep his hands off Bailey. "You look so fucking sexy, baby," he told her.

Bailey opened her eyes and smiled at him, and he growled. He fucking growled. What the hell was that? She reached over and touched his dick.

"I want to suck your cock," she told him.

His brain must have short-circuited because he couldn't possibly have just heard her say that. "Huh?"

"Come up here so I can suck your dick."

His eyes flashed back to the toy sucking away on her clit. "This is supposed to be about you," he told her.

She moved the toy off herself. "This is supposed to be about me showing what I like. I think it would be really hot to have something sucking my clit at the same time I'm sucking you."

His cock practically jumped, it throbbed so hard. "Jesus," he muttered.

"Please," she practically begged.

He scurried up the mattress. Kneeling above her face, he held his cock as he looked down at her. His chest tightened like it had when he'd first seen her in his bed tonight. "You have any idea how perfect you are?"

Bailey's lips curled into the little smirk of a woman who knew she had the upper hand. "What is it with men and blowjobs?"

He cupped the back of her head and threaded his fingers through her hair. This was anything but just a blowjob. This was about so much more, but he sure as hell wasn't ready to examine what. "Turn on the toy, Bailey," he said and placed his cock against her lips.

Her tongue dipped out and she ran it along the seam of his cock. "Mmm," she said, then the rose began vibrating again. Bailey sucked him in deeply. And he hissed out a breath as her hot mouth closed around him. Torn between watching Bailey suck his cock, or watching her play with the toy, he didn't know where to look. His senses were on overload and judging from the noises Bailey was making, she was feeling the same way. Her little moans vibrated against his cock and he fucking loved it. Bailey's mouth gaped and his dick popped from her mouth as her orgasm tore through her. He'd never seen anything more beautiful. He leaned back on his heels and just watched her until finally her eyes opened. She flicked a glance at his still erect cock.

"Sorry," she winced.

"You don't have a single thing to be sorry for, Bay. That was the hottest thing I've ever seen."

She smiled. "You need to get out more."

"I've seen plenty and that was by far the top of the list." He brushed her hair away from her face. "I've never seen you look more beautiful."

She grabbed his hand and kissed his palm. "Thank you, Gonz. I've never felt more beautiful."

"That's because you are," he said.

A slow, seductive smile spread across her lips. Bailey sat up and pushed her hand against his chest. "Lay back, Gonzo." She continued to push against his chest until he lay on his back, then straddled his waist.

"What are you doing?"

"I thought maybe today I'd be on top."

Holy shit. She never went on top. They'd come a long way in her confidence, but so far, it hadn't extended to this.

When he didn't speak, she bit her bottom lip. "Is that okay?" she asked.

"I can't think of anything better." He reached over and grabbed a condom off the bedside table. "Put it on me," he ordered.

Bailey eased her body back on his thighs, and his cock sprang up in front of her. He bit back a groan as she slowly slid the condom down his length. With the condom in place, Bailey pushed up on her knees and grabbed his cock. He watched her as she positioned him where she wanted him and slowly sank down. She shifted her weight and he slid a little further inside, then suddenly she took him all the way in.

"Oh Jesus," he groaned as her wet heat fully engulfed his cock.

She eased back up, then down, and stopped. Her nose wrinkled up.

"What's the matter, baby?" he asked.

"I don't really know what to do up here. I've never been on top before."

"Ever?" He couldn't keep the shock from his voice. He knew she said she didn't feel comfortable being on top, but it never occurred to him she'd never even tried it.

"No." She shifted like she was going to get off and he clamped his hand down on her thigh.

"Where you going?"

"I suck at this."

He disagreed. His dick was still buried deep in her pussy. Hell, they could just stay like this and he could die happy. He shifted his hips and she sucked in a breath. "You feel pretty fucking fantastic to me."

"I don't know what I'm supposed to do," she admitted.

"Just try a couple of things and see what feels good."

"What do you mean, try a few things?"

"Go up and down, lean back, lean forward, swivel your hips." He rubbed his hand along her thigh. "Use me to make your body feel good." He held her hips down as he shifted his own. The movement drove her clit against his pubic bone, and she gasped. "You like that?" he asked.

"Mmm-hmm." She nodded.

He swiveled his own hips slowly to the left, then around to the right, watching Bailey's face the entire time. Her mouth dropped open. He continued the motion and her breath turned into a pant. He pulled her forward so her breast touched his mouth and he flicked his tongue against her nipple. "See? Just move your body and see what you like."

"You're doing just fine," she said.

He chuckled. "Imagine how much better it would feel if you were controlling the movement, taking what you want, how you want it, just like you did with your toy."

Bailey's hips shifted like she was grinding her clit against him, and he grinned. "That's it, baby, use me to get you off."

Bailey sat up and pressed her hands against his chest. She pushed herself up till he almost popped out, then slowly dropped back down. He groaned. Bailey smiled, then did it again. Her eyes never left his face as she continued to move her hips in various ways. When she hit something she liked, her eyes widened.

Suddenly, her movements changed. It was like she forgot to be nervous or unsure and became a woman who knew exactly what she wanted. He couldn't look away as she rode him hard. Her back arched, thrusting her breast forward. Bailey reached up and pinched her own nipples and he couldn't hold back. He gripped her hips and bucked into her. Bailey's grunts and moans matched his own. His balls pulled up tight. He was so fucking close. He reached between them and found Bailey's clit and pressed against it with his thumb. Her pussy clamped down tightly on his cock as she screamed out her orgasm, dragging him along in the wake. Bailey collapsed against his chest and he rubbed his hands up and down her back as he tried to catch his own breath.

"Holy shit," Bailey mumbled against his chest.

"You're a fast study Bailey Reynolds."

"I had an excellent teacher."

He continued to rub his hands up and down her back. The next thing he knew, she made a little baby snoring sound like she'd fallen asleep. Smiling to himself, he tossed the condom in the garbage can at the side of the bed then shifted her slightly so he could get more comfortable. She sniffled and burrowed deeper against him. Not wanting to let her go, he tightened his arms slightly and drifted off to sleep.

# CHAPTER TWENTY-ONE

The following week, Bailey glanced around the nearly empty coffeeshop. No sign of Kia yet. She walked up to the counter and ordered an iced coffee. The barista set the drink on the counter and still no sign of Kia.

With drink in hand, she sat down at a table near the window so she could watch the people walking by. Several minutes later, Kia rushed into the cafe. "Oh my god, I'm so sorry." She flopped into the vacant chair across from her. "Max stepped in dog poop and there was no way I was letting him into my car with that on his shoe. Then it became a whole thing." She sighed.

"Yuck. I didn't know you had a dog."

"We don't. The neighbor does and since Jeff's front yard doesn't have a fence, the neighbor thinks that means it's fair game to let his dog wander over."

Bailey wrinkled her nose. "Gross. I imagine you don't live in one of those neighborhoods where it's acceptable to flick it back in their yard."

Kia snorted. "No, I don't think that would go over well."

"Bummer."

"Although now that you mention it. I'm sure Jeff would love to tell the neighbor that's what's coming down the pipe if he doesn't start cleaning up after his dog." Kia pushed away from the table. "I'm just going to grab a drink and I'll be right back."

Bailey watched the other woman as she strolled up to the counter. Everything about Kia just screamed cool. From the tattoos to the edgy wardrobe, to the confident way she walked across the room like she didn't give a shit what anyone thought of her. On the outside, they didn't look like they would have much in common, but the more time she spent with Kia, the more she liked her.

Kia dropped back into her seat and took a long sip of her coffee. "Ah, now I feel human." She closed her eyes, still holding her cup up near her mouth after taking a sip. Her eyes popped open and she took another sip before setting the cup down on the table. "Sorry. We have this ridiculous fancy coffee maker that Jeff had before we got together and the thing was on the fritz this morning and I couldn't get it to work. I'm pretty handy, but I swear you need a freakin' space degree to operate the thing. I'm digging my regular old Walmart special out of storage when I get home. I don't care if he likes it. It's unnatural not to have coffee first thing in the morning."

"Agreed. I have caffeine running through my veins. I'm surprised they allow me to donate blood."

"You donate blood? That's cool. What made you decide to do that?"

"I've been doing it for the past decade, ever since my sister's surgery."

"Your sister needed a blood transfusion?"

"She needed part of my liver," Bailey replied. "But when we were going through the process, I learned how much they needed blood, so..."

"Hold up." Kia held up her hand. "You gave your sister part of your liver?"

Bailey shrugged. Why did people always look at her like that when they heard? It was her sister. Of course, she'd given her part of her liver. It grew back. Why wouldn't she? "Yeah, she needed it."

"Wait, wait, wait," Kia said. "You say that like it's nothing. It's your freakin' liver."

"It grows back," Bailey said.

"Well, yeah, but still. That's like some major surgery."

Deliberately misunderstanding, she nodded. "It was a long road for her, but she's doing really well now."

Kia blinked at her. "I'm just trying to wrap my head around the fact you donated part of your liver."

"It's really not that big a deal. My sister was really sick. She needed it. I was a match."

"You were like what? 18?"

"Yeah."

"Holy shit. How old was she?"

"21."

"Wow. That's amazing." Kia leaned back in her chair and stared at Bailey for several seconds. "I can't imagine anyone in my family doing that for me."

"You'd be surprised what people will do for their loved ones when push comes to shove."

Kia laughed, but it sounded hollow. "Yeah, I think we have very different families."

"What do you mean?"

"Mine practically disowned me when I had Max, so I don't think a liver would be on the table."

"Are you kidding me? Why would they…" She didn't even know how to finish that sentence. She couldn't imagine her family disowning her. If her sister's illness had shown her anything, it was how amazing her family was. Every single person in her family had been tested as a donor. Bailey had been the closest match.

"Like I said, we obviously had different family situations. But I'm doing everything I can to make sure Max has a family like yours." Kia's eyes welled up, and she blinked rapidly. "Shit."

Bailey reached across the table and squeezed her new friend's hand. "From what I hear from Gonzo and what I've seen so far, you're doing an amazing job with him."

"Thank you." Kia stared at her and shook her head slowly.

"Okay, you need to stop looking at me like that." She pointed a finger at Kia. "Don't make me regret telling you."

"I won't. I promise. That's just very cool. I knew I liked you, but now I like you even more."

"Well, you've never tried to get between me and a chocolate bar when I have my period. It's not pretty."

"I'll be sure to keep that in mind." Kia took a sip of her coffee. "Thanks for doing this with me. I'm not really a formal dress kind of girl."

"No problem. I'm surprised you didn't ask Peyton or Kendall to come with you."

"I thought about it, but I figured this would be a good chance for us to get to know each other better."

"I love looking at all the pretty dresses. I can't wear most of them, but I enjoy looking."

"Why can't you wear them?"

"Honestly? Most of the stores don't carry my size."

Kia's forehead wrinkled. "That can't be right. They have to."

"Mmm. Not in my experience. I'm not exactly the average size."

"True. How tall are you, anyway?"

It sucked that her first thought when Kia had said true was that she was talking about her weight. "5ft8."

"I'm barely 5ft5."

"Perfectly average."

"Yep, that's me, average." Kia agreed.

"Other than your height, I'm pretty sure there's nothing average about you."

"Ah, aren't you sweet?" She pushed off from the table. "All right, you ready to do this?"

"Yep."

They tossed their cups in the garbage on their way out of the cafe and onto the street out front.

"I figured we'd start there?" Kia pointed at a boutique shop with beautiful dresses in the window.

"Sounds good." Bailey looked both ways for cars before jaywalking across the deserted street. As she pushed open the door, a little bell dinged, announcing their arrival.

The woman working in the store glanced up as Bailey walked in ahead of Kia. The woman's gaze quickly scanned Bailey, then recoiled. It was like the derision on her face was so strongly offensive every sense felt the need to jump in and participate in its attempt to make sure Bailey knew she didn't belong here. Fantastic. Looked like it was going to be one of those days. Thank god she wasn't the one needing a dress.

Kia stepped into the store, and the employee tilted her head in acknowledgement.

As they walked past a rack of dresses, Bailey fingered the fabric of a beautiful purple silk dress. The color reminded her of the lavish bedding in Gonzo's spare bedroom.

"You should try it on," Kia said.

Bailey snorted. "I don't think so." In her experience, sheath dresses were not cut for curves, at least not her curves.

Kia wandered deeper into the boutique. She picked up a dark gray dress that at first glance appeared charcoal, but as the light hit the fabric, it shimmered like a crystal.

"That would be gorgeous on you," Bailey said.

"You think?" Kia chewed on her bottom lip. "I'm supposed to be thinking color, not my normal black and gray."

Bailey ran the shimmering fabric between her fingers. Up close, it definitely looked gray. She plucked it out of Kia's hand and angled it slightly. The light hit the dress and it looked more green, then blue, then pink.

"Oh, it's like a hologram," Kia gasped. "I'm definitely trying that one on." She draped the dress over her arm, then reached out and shifted through a few more dresses on the rack. As she pulled out a new dress, she turned toward the employee who was sitting at the counter playing on her phone. "Any chance you can start me a room?"

The girl rolled her eyes as she stood up. "Sure," she sighed.

Kia made eye contact with Bailey. "Must suck to have to actually do your job," she whispered. "Now I kind of want to make her work." Kia's tongue poked out between her teeth, and she grinned mischievously.

With three more dresses picked out, Kia made her way back to the change room. Bailey sat down on the plush lounge chair that was strategically placed facing the floor to ceiling mirror outside the dressing room.

"I want to see it," Bailey called out. She turned her head and caught sight of herself in the mirror. Instantly, her hand shot out to fluff her hair even though there was nothing wrong with it. The light made her hair look more orange than its normal red. Frowning, she tilted her head slightly, allowing the light to catch her highlights and fluffed her hair again. That was better.

Kia walked out of the change room in a black sheath dress.

"Wow, that looks amazing on you," Bailey said.

"Thanks." Kia stepped in front of the mirror and ran her hand down the front of the dress, then cocked her head to the side as she studied herself. "I'm not sure."

"We have a similar dress, but the neckline is much higher, so it would cover your chest tattoos. It might be more what you're looking for," the employee said.

Kia's eyebrow arched. "Why would I want to cover up my sternum tattoo?"

Confused, the woman blinked at Kia. "I just thought it might be more appropriate for the event you were going to."

Kia snorted. "I don't attend that kind of event. Where I go, my tat's go."

Wow. Bailey was so envious of that kind of confidence. "The dress looks beautiful, but I thought you wanted some color?"

Kia adjusted the strap of the dress and studied herself in the mirror. "Yeah, I do. You know this would be more fun if you tried something on as well."

"Somehow I think the dress would look a little different on me," Bailey said.

"Well, of course it would, because your boobs are freakin' insane. I'm so jealous."

She was jealous of Bailey? That was a laugh. Kia looked amazing in the dress. There was no way Bailey wanted to attempt to slip into a dress, knowing how good her friend already looked in the same style.

Kia turned to the saleswoman. "Can you grab the purple dress like this you have out front for my friend?"

Bailey winced. "I don't really know that this cut is the best one for me."

"I agree," the saleswoman said.

Kia glared at the saleswoman. "Isn't that the whole thing with paying extra money for a dress like this? The quality of the fabric, the cut." Kia flapped her arm. "Isn't that the reason people shop at your store because quality covers a multitude of sins? Otherwise, people could just go to the mall."

"Well, of course. There's a tremendous difference in how a properly designed dress fits vs the cheap knock-offs that come off an assembly line." The woman looked at Bailey. "But not all dresses look good on all body types."

Bailey crossed her arms over her chest. "I don't really want to even try anything on."

"Tough." Kia glanced at the saleswoman. "Okay, I'll give you that not every dress looks good on every body. I know I sure can't pull off a mermaid cut. So you know your store. Can you grab something that will look good on her?"

"We wouldn't have anything."

"What?" Kia's face wrinkled in confusion and Bailey slunk deeper into her seat.

"We don't carry plus sizes," the woman sneered.

"Plus size? What the hell?" Kia snapped, then flicked a glance at Bailey. "Oh, you weren't kidding that they wouldn't even carry double digits."

"Nope." Bailey muttered.

"Holy shit." Kia looked at the salesperson and shook her head in disappointment before turning on her heel and walking back into the change room. A moment later, she stepped back out, dressed in her street clothes.

Bailey hopped out of her chair. "What are you doing?"

"We're out of here. Let's go." Kia grabbed Bailey's elbow and propelled her forward.

Bailey's mind raced to catch up. "Why? You still haven't tried on all the dresses."

Kia turned to the saleswoman. "You work on commission, right?"

"Yes," the woman replied.

"Big mistake. Huge." Kia linked her arm with Bailey and pulled her toward the exit. Once they were on the street, Kia just grinned at her. "I feel like Julia Robert's in Pretty Woman."

"What?" What had just happened in there? One minute Kia was trying on dresses, the next they were out here.

"Pretty Woman? Come on." Kia splayed her hands in front of her. "Are you kidding me? I freakin' crushed that quote and you don't even know what I'm talking about?"

"I'm still trying to figure out why you aren't trying on that gray dress you loved. Just because they don't have my size doesn't mean you shouldn't shop there. Lots of stores don't carry my size."

"Bailey, you're what, like a size 14? 16? That's not even big. It's fucking ridiculous in this day and age that a store doesn't carry a range of standard sizes. Of course, they aren't going to carry everything in every size, but come on. Not carrying any double-digit dresses is ridiculous. There are lots of stores out there. I don't need to give my money to this one."

"But—" Bailey stammered.

"No, I'm still trying to figure out how you didn't get my movie reference. You've seen Pretty Woman, right?"

"Of course I have." Bailey rolled her eyes. "I just didn't really like it."

Kia slapped her hand across her chest and stumbled backwards like she'd been shot. "What? How is that possible?"

"I don't know, it just wasn't very realistic."

"Wha—" Kia blinked as her mouth opened, then closed, and opened again. "I just—" She brought her hands up to her head and made an explosion sound like her head blew up. "It's Pretty Woman."

Bailey chuckled. "I know and you can keep saying it, but it's not going to change anything. It was just a little too farfetched."

"But that's what made it so great."

"Nope, sorry, that kind of stuff is what makes women buy into these unrealistic ideals about finding Prince Charming and all that bullshit." Bailey wrinkled her nose. "No. In real life, the hooker doesn't get the billionaire, the jock doesn't date the brain and the hero doesn't pick the fat girl. It's just not how it works." And she'd do well to remember that. She'd been spinning all these dreams around her and Gonzo and she was just kidding herself.

"Well, that's just sad," Kia muttered. "And I don't buy it. I mean, look at me." She flicked her hand toward her body. "Do I look like the stereotypical professional athlete's girlfriend?" Before Bailey could even respond, Kia pressed on. "No, I don't. I look like I belong in some biker bar or waiting outside a jail to pick up my boyfriend. Just ask my parents. But I'm not. I'm living in a house on the beach with my son and his father, living a dream I never imagined was possible. So no, I'm not going to stop believing in fairytales and you shouldn't either." Kia stepped in closer to her. "Bailey, I don't know what made you so cynical, but what I do know is once you stop believing something is possible, it becomes impossible." Kia nudged her with her hip. "Let's go find another store."

"Okay, but I think your little pep talk was enough for one day, so can we please just skip me trying on dresses with you and forgo the whole making stores see the error of their ways?"

Kia stared at her for several seconds. "Fine, but only if you promise to think about what I said."

She didn't think she'd be able to think about anything else. "I promise."

"Good. Let's go."

# CHAPTER TWENTY-TWO

Hoisting his bag on his shoulder, he strolled down to his bedroom. On auto-pilot, he followed the mundane routine of unpacking from a road trip, dumped his laundry in the basket, and wandered into the bathroom with his overnight kit. Gonzo pulled open the glass door of the shower and turned on the water and closed the door. Within seconds, steam filled the shower enclosure. He quickly flicked on the heated towel bar so his towel would be warm when he got out. Reaching behind his head, he pulled his shirt off and dropped it on the floor, his pants and underwear quickly followed suit.

God, it felt good to be home. As much as he loved playing ball, there were days when the travel got exhausting. He pulled open the shower door and stepped inside. The hot water hit him from every direction. Installing this shower had been one of the best investments he'd made when he'd bought the place. There was nothing like a steam enclosed shower. He dropped his head back and let the water pelt against his tired body.

He opened his eyes and saw Bailey leaning against the bathroom door, watching him. Damn, he'd missed her. "You gonna just stare at me, or you gonna get in here and join me?"

Bailey licked her lips and her gaze trailed down his body. "I'm kind of enjoying the view."

His cock twitched under the scrutiny. "With the steam you can barely even see, and I can promise you, it looks a lot better in here." Watching her, he fisted his cock, then slowly slid his hand down the shaft.

Her chest rose and she sucked in a breath. Her teeth dug into her bottom lip as she watched him. "I don't know. It looks pretty spectacular from where I'm standing."

He pushed open the shower door and stalked toward her. Bailey backed up. "You're all wet," she squealed when his hand snaked around her waist.

"And I'm gonna make sure you're nice and wet, too." He pulled her against his body. "Hi, baby," he whispered as he looked down at her.

"Hi." She cupped the side of his face. "I'm glad you're home."

"Me too." Threading his hand around the back of her head, he brought her mouth to his. He pressed his lips against hers. She melted against his body as he deepened the kiss.

"You're letting all the steam out of your shower," she murmured against his mouth.

Gonzo reached down and gripped the edge of her T-shirt and swiped it over her head, making Bailey gasp. "What are you doing?"

"I'm getting back in the shower." He pressed a kiss against the top of her shoulder.

"This feels more like getting me naked." She tilted her head to the side, exposing her neck. Taking the hint, he ran his tongue up the side of her throat and sucked her earlobe into his mouth. "I thought you'd prefer if I took your clothes off out here."

Bailey pressed her hand against his chest. "I'm not showering with you, Gonzo."

"What? Why?"

She stepped back and crossed her arms over her bare stomach. "Come on, Gonz, please," she pleaded.

"Please what?" He watched her closely, trying to figure out what the hell was going on.

"I just..." She flicked a wrist at her body.

When she wouldn't make eye contact with him, he pushed his finger against her chin to force her to look up. "You just what?"

"Please." Bailey closed her eyes. "God, this is embarrassing."

"Talk to me, Bay."

"I just...I don't look good naked."

This again? They'd been having sex for weeks. He thought they were over all this. "I've licked every inch of your body. I'm pretty sure I know what you look like naked."

She shifted uncomfortably on her heels. "Yeah, but there's bedroom naked and there's shower with all the lights on naked."

"What?" Where they were was irrelevant. Naked was naked, and Bailey naked was always a good thing.

She let out an exasperated huff. "You know what I mean."

Unfortunately, he did. While he loved her body. She clearly still didn't. Bending his knees, he squatted so they were eye level. "Bay, trust me, you have nothing to worry about. I love the way you look." He ran his hand down her hip and cupped her ass. "And now that I've started thinking about fucking you in the shower, I can't imagine anything better."

She snorted. "Yeah right."

He leaned back and looked her in the eye. "I'm serious. I've seen you in the hot tub, so I know how good you look wet. It'll look even better when I can see all of you."

She chewed her bottom lip and dropped her eyes. "What if you don't like it?"

"Bay, there is not a fucking thing about your body I don't like. Light, dark, I know what your body looks like. You turn me on more than anyone I've ever been with because it's you."

"But you'll be able to see better in the shower."

"I know, and it's going to be fucking great." Knowing how much she liked it when he talked dirty to her, he trailed his finger over the curve of her breast. "I'll be able to see the way your skin gets those little goosebumps when I blow against your nipple, and how it pulls up tight and gets hard."

He crouched further and kissed the scar on her stomach. She tensed briefly, then relaxed when he ran his tongue around her belly button. Trailing his hands down her hips, he cupped her ass and pulled her toward him. He exhaled hard against her mound, hoping the heat of his breath would get through her leggings. When she shivered, he grinned.

Bingo. He teased his finger up her inner thigh and nudged her legs apart, then opened his mouth over her clit, and pressed his tongue firmly against her through her pants. Bailey's head dropped back against the door. "I'll be able to see how your clit likes to tease me by poking its head out and then when I've really got you turned on how it stays out, just begging me to suck it."

Bailey shifted her weight and made a little mewing noise. God, she was so fucking sexy. How could she doubt for one second how beautiful she was? He flicked his tongue against her core, and she groaned in frustration.

Kneeling, he looked up at her. "Shower with me, Bay. Let me show you how fucking sexy I think you look."

She watched him for several seconds, took a breath, then nodded.

God, she blew him away. He knew how hard this was for her. The way she trusted him was humbling. "Yeah?"

"Don't hurt me, Gonz," she whispered.

He stood up and placed a kiss against her lips. "Never." He hooked his hand on the edge of her leggings and pushed it down her thighs. "I'm gonna fuck you so good, you'll never doubt how fucking sexy you are ever again." Kneeling, he pulled her right foot from the pants.

Bailey snorted. "Good luck."

"Is that a challenge?" He raised his eyebrow as he picked up her left foot to pull her pants the rest of the way off her body.

She smirked at him. "Take it however you want to."

He pushed himself upright. "Oh, it's on." Waggling his eyebrows at her, he pulled his bottom lip between his teeth. They weren't leaving this bathroom till she'd come multiple times in the bright light.

With a flick of the wrist, he unhooked her bra and dropped it on the floor. Bailey's arm moved like she was going to cover herself.

He hated she felt like she needed to cover herself in front of him. "Don't." He grabbed her hand. "Let me look at you." He stepped back and let his gaze trail down her luscious body. "Fuck," he groaned as he looked at the best set of tits he'd ever seen in his entire life. From where he was standing, she didn't have a single thing to be shy about. He was a visual guy, and seeing her in the bright light of the bathroom just made him want her more. "How'd I get so lucky?" he asked.

A shy smile and blush covered Bailey's cheeks. "Thank you, Gonz," she whispered.

Jesus, it was like a punch to the sternum. He was gone for this woman. "You never have to thank me for that, Bay." Needing to lighten the mood, he grabbed her hand and pulled her toward the shower. "Now, the orgasms you're about to have, you can definitely thank me for after." He paused and looked around the bathroom. "Shit, I need to get a condom." Maybe he had one in his overnight case. He moved to go look but Bailey pulled against his hand.

"You don't need one."

"Wha—what do you mean?" He was surprised her could even talk let alone ask a question with the way his brain had just short circuited at the thought of feeling Bailey against him without any barrier.

Bailey smiled shyly. "I went on the pill when we started dating so we don't have to use them unless you want to."

"Holy shit." He wrapped his arms around her. "I definitely don't want to." Stepping inside the shower, he pulled the door shut behind them. Most of the heat had left the shower since he'd stupidly left the door open. Thank god, he had a tankless water heater and could run his shower all day. He wrapped his arms around Bailey and stepped them both under the spray while they waited for the stall to heat back up. "What'd you get up to while I was away?" he asked as he rubbed his hands up and down her arms to warm her up.

"I'm pretty sure you didn't bring me in here to talk."

"Absolutely not. I just thought you might need a minute now that we're in here."

She wrapped her arms tightly around his waist and rested her head against his chest. "Thank you, but I'm good."

It was like she'd waved the starter's flag at his dick. It instantly jumped to attention. Bailey giggled. "Guess you are too." She shifted her body and her stomach dragged against his cock.

"You're not fighting fair, Bay," he groaned.

"Who said anything about fair?" Her hand snaked down and wrapped around his shaft.

"Jesus." He dropped his head back into the shower spray. The hot water cascaded down his face. Widening his stance, he simply enjoyed the way the blood rushed to his cock as she stroked him. The confidence in her touch made him want to just stay still and enjoy. It was such a contrast to how unsure she felt about herself in other areas.

With a groan, he stayed her hand. "You better stop. I've been thinking about fucking you all week. I'm not gonna last like I want to if you keep doing that."

Bailey ran her tongue up his neck. "Maybe this shower round should just be about you."

"Nice try, honey, not happening. If anyone is coming in this shower, it's you."

"I don't mind." Bailey looked up at him through wet lashes.

Gonzo shifted their bodies so the spray moved off her head. "I mind. When I said I've been thinking about fucking you, you'd better believe I meant with my tongue."

Her eyes widened, then darkened as she looked at him.

He glanced around the shower for the best place to position her. The steam nozzles strategically lined the walls of the shower but made pressing her up against the back wall a challenge. He nudged her toward the bench. "Sit," he ordered when her knees hit the seat.

Bailey dropped onto the seat. Her arm instantly covered her lower abdomen. He wanted to yank her hand away and her insecurity with it, but unfortunately, he couldn't control that. All he could do was show her how beautiful she was.

Cupping the back of her head, he took her mouth in a hot, searing kiss, putting all the desire he felt for her into it. He fucked her mouth with his tongue, giving her a little preview of what he planned to do to her pussy.

Her arms curled around his neck as she pulled herself closer to his body. No one made noises like Bailey. The little frustrated, aroused sounds she made as she tried to get her clit in contact with him properly made it really tempting to make her suffer, make her want it more. Unfortunately, he wanted the contact just as badly as she did.

Pushing up on his knees to brace himself, he pressed his cock against her seam and shifted. The motion dragged his cock against her wet heat, making Bailey suck in a breath. Breaking the kiss, he licked his way down her body. When her hand moved toward her stomach again, he threaded his fingers with hers and held her hand against the bench. With his other hand, he pressed lightly against her chest to get her to lie back. The movement exposed her beautiful pussy completely. Gonzo shifted his body between her thighs, widening her legs even more.

He licked his lips as he stared at the pink folds that were just begging him to kiss them. Letting his gaze trail up her soft stomach, he pressed a kiss against her belly.

"Gonz." The warning tone in her voice made him press another kiss just below her belly button.

"Shh," he said. "You're distracting me. I'm trying to decide where to start, since it all looks so fucking good."

That must have been the right thing to say, because Bailey's hips shifted and she moved her pelvis toward him. "I've got a suggestion," she murmured.

"I'm sure you do, but once I taste that sweet pussy, I'm not going to stop until you're coming all over my face and I don't want your tits to feel neglected."

"Mmm, you think they'll mind, do you?"

He ran his tongue up her abdomen to the underside of her right breast. "Absolutely, they'd mind. Look at those nipples, all hard and ripe, just begging for me to bite them." He swiped his tongue around one red bud, and Bailey squirmed against the seat. "You wouldn't want me to neglect one inch of this luscious body, would you?"

Bailey's mouth curled up with amusement. "I guess not, no."

"Turn around," he ordered.

"Gonzo," Bailey warned.

"Bay, turn around and put your hands on the wall. Kneel on the bench and let me see that gorgeous ass."

Bailey looked at him for several seconds. He wasn't sure she was going to listen. His cock throbbed in anticipation as it waited for her to decide. Finally, she turned around and crawled onto the bench.

"Jesus," he groaned.

Bailey whipped her head around and looked over her shoulder. "What?"

"I thought your tits were the best thing about your body, but fuck...your ass. Jesus, Bay." He ran his hand along the curve of her ass cheek, then over to the other side. His dick throbbed impatiently as he looked at her body.

He pressed his cock against her pussy. Bailey pushed back and he slid inside. Gonzo dropped his head back and just enjoyed the sensation of being buried deep inside Bailey. Her hot wet pussy clamped around his cock. Holy shit, he'd just died and gone to heaven. He'd never felt anything more incredible in his life.

After a second, she wiggled her hips to get him to move. He thrust deep, making her moan. He couldn't stop watching the way his dick moved in and out of her pussy. His balls pulled up tight. Fuck, he wasn't ready to come. He wanted to keep watching. "We are never fucking in the dark again. Holy shit," he groaned.

Bailey pressed back against him and moved. Her pussy clenched around his cock. "Oh, Jesus." This was gonna be quick. He wasn't going without her. Reaching up, he grabbed the handheld shower head from above him and aimed it at her clit.

"Oh my god," Bailey moaned.

The widened spray hit his balls with warm water. With one hand occupied with the shower nozzle, he couldn't grip her hips the way he wanted. Damn it. He grabbed her long hair and wrapped it around his hand, pulling her head back. The way she threw her head back, arching her spine gave him a clear view of her breasts over her shoulder. He didn't know where to look, her tits, her ass. His gaze flitted between the two as he thrust into her.

Suddenly, Bailey grabbed the shower nozzle from his hand and moved it closer to her clit. Fuck yeah, he loved his girl taking control of her own orgasm. "That's it, baby, put it where you need it," he said.

Releasing her hair, he gripped her hips in both hands and fucked her. Hard. His eyes never left her ass as he drove in and out.

"Oh my god, oh my god, oh my god," Bailey moaned a second before she screamed out her orgasm.

"Fuck," he growled as her pussy clenched against his dick with the post-orgasm spasms. There was no way he could hold out any longer. His balls pulled up tight and he threw back his head as he came.

The hot spray of the shower hit the back of his head and shoulders, relaxing his muscles as he tried to suck air into his lungs. Finally, after several deep breaths, he felt more steady on his feet. Dimly aware of the water hitting his legs at a weird angle, he glanced at the discarded shower nozzle lying on the bench where Bailey had dropped it. Her head hung down between her shoulders. He ran a hand down her spine. "You okay?"

She glanced over her shoulder and smiled. "Yep, you?"

"Fuck yeah,"

Bailey shifted to stand and winced. "Oh," she groaned as she hobbled to stand upright.

"You all right?"

"Yeah." She winced. "That marble looks nice, but it's not very forgiving. Ow." She picked her foot off the floor and straightened her leg, then did the same with the other.

"Come here, baby, get under the water and let it loosen things up."

He grabbed the nozzle off the bench and hung it back up, then directed the spray from it toward them. Bailey moved fully into the middle of the shower and he stepped up behind her and wrapped his arms around her waist. When she didn't flinch when his arms touched her stomach, he couldn't help the smile that spread across his face. Bending, he pressed a kiss to the side of her neck. "That was a hell of a welcome home. Thank you."

She wrapped her arms over his and squeezed as she leaned back into him. "Agreed. I now see what all the hype is about shower sex."

"That the first time you've done it?"

She turned her head slightly so she could see him. "Wasn't it obvious?" she asked.

"Are you kidding me? Not even close."

"Good." Her shoulders bounced happily as she spoke. Bailey turned and wrapped her arms around his waist. "Thank you for making me feel safe enough to try things with you."

He ran his hand down the side of her cheek. "Nothing about sex with you is a hardship, Bay. I am more than happy to be your guinea pig for anything you want to try."

She leaned back and raised her eyebrow at him. "Anything?"

Oh shit, why did she have that look on her face? "Umm, hang on, I retract that. I've seen some of the books you read. I'm up for trying anything between you and me, but there's not a chance in hell I'm letting another man touch you."

"What about a woman?" she asked.

"Ugh…" He stumbled and damn near swallowed his tongue. Bailey liked girls?

Before he could even formulate a coherent thought, she smacked him in the chest. "Oh my god, what is it with guys and girl-on-girl shit?"

He shook his head. "No, hang on, hang on." He held up his hand. "Did my mind instantly picture you with a girl? Yes. But do I want to share you with a woman? Honestly, no. I don't want to share you with anyone. Period. The only person I want to see touching that pussy besides me is you."

"Good, because the only person I want touching you is me."

He wrapped his arms around her waist and picked her up so he didn't have to keep squatting to be eye level. "Good."

Bailey slapped his shoulder. "Put me down, I weigh too much. You're gonna hurt yourself."

"Bay, the minute picking up my girl hurts me, there's a problem."

She tensed. Shit, he'd meant he was a wimp if he couldn't hold her, not that there was something wrong with her. He backed her up to the wall and pressed her back against the glass. He hoisted her so she had to wrap her legs around his waist, allowing him to lean back slightly to look at her. "Don't do that, Bay, there's not a fucking thing wrong with your body. I love everything about it, and I'm pretty sure what just happened in here proved that."

He watched her. Finally, she nodded. "It did."

"Good. I work out, Bay. Hard. The only way I'm not going to be able to pick you up is if I have an injury and then it wouldn't matter if you were a kid, I wouldn't be able to pick you up. Just because every guy you've been with before has been soft, doesn't mean I am. Now if you don't like being picked up and carried, that's one thing, but like I told you before, if it's because you're worried I'm like those other guys. Don't be. I've got you and I'd never let you fall."

Her legs tightened around his waist. "I know you wouldn't." She ducked her head and rested it in the crook of his neck. "I love you, Gonzo."

His body tensed. Did she just say what he thought she did? He pulled back and looked at her. Bailey watched him warily. "Is that okay?" she asked.

"No."

"No?" Bailey's eyes widened and she scrambled to get out of his arms.

He held her tight and pressed firmly against the wall to keep her from going anywhere. "I feel like if the woman I love says she loves me, then maybe she should call me by my given name at least at a time like this."

"The woman you love?" Bailey whispered.

"Jesus, yeah, Bay, obviously I love you. How could I not?"

"You've never said it before, not like this, anyway." Her head tilted to the side as she shyly watched him.

"You've never said it either." His heart pounded in his chest. He'd never told a woman he loved her in this kind of context before. "I think the first time you say it you should call me Ramon."

"I thought you said it was too intimate for someone to call you by your given name." She trailed her finger down his chest.

"Doesn't get much more intimate than what we're doing, Bailey."

"I love you, Go...Ramon." Bailey smiled at him.

It sounded really weird hearing her call him Ramon, not like them at all. "Maybe just Ram instead."

"Ram, not Ramon?" Bailey smirked at him.

"Yeah, Ramon's too formal." Ram should work. It was his name, but not one anybody else called him. At least not anymore. As soon as he'd started elementary school, he'd been called Gonzo and everyone, including his family, had called him that. The only time anyone called him Ramon was when he was in trouble.

Amusement curled up in the corners of her eyes. "Okay, Ram."

He wrinkled his nose. Still sounded weird because she'd never called him anything but Gonzo since they were six years old. "Let's try it again."

"Ram."

"Hmm." Why'd it sound weird?

Bailey cupped his cheek, her eyes warm with emotion as she held his stare. "I love you, Ram."

His chest clenched. "It's getting there. Might have to hear it a few more times to get used to it."

"Oh, yeah?" Bailey smirked at him.

"Absolutely."

"So you want me to call you Ram now?"

"No, it's too fucking weird, but maybe every now and then in bed or when you say you love me or something, when it's just us, it might be cool. Kinda like a little thing just between us."

Bailey smiled, then pressed a kiss against his lips. "I can do that."

"Cool." Why it mattered to him, he had no idea. He'd never wanted to be called by his given name before. He liked how everyone called him by his nickname, even his family, for the most part. He sure as hell had never wanted a woman to call him it before. Why he did now, he had no fucking idea. He just knew in this moment, with Bailey, he did.

She patted his cheek. "Okay, you big lug, put me down before you break your back."

"Bailey," he growled.

"What? I'm just saying you've been holding me for a long time, so put me down before we turn into a couple of prunes."

"Fine, but only because I like your skin all soft and silky, not like a raisin."

"Fair enough." She rolled her eyes.

Gonzo set her down on the floor then grabbed the shampoo bottle off the built-in shelf. He squirted some in his hands. "Turn around," he told her.

"You're gonna wash my hair?"

"Yeah, so turn."

"Oh, Ram," she sighed.

Okay, yep, it was definitely growing on him. He cleared his throat. "Don't make a big deal about it. It's just hair."

Bailey smiled indulgently at him. "Okay, thank you."

"Mmm-hmm." When she finally turned around, he rubbed his hands together to get the shampoo on both palms, then placed his hands against her scalp. He dug his fingers in as he massaged the shampoo into her long, red hair.

"Mmm," Bailey groaned in a way that sounded decidedly close to what she sounded like when she came.

His dick gave a little jolt as it clocked the sound as well. Damn. "Okay rinse, then I'm taking you back to bed."

"Oh, you are, are you?"

"Abso-fucking-lutely." He gave her a little push under the spray to rinse her hair.

She sputtered as the water hit her mouth. "Hey Mr. Impatient I'm still gonna need conditioner."

"Je-sus," he muttered.

Bailey giggled and wrapped her arms around his waist. "I'm really glad you're home," she said.

"Me too, babe. Me too."

# CHAPTER TWENTY-THREE

Still riding the high from his meeting with his agent, Gonzo pushed open the apartment door, eager to see Bailey. When he saw her sitting on the floor at the coffee table, papers spread out in every direction around her, he smiled. "We do have a table, you know," he teased.

Bailey looked up and smiled. "I know, but I like to have everything within arm's reach when I'm marking and sitting on the floor makes it feel less like work than being at a table."

He leaned down and pressed a kiss to the top of her head. "Has anyone ever told you you're weird?"

"Just you." She scrunched up her nose, her eyes twinkled with amusement as she looked up at him. Bailey shifted herself so her back rested against the sofa. "How come you look so happy?"

"My agent stopped by the stadium this morning and we grabbed a quick bite after my workout."

"Does he normally do that?"

"Yeah, Brian usually stops in whenever he's in town, and we grab a beer or something."

"That's nice. So what did he have to say that has you looking like you're about to bounce out of your shoes?"

"I'm not ready to bounce out of my shoes," he grumbled. But he would be if what Brian said was true. "So not sure if you remember I'm a free agent after this season."

Bailey's spine stiffened. "No, I didn't."

"Right, well, I am. So the fact I'm having the best season of my career couldn't be coming at a better time and Brian wanted to run some scenarios by me to start thinking about."

Bailey pushed off the floor and onto the couch. She placed her hands in her lap nervously. "Scenarios? So, like possibly moving?"

Why'd she look so nervous? Did she really think he'd consider moving anywhere without her? He pulled the coffee table across the carpet closer to the couch and sat down on it, so he was facing her. Adjusting his thighs so they were on either side of her legs, he moved closer and picked up her hands. "This is a good thing, babe. You don't need to look worried."

"You possibly moving is a good thing?"

"I don't know what's happening yet. We won't even start discussions until after the season is over, but Brian was in town and wanted to get a feel for what I was thinking."

"Okay? And what are you thinking?"

"From what Brian said with the past couple seasons for the Hawks and my record, I could lock into a career making contract." He couldn't help the smile that split across his face. "He's talking insane money." He chuckled and wrapped his arms around her waist and pulled her toward him. "If I can pull in even half of what Brian thinks he'll be able to get me, this would be more money than I ever dreamed of making playing ball."

After a couple seconds, he registered Bailey was slightly stiff in his arms. He set her back against the couch. "What?"

"So you'd be leaving San Diego?"

"Yeah probably, I don't think San Diego will offer me the kind of money Brian is talking about."

Bailey's mouth tightened and she nodded her head slowly.

He grabbed her hands. "Bay, of course I want you to come with me wherever I end up."

"You want me to come with you to wherever you end up?" She slowly spoke the words in that way she did before she blew up.

What the fuck? Why was she pissed? He'd just told her he wanted her to move with him.

"Well, yeah, of course. Did you really think I'd want to move without you?" he asked.

Bailey cleared her throat. "Do you have any idea where you think you might end up?"

He eyed her cautiously. She still sounded pissed. "Umm...Not really, Brian floated a couple of possibilities out, but it's only the end of August. We've got some time before he starts negotiating, but he's really hopeful."

"Let me get this straight. You want me to move with you to who knows where for next season?"

"Umm, yeah," he said warily. The vein in her forehead pulsed. That couldn't be good. "Why are you upset?"

"Are you kidding me?" Bailey smacked his hands away from hers and stood up. Her knee bashed against his as she shoved past him.

He watched her pace around the living room. "What? I don't get why you're pissed. I just told you I wanted you to move with me. That shouldn't make you mad. I kind of thought you'd be happy."

"You thought I'd be happy that you just expect me to walk away from my job and follow you somewhere, who knows where, on a moment's notice."

"It wouldn't be a moment's notice. We'd have a couple months," he grumbled.

"Oh well, then." She threw up her hands. "You're unbelievable."

"I'm unbelievable?"

She stopped in the middle of the room and spun to face him. "Yes, you're unbelievable. Do you not know me at all?"

"What the fuck? Of course I know you."

"Do you? What do I teach, Gonzo?"

"Are you fucking kidding me?" he growled.

She placed her hands on her hips and stared back at him like she was waiting for him to answer.

"Sociology."

"What's my specialty?"

"Gender equality."

"Exactly. So why the hell would you think you could just come in here and demand I abandon my career to follow you somewhere?"

"Jesus, I didn't demand you abandon your career. I fucking came home excited and wanted to share it with you."

"Seriously, Gonzo?"

"Yeah, seriously. I just fucking told you I wanted you to move with me because I can't imagine living my life without you and this is how you act? What the hell?"

"You came home and announced we'd be moving."

He closed his eyes and took a breath to rein in his temper. "I didn't announce anything, Bailey. I told you what my agent said. Shoot me, I'm excited about the possibility of a kickass contract. Obviously, when the time comes, we'd discuss our options and where we wanted to move."

"Would we?"

"Fuck," he grumbled and shoved his hands through his hair. "Of course we would."

"Do you have any idea how hard it is to find jobs in my field?"

He shifted uncomfortably on the sofa. Okay, so maybe finding a job in her field might take some time, but if they ended up in some place like New York, there were tons of schools. Surely someone would be hiring. "It might be tricky to find a job teaching exactly what you want, but most of what you're teaching right now isn't what you want to be teaching, anyway. And the kind of money I'd be making you could teach part time or hold out till something better opens up."

Bailey glared at him. Her nostrils flared. "Oh my god, you did not just say that."

"What?"

"Gonzo come on." She stared at him like he just asked what 1+1 equaled. It wasn't like it was a stupid suggestion. He was being nice. The last thing he wanted was for her to take a job she hated just to be with him.

When he didn't say anything, she rolled her eyes. "First, I'm not going to let some man support me. Ever. Not a chance."

"Okay, so you work. I don't really see what the problem is here."

"Agh," Bailey growled. "You know what it was like for me moving here. How messed up I was about what happened with Brad."

His spine stiffened. How the hell did him suggesting she let him pay for things become anything close to what that douche did to her? That was just insulting. Feeling his temperature spike, he took a deep breath. "Maybe you should explain that to me."

"I'm not moving to another city with you. I can't."

The muscles in his spine tensed as her words hit him like a punch. "So let me get this straight. You were willing to move to San Diego for Brad, but you're not willing to move someplace for me?" He paused and pressed his lips together tightly, then exhaled. "Wow. Okay, good to know."

"And look where that got me," she yelled.

"Seems to me it worked out pretty fucking well, since the only reason we're together is because you moved here."

"Yeah, we're great, but so were things with Brad." She shook her head. "I made that mistake before. I'm not doing it again."

"Moving with me would be a mistake?" Jesus, that hurt. He swallowed past the lump in his throat. "So you aren't even willing to discuss it?"

Tears welled in Bailey's eyes. "I'm sorry Gonzo, I can't."

He scrubbed his hand over his face. "Jesus, I'm a fucking idiot," he mumbled. The entire drive home he'd been picturing this life they could have together, exploring a new city, picking out a place together that was just theirs and she didn't want any of it.

"You're not an idiot, Gonzo. I just can't move with you."

"No, you mean you won't move with me." The irony of the situation wasn't lost on him. She'd shown up at his house, broken. He'd put her back together and now he was the one broken.

"Same thing," Bailey replied.

"Yeah, it really isn't." He sighed. His watch buzzed, letting him know it was time to head to the airport. He pushed off the couch. "I gotta go."

"Go? Now?"

"I got a plane to catch." He walked toward his bedroom.

Bailey raced after him. "But we aren't done talking."

He grabbed his overnight bag off the floor where he'd left it this morning. Thank god he'd packed last night. "If we keep talking, are you going to move with me?"

"No," she whispered.

"Then not much point in talking, is there?" Pissed off, he slung his travel bag over his shoulder and tried to step around her.

"Gonzo don't leave like this. I love you."

"Not as much as you loved, Brad, apparently."

Bailey reared back. He took the opportunity to step around her.

"How can you think that?" she asked.

"Umm, maybe because you were willing to change your whole life for him and move here, but you aren't even willing to discuss moving someplace with me. Fuck, for all I know I could end up here still, but I don't know, and you won't even fucking discuss it."

At the front door, he spun around. "What does that say to you? Because to me it says a hell of a lot." He grabbed his keys out of the bowl.

Pulling open the front door, he paused. "Maybe you should start looking for a place of your own to live. I don't know where I'm going to end up, and I sure as hell wouldn't want you to be depending on some guy."

Bailey gasped at the dig like he'd intended. Good, he hoped that hurt because Jesus, she'd fucking decimated him. Without waiting for her to reply, he slammed the door behind him. He punched the elevator button. "Fuck," he cursed when he saw it go from G to 2 and stop. He stormed to the stairwell. It would probably do him some good to take the stairs.

The entire way down the stairs, he ranted to himself. By the time he hit the parking garage, he'd almost convinced himself he was better off without her. Almost. He clicked the button on the key fob and his trunk opened as he walked up. Bailey's jacket lay on the floor of the trunk. He fingered the fabric. Who was he kidding? He wasn't even close to feeling like he was better off without her.

Jesus, how could he have been so stupid? He'd known it was a risk getting involved with his best friend, but he'd honestly thought when they finally crossed that line it was because what they had meant something. That they had what it took to go the distance. Apparently not. He'd been working so hard to prove he was more than his reputation and in the end, that's all she'd wanted him to be. Fuck.

He chucked his bag in the trunk. Needing the satisfaction of slamming the door, he reached up and pulled the trunk. The door resisted. Fucking technology didn't even let you do a good rage slam anymore.

With a growl, he pushed the button on the trunk and watched the trunk slowly shut. Holy shit, that was unsatisfying. He opened the driver's side door and slid behind the wheel. He pulled the door closed roughly. Then opened the door and slammed it shut again. Slightly better.

Maybe he could convince the guys to see if they could find some kind of bar that let you wreck shit when they landed. It was New York, after all; they had everything, so there had to be some place like that. One more reason not to cross it off his list of potential places to move. If Bailey and he broke up, he sure as hell was going to need to move some place where he could wreck shit. It was either that or curl up in a ball, and that wasn't an option.

# CHAPTER TWENTY-FOUR

The next morning, Bailey groaned as she rolled over in bed. She'd tossed and turned all night long and still was no closer to an answer. Several times throughout the night she'd picked up her phone to text Gonzo, but what was she gonna say? *Were you serious about me moving out?* She couldn't ask that. Nor could she ask if he couldn't just stay in San Diego.

As much as his dig hurt, after she'd cooled off, she'd known he hadn't meant the comment about her getting her own place. That wasn't Gonzo. But knowing that didn't make it any easier for her to know what to do next. How the hell was she supposed to even think about uprooting her life again when everything in her body recoiled at the thought of it? What if she moved and lost him anyway, just like Brad?

But not moving guaranteed she'd lose him. Damn it. She looked up at the ceiling and screamed. What was she supposed to do? And how were they supposed to figure it out when he wasn't even here to talk to?

After several minutes, she pushed herself upright on the bed. She couldn't just sit around here all day. Grabbing her phone, she pulled up Kia's number.

BAILEY

Hey, what are you up to today? I need to get out of the house.

KIA

Max and I are hitting the beach. Wanna come?

BAILEY

Definitely.

KIA

We'll wait for you to get over here.

BAILEY

On my way.

Hanging with Max would be the perfect distraction. It was hard to be depressed around that kid.

Bailey quickly threw on her bathing suit and covered it up with shorts and a T-shirt. She threw a towel and underwear in her beach bag, dropped in a book and sunscreen, and headed for the door.

As she got behind the wheel of Gonzo's SUV she'd been driving for the past few months, she sighed. She'd become so dependent on him since she moved here. Their lives were totally intertwined. She relied on him for a car, a place to live. Her entire friend group was made up of his friend's partners. She hadn't made a single friend of her own since she moved here. Sure, that hopefully would change once they got into the swing of fall semester and she was actually working regularly and meeting people, but at the moment, her entire life revolved around him.

This was exactly what she'd said she didn't want to happen. When she'd been with Brad, he'd controlled everything. What she wore, who she hung out with, what she ate and now look at her, she'd let herself do the same thing.

Bailey pulled up in front of Smitty's beach house. While Gonzo's place was amazing, there really was something about a house on the beach. The location wasn't nearly as convenient as Gonzo's, but the view...unbelievable.

She rang the bell. A moment later, the door swung wide. Kia answered in a pair of shorts and a bikini top. Bailey stared at the tattoos covering the other woman's body. She'd known Kia had a lot of tattoos but seeing them like this was eye opening. "Wow," Bailey said.

"Not for the faint of heart." Kia chuckled.

Bailey forced herself to stop staring. "Sorry, that was rude. My little sociological brain kicked into high gear there."

"What?"

Embarrassed, she ducked her head. "I didn't mean to stare. I saw all your tattoos and I instantly started thinking about a lecture I could do on body art and the wheels were spinning."

"A lecture on body art?" Kia laughed. "Wow, our brains really do work differently." Kia held open the door and stepped back. "Come on in."

Now that her brain had started down this path, she couldn't turn it off. "How do you feel about public speaking?"

"What?" Kia blinked at her.

"Public speaking. Yay or nay?"

Kia eyed her warily. "Umm. I guess it depends on how many people we're talking about and why I'm talking?"

"Would you have any interest in coming in and talking to my class about tattooing?"

Kia puffed out her cheeks and audibly exhaled. "How big is your class?"

"It's not too big, maybe around seventy-five people."

Kia's eyes widened. "Seventy-five? Umm...can I be honest?"

"Of course," Bailey replied.

"That sounds awful. I was thinking like Max's class size and even that would be pushing my comfort zone since this would be adults, not kids. But seventy-five? No, thank you. Sorry, you're gonna have to find some other tattooed body to discuss."

"No, no, no, I wasn't wanting to discuss your body. Well, not exactly. I was hoping you could talk about why you like it both as an artist and as someone who clearly enjoys getting tattoos."

"Nope, seventy-five is far too many judgy little eyeballs looking at me." Kia shook her head. "Honestly, I don't know how you do it. That would absolutely terrify me."

Bailey shrugged. "You get used to it. Besides, despite what they might think, I still know more than they do."

"I guess, but still, public speaking is not for me. It's listed as one of the top ten fears for a reason."

"I guess," Bailey mumbled. Public speaking was fine. But the idea of following Gonzo to some unknown city, relying on him and then things not working out absolutely terrified her. What happened with Brad was bad enough, but at least she'd had a job to fall back on. If push came to shove, she could support herself, at least. The idea of depending completely on someone else financially made her feel sick.

"You okay?" Kia asked. "You look a little pale all of a sudden."

"Yeah, just thinking."

"Mom," Max called. "Can we go to the beach now?"

"Yep. Grab your stuff."

A moment later, Max came tearing down the hallway with his towel dragging on the floor behind him. "Here," he said, thrusting his towel at his mom as he hopped into his flip-flops.

Bailey grinned as Kia looked at her son, her face a mixture of amusement and exasperation. "Manners, dude, say hi to Bailey."

Max glanced over his shoulder. "Hi Bailey, can we go now?"

Bailey chuckled. "Let's do it."

Max whipped open the door and raced toward the beach. Bailey couldn't do much more than follow in his wake.

She spread out her towel on the sand and plopped down with a sigh.

"You okay?" Kia asked.

"Not really, no," she mumbled as she looked out at the water.

"You want to talk about it?"

Out of the corner of her eye, she saw what looked like parachutes drifting through the sky.

"Bailey?"

She pulled her attention off the skydivers.

"You want to talk about it?" Kia asked.

"What?" she absently replied as her gaze shot to the parachutes once more. An idea taking hold. "I'm going skydiving," Bailey announced.

"What?" Kia's head whipped around. "What do you mean you're going skydiving? When?"

Bailey stood up. "Now."

"Whoa, hang on." Kia grabbed her arm. "What's happening here?"

Bailey scooped up her towel. "You can come if you want to, but I'm going."

"Holy shit, okay, wait." Kia scrambled to her feet. "Max, let's go," she yelled.

Bailey tapped her knuckles on her knee as Kia pulled up to the hanger at SoCal Soar Skydiving and parked the car.

Maybe this wasn't the best idea.

"Is this where you jump out of the plane?" Max asked from the backseat. "Will I be able to see you?"

"Yep, this is it, buddy." Kia turned in her seat to look at her son. "We have to stay on the ground when Bailey jumps, but we'll try to guess which one she is when she's coming down."

"Let's go." Max unhooked his seatbelt, stood up, and poked his head between the seats. "Are you scared?"

"Umm a little." Bailey eyed the plane near the hangar. It somehow seemed both bigger and smaller than she'd expected. She took a deep breath and let it out. Squaring her shoulders, she pushed open her car door. "Let's do this."

As she walked to the hangar, Bailey dimly listened to Max pepper his mom with questions. How fast did the plane fly? How fast would it be going when she jumped out?

Kia pulled open the hangar door and held it. As Max walked in, he asked, "What if there's a bird?"

Kia winced and mouthed sorry to Bailey, before saying to her son, "There won't be a bird and if there is, it'll move."

Bailey's heart jumped. What if there was a bird? That had to be bad, didn't it? Was death by bird a thing? She put her hand on her pounding chest. She was too old for this. Maybe she didn't have to literally jump out of a plane to take a leap of faith with Gonzo.

Kia grabbed Bailey's forearm. "It's completely safe. You got this. No guts, no glory."

Right, like her mom always said, fear was just a lie you told yourself.

"Hey guys." Sloane stood up from behind the desk in the corner and walked toward them. "Hi Max, you here to watch Bailey jump out of the plane?"

"Yeah, but she might chicken out."

Geez called out by a child. That was rough. Was it that obvious? Now there was no way she could back out. "I'm not gonna chicken out," she told him.

"You sure? Cuz you kinda look like you wanna puke."

Bailey pretended to sneer at the little boy. "I'm not gonna puke."

Max cocked his head to the side and wrinkled his nose as he looked at her. "You sure?"

"Positive." She stood up straight. "All right, Sloane, what do I need to do?"

"First, we need to fill out some paperwork. Then we have a video and a bunch of safety stuff to go through." Sloane guided them back toward the desk.

"Whoa." Max stared wide-eyed at the open parachute attached to the back wall of the hangar. The colorful fabric looked like a mural with a beautiful butterfly in the middle.

Bailey glanced at Kia. "You don't have to stick around for all this. He's gonna get pretty bored."

"Nah, it's cool. He's got his heart set on seeing you fly through the sky. We have books in the car to read while we wait, so we're good."

"Can we go look at that?" Max pointed to the parachute.

"Absolutely," Sloane replied.

And like a shot, Max ran toward the opposite wall, with his mom trailing behind him.

"So what made you wake up this morning and want to jump out of a plane?" Sloane asked.

"How do you know I haven't always wanted to do this?"

"Besides what you said that night in the bar?" Sloane held out the clipboard with a waiver form on the top. "I've been doing this a long time. I can tell the difference between a bucket list and someone who's battling some demons."

"That obvious?"

"Kinda. You want to talk about it?"

Did she want to tell a virtual stranger that she was scared she'd lose herself if she followed Gonzo? That despite everything he said, she was terrified she didn't have what it took to hold on to him long term? Hell no, that was not a conversation she wanted to have. "I'm good, thanks."

"You're gonna be jumping out of a plane strapped to my chest. Emotions often come up for people. Sometimes it's easier to work through a few things down here."

Bailey's mouth dropped open. How was that gonna work? "Hang on, I'm gonna be strapped to your chest? But you're tiny. I'll crush you."

Sloane chuckled. "I'm a lot stronger than I look."

She'd have to be. From what she could tell, there wasn't an ounce of fat on the other woman. Bailey had her by a good 3-4 inches and at least 50lbs. "Umm, no offense but..." Bailey waved her hand, gesturing to her own body. The other woman had to see how this would be a problem.

"I got you. There's nothing to worry about. I've jumped with some pretty big dudes and stuck the landing."

"Okay," Bailey mumbled. Grabbing a pen, she started filling out the paperwork. "Hang on. Why do you need to know my weight?"

"Oh, you're there already? Hang on, let's get you on the scale."

"You need me to get on a scale? Why?" Geez, writing it down was bad enough. Having Sloane see her standing on a scale was mortifying.

"We've just found people don't always accurately know their weight, so the scale ensures we have the best number."

"Umm..." Bailey eyed the torture device in front of her. How many diets had her mom put her on as a kid? The scale had become something she dreaded and avoided at all costs. Her heart pounded in her chest. The drumbeat was so loud it was like she'd already jumped out of the plane.

"Bailey you okay?" Sloane asked.

"Uh, yeah sure." Bailey eyed the scale again. She couldn't do this. "I think I changed my mind."

Sloane's hand snaked out and grabbed her wrist. "Come sit down for a second." Sloane pulled Bailey into an office and closed the door. Bailey paced around the small office.

"Bailey talk to me. What's going on?"

"I just—" How the hell was she supposed to explain this?

"You know we're not so different, you and I," Sloane said.

Bailey raised her eyebrow as she looked at the other woman. "How do you figure?"

"The first time I came skydiving it was because I was terrified of heights."

"You're scared of heights?" Why would someone do this for their job if they were afraid of heights?

"Turns out I'm not really. I mean, yes, I have the normal, healthy caution around heights, but not actual fear."

"Okay?" Where was she going with this?

"What I'm saying is my fear wasn't about the height, it was about control. Losing control, not being able to control the outcome. All of those little what ifs that scared the beejeezus out of me."

The kindness and understanding on Sloane's face made Bailey's chest tighten. Did she understand? Could she?

"So what is it about the scale that scares you, Bailey? Because it's not me seeing your weight."

Okay, apparently she didn't understand at all, because it was definitely about the weight. Bailey snorted in reply.

"It's not. That number means nothing to me other than for safety. That number matters to you. Your actual weight doesn't change just because you happen to know the number. Your pants still fit the same. Who you are is still the same. What changes is the power you give that number."

"Okay, not to be rude, but I came here to jump out of a plane, not have a counseling session."

"Fair enough, and I'm not trying to psychoanalyze you. I've just been doing this long enough to have seen the catharsis that can come from doing something that scares you and the healing that can come after. You came here for a reason, Bailey. You either wrangle the fear or it wrangles you. Up to you. I can't do it for you, but in this case, it doesn't get much closer than being strapped to you to support you through it. Like I said,

I'm stronger than I look and I think you are too." Sloane stood up. "I'll give you a minute," she said and closed the door behind her.

Bailey dropped into the open seat. Damn it. This was supposed to be simple. Just jump out of a plane and live to tell about it. Rah, rah, female empowerment shit. Not something that dug into a bunch of her inner child lifelong body image issues. This was so not what she'd thought she was signing up for.

Resting her elbows on her knees, she dropped her face into her hands. Did she want to deal with this today?

Shit. She'd come so far already on this issue with Gonzo's help, but if she was honest with herself, truly honest, part of why she thought things wouldn't work with them was because of her body image crap. If her own mother hadn't thought she was good enough and judged her on her body, why wouldn't everyone else? Before Gonzo, every man she'd chosen had criticized her body, said she was pretty but...

Was Sloane right? Was Gonzo? "Agh," she growled. "Fuck it." Bailey pushed to her feet. It looked like she was jumping out of a goddamn plane after all.

She opened the office door and marched over to the scale. "Let's do this."

"Atta girl," Sloane whooped.

Bailey stepped up to the scale. "I'm doing this, but don't say it out loud, okay."

"No problem," Sloane agreed.

After one deep breath, Bailey stood on the scale. She eyed the number, winced, and closed her eyes. It's fine, it's just a number, she told herself.

"Got it," Sloane said. "You can step off now."

Bailey hopped off and looked over at Sloane. The other woman looked at her exactly the same as she had before she'd been weighed. "Thanks," Bailey murmured.

"Of course. Now let's go get this video watched and start talking safety so we can get you up in the air."

"All right, I'll follow you."

An hour later, Bailey suited up and followed Sloane to the plane.

"We'll meet you at the drop zone," Kia told her.

"Thanks for sticking around. I know this was a little boring for you both."

Kia rubbed the top of Max's head. "It's all good. He's pumped to watch you and now that he met everyone in your group, he's even more excited."

"I'll try not to land on you, Max," Bailey teased.

The little boy's eyes widened. "I'm not standing on the button. Sloane said I had to be outside the target."

Bailey chuckled. "Yep, you do. I was just teasing you."

"Oh, good one," he laughed. "High five." He held up his hand for her to smack. She smacked his hand, then turned to her friend and gave her a quick hug. "Big girl panties, right?"

"Absolutely, you got this. I don't know what made you have to do this today, but whatever it is, let the wind rip that shit off and leave it behind," Kia said.

"That's the plan." Bailey gave her one more tight squeeze. She'd watched the video. She knew the stats on how safe tandem jumps were, yet that didn't stop the buzz of nerves coursing through her veins.

Bailey and Sloane followed two other tandem groups onto the plane. At the metal bench, Sloane sat down, got herself situated, then patted her legs. "Have a seat and we'll get you strapped to me."

A wave of embarrassment crashed into her chest. She knew she'd have to sit on Sloane's lap the entire flight, but now that it was here, she really didn't want to. Damn it, how stupid she was more nervous about putting her full weight on someone's lap than she was about jumping out of a plane. Clearly, she needed some flippin' therapy or something. This was ridiculous. Bailey chastised herself, then sat on Sloane's lap. With a couple of deft moves, they were strapped together.

Sloane tapped her shoulder and pointed at the guy who was going to be taking photos of the jump and flashed him a thumbs up. Bailey pasted a grin on her face. This was it.

As the plane rose into the sky, nervous excitement replaced the previous anxiety.

"How are you doing?" Sloane asked.

"I'm good. Excited."

Sloane squeezed her arm. "You're gonna have a blast."

A couple of minutes later, the pilot let them know they had leveled off. The photographer stood up and opened the door. "We're up," Sloane told her.

"We're going first?" Bailey squeaked. She'd kind of been hoping to watch someone else go first, but maybe this was better. They lined up at the edge of the door.

The photographer hung out of the plane facing them and yelled, "Smile!"

"Cheese," Bailey yelled back. Holy shit, this was really happening. Her heart pounded in her chest. She sucked in a breath. "Oh, boy." Her breath exhaled in a whoosh.

She closed her eyes, took a deep breath, and nodded to Sloane to let her know she was ready.

They sat down on the edge with their feet dangling. "On three," Sloane said and Bailey nodded to let her know she'd heard. "One." The photographer dropped out of the doorway, leaving Bailey on the edge. "Two." Bailey glanced down. Oh god, they were going to die. "Three."

As they slid off the edge, a scream tore out of Bailey's mouth, followed by a laugh from Sloane.

"Open your eyes," Sloane told her.

She hadn't even realized her eyes were closed. Bailey peeled her eyes open. Her first thought was fuck. Quickly followed by awe at the sight in front of her. "This is amazing," she yelled.

"Told you."

Bailey threw her arms out wide. She was flying. And she'd never felt more free in her entire life. She looked at the little video recorder strapped to Sloane's wrist and grinned.

After what felt like no time at all, Sloane tapped her hand to let her know it was time to pull the cord for the parachute. The shoot deployed and suddenly they were floating instead of soaring. Sloane guided her to steer the parachute, so they stayed on course to hit the target when they landed.

Before the chute opened, she hadn't even been aware of their surroundings. She'd just been basking in the powerful feeling of freedom unlike anything she'd ever felt.

The freedom she felt now was so different from what she'd felt before the chute opened. That had been spectacular, but this? This was so incredible in its own right. She truly understood the expression "being on top of the world." She could see for miles in every direction.

They glided through the air for a couple of minutes. The only words spoken between them were directions from Sloane to keep them on track. After a couple minutes, Sloane took control of their shoot to guide them the rest of the way in.

Trusting that Sloane was fully in control, Bailey closed her eyes and just let the breeze hit her face as she enjoyed the feeling of being weightless in the sky. She'd expected to have a bit of nerves about her feet dangling at the height, but she didn't, she felt completely safe. In this moment, she didn't need to worry about a single thing, not her job, not her relationship, not her finances, nothing. Her eyes popped open as she felt Sloane change their angle. They'd be coming in for their landing any second.

"Legs out," Sloane ordered.

Bailey put her legs in the landing position, and Sloane set them down safely on their butts. Her body took a second to register it was back on solid ground. She unclipped her harness and popped up and spun to face Sloane. "Oh my god, that was amazing."

"Told you." Sloane chuckled. "Was it everything you were hoping for?"

"Oh, it was so much more." She couldn't even begin to explain what she was feeling.

Sloane scooped up their parachute and pointed to the spectator area outside the landing zone. "Looks like you impressed your cheering team."

Bailey glanced over at Max, jumping up and down, waving his arms. She flashed him a little wave and headed in their direction with Sloane.

"Thank you so much for this, Sloane. I'm glad you didn't let me chicken out."

"Good. You feeling like you have a little more perspective?"

She didn't know what she was feeling at the moment other than high. "Too soon to tell, but I do feel amazing."

Sloane grinned. "Yeah, that's pretty normal."

"Is this what you feel like every time?"

"Nah, there's nothing like the first jump, but I'm not going to lie. It never gets old."

"I can't imagine feeling like this every day. No wonder you do this job."

"It is pretty outstanding. But you're welcome to come back anytime. Maybe eventually get you to do a solo jump."

The sky drew her gaze. It looked so open with endless possibilities. "Yeah maybe."

As they walked closer to Max and Kia, Max yelled, "That was awesome!"

"I know, right?" Bailey widened her eyes and flashed him a big toothy grin.

Sloane looked at Kia. "So what do you think, wanna go?"

Kia glanced at the sky, then at Max. "No, I've got enough excitement right here on the ground."

"Well, if you change your mind," Sloane replied, then turned to Bailey. "Anytime you want to go again you've got my number."

Bailey wrapped the other woman in a hug. "Thank you."

Sloane squeezed her tight and patted her back. "Anytime."

Bailey watched the other woman walk away, then turned to Max. "Who wants ice cream?"

# CHAPTER TWENTY-FIVE

"That was one hell of a game, boys," Ryan yelled as they walked off the field. He slung his arm around Gonzo's shoulder. "Looks like somebody's shooting for Heavy Metal this year. A dinger and a sweet snag for a DP in one game."

Pete walked up to Gonzo's other side. "Nice catch, man. How am I supposed to win Golden Glove again this year when you do double plays like that?"

"Guess you'll have to work a little harder to keep up."

"Fuck you. That glove is mine." Pete laughed. "I'm gunning for you, asshole."

"You can try." Gonzo waggled his eyebrows at his friend. "But you don't have the lightning moves I do."

"Sometimes you gotta take it slow and drag it out more, hasn't Bailey taught you that?" Pete tossed out the dig and carried on toward his locker.

Bailey had taught him a lot of things. He tossed his glove in his locker, dropped on the bench, and rubbed his hands across his face.

What the hell was he going to do? Baseball was everything to him. Everything. But so was Bailey.

And having both of them for the past few months? He'd never dreamed his life could feel like this. And in a few months, if he got offered the kind of deal he'd always dreamed about and took it, then it could all disappear. Now that he'd had a taste of what life could be like with her, he couldn't imagine baseball alone would ever be enough.

How was he supposed to choose between the life he'd always dreamed of and the woman he loved? Fuck.

Smitty sat down on the bench beside him. "That was a hell of a play to end the game, Gonz."

He flicked a look at his friend. "Thanks."

"So how come you're sitting over here like your dog just died?"

"I don't know. Just got a lot on my mind, man." He untied his shoes and pushed them toward his locker before peeling off his sweaty socks.

"This have anything to do with whatever had you being all mopey yesterday on the plane?"

"I wasn't mopey. I just didn't feel like talking and hanging out."

"You always want to hang out, especially when we're on the road."

"That's because it's the only time you assholes want to hang out anymore."

"Whoa." Smitty's shoulders snapped back. "Where's that coming from?"

"Nowhere, fuck, forget it." He stood up and peeled the rest of his uniform off his body and stalked toward the shower. The locker room was the last place he wanted to have a conversation about his fucking feelings.

He stepped beneath the shower spray and let the hot water hit his shoulders. He cranked it hotter, so it sat just at the edge of too hot and dunked his head under the spray. He turned around, dropped his head, and placed his hand on the wall to brace himself as the burning heat pelted his scalp.

"Fuck," he yelled as a pain seared his ass. He whipped around to see Charles standing there laughing with his towel in his hand. "What the hell, Chuck?" The fucker had snapped his towel on his ass.

"Stop calling me Chuck," the man complained.

"Well, stop being an asshole." Gonzo rubbed his ass cheek.

Charles stepped toward him. Was the fucker seriously challenging him? Not a smart idea in the mood he was in. Game on, asshole. Gonzo took a step.

The next thing he knew, Smitty jumped between them. "Are you fucknuts seriously making me get between you butt-ass naked? Jesus," Smitty muttered. "Grow the fuck up." Smitty glared at Charles. "It was a fucking nickname, dude," he said before turning to Gonzo. "And what the hell? It's a towel snap. How many times have you done that to me?"

"It's different," Gonzo muttered.

"How's it different? Because you're in a bad fucking mood?"

He glanced at Charles. No. Because it was different when it was your friends, but he wasn't going to say that.

He rubbed a hand across his face. This shit with Bailey was doing a number on him. Maybe what he needed was some perspective. Surely the guys had talked to their women about this shit. "Can we grab the guys and get a beer?"

"You okay?" Smitty pressed.

"I don't know." He sure as hell wouldn't be if Bailey and he broke up.

"Let me grab a quick shower and we'll grab the guys. We got you, man."

"Thanks," he mumbled, then walked back under the spray to wash off.

Half an hour later, Gonzo slung his bag over his shoulder as he walked off the bus at the hotel.

"Is this a pub across the street, or beers in the room, kind of conversation?" Ryan asked.

"I'm not gonna cry if that's what you're asking," Gonzo muttered.

Ryan's shoulder bobbed. "I don't know. You want everyone to spill their shit, but you don't spill yours."

"Normally, I don't have shit to spill."

Ryan's eyes widened. "Do you, now?"

"No. I don't know." He adjusted his bag. "Just shit with Bailey I could use some advice on."

"I'm great at handling woman shit," Ryan said.

"Oh my god," Smitty snorted. "Are you kidding me? None of us are great at it, but between us, we can probably figure it out. Let's drop our bags and we'll head over there." He pointed at the Sherlock Holmes pub across the street.

In his room, he set his bag on the floor by the door and pulled his phone out of his pocket. Still no text from Bailey.

Damn it. He didn't want to be the one who reached out first. She'd hurt him, not the other way around. If anyone should text first, it was her.

He shoved his phone into his pocket. Screw it. He needed a beer.

Ryan and Smitty were already in the lobby when he got there. "Where's Pete?"

"On the phone with my sister." Ryan rolled his eyes. "I told him to let it go to voicemail, but for some reason, he always wants to talk to her."

"What the hell?" Smitty mumbled.

Following his gaze, Gonzo watched as Pete stumbled toward them like he'd just sucked down a cannister of laughing gas. His face split in some weird Joker-esk grin, one part happy, the other part crazed.

"Good talk with Kendall?" Gonzo asked.

"Everything okay with my sister?"

Pete blinked several times, then chuckled. "Yeah, fuck, umm." He laughed again and looked at Ryan. "Ken's pregnant."

"Holy shit," Ryan whooped, then grabbed Pete and picked him up.

Gonzo's chest tightened. He was happy for his friend, he really was, but Pete's news was like a neon sign showing the differences between where they were both at in their lives.

When Ryan set Pete down, Smitty hugged him. "Welcome to the club, brother."

"Thanks. I'm still trying to process it." Pete slapped Smitty on the back, then turned to Gonzo.

Another one of his friends was going to be a dad. "I'm happy for you, man. Looks like I'll get a chance to be the favorite uncle again."

"Fuck you. If anyone is going to be this kid's favorite uncle, it's me," Ryan told him.

"We'll see," Gonzo taunted. "You obviously just found out?"

"Yeah, yeah, she just told me." The goofy smile on his face changed to a laugh. "Holy shit."

"Kendall is way more chill than my sister was," Gonzo said. "When Ramona got pregnant, she wouldn't let anyone know till she was something stupid, like three months along or something."

Pete's eyes widened. "Umm yeah, I might have fucked up there."

"What do you mean?" Gonzo watched his friend and chuckled when Pete winced. "Oh shit, were you not supposed to tell us?"

Pete's wince turned into a grimace. "Maybe not."

"Maybe not?" Ryan asked.

"Definitely not." Pete sucked in a breath through his teeth. "Kendall's gonna kill me."

Ryan smacked him on the arm. "Why'd you tell us then?"

"I didn't mean to. I was fucking standing over there when she told me." He pointed to where he'd been standing a couple of minutes ago. "It hadn't even sunk in when I saw you guys. It just kind of slipped out."

"It slipped out?" Ryan growled.

"Apparently not in time," Smitty joked.

Gonzo snorted, then covered it with a cough when both Ryan and Pete glared at the other man.

"I'm just saying," Smitty mumbled.

"Can we just pretend I didn't tell you guys? Then when Kendall gives me the all clear, you can act all excited?" Pete asked hopefully.

Ryan glanced at him, then back at Pete. "Do you really think this guy can pull that off?" He flicked his thumb toward Gonzo.

"Hey," Gonzo complained.

Ryan raised his eyebrow at him. "Am I wrong?"

"No, probably not," he grumbled. "What? I'm excited to be an uncle again."

"I know and you fucking suck at keeping secrets."

"No, I don't. I'm just not good at keeping the good ones. I get too excited." He looked at Pete. "Sorry, man, there's no way she's not gonna know."

"Yeah, I know. It's all good." Pete wrapped his arm around Gonzo's shoulder. "If you think about it really, it's her own fault. What was she thinking telling me when I was on the road? It's almost like she was begging me to tell you."

"Exactly, she's got no one but herself to blame," he agreed.

Ryan rolled his eyes. "I'd love to hear you explain that to my sister."

Pete winced. "I might not say it exactly that way."

"No shit," Ryan chuckled.

Smitty wrapped his arm around Pete's shoulder. "All right, boys, let's go get that beer."

Between tonight's win and Pete's news, he should be flying high. But he wasn't. Yeah, things with Bailey were fucked up, but in the other areas of his life, they were pretty good. He swallowed past the lump in his throat. Somehow, the Bailey piece felt bigger than all the rest.

Inside the pub, he scanned the room. The place was practically empty. Eying a table in the corner by the window, he led the way through the pub. Gonzo slid onto the bench and Smitty took the seat beside him.

He picked up the cardboard coaster on the table, absently noted the name of the beer and tapped it against the wood. His phone burned in his pocket. What if his sound wasn't turned on and Bailey texted?

A brunette in a tight black T-shirt walked up to their table. "You eating or just here for drinks?" she asked as she held up the menus in her hand.

"We're just having beer," Smitty replied.

"What can I get ya?" she asked.

Smitty snaked the coaster out of Gonzo's hand. "Is this any good?"

"It's pretty dark, kind of like a cross between a stout and a dark ale."

Smitty glanced around the table, then looked back at the server. "Sounds good. Let's do a jug of that."

"Coming up." Order in hand, she turned and headed toward the bar.

"Okay, so." Smitty turned in his seat to face him. "You gonna tell us what's going on with you?"

"Nah, it's fine. Pete just found out he's gonna be a dad, I don't want to bring that down."

"It's fine. I need to chill out about this anyway, otherwise I'm gonna announce it to some reporter or something and then Kendall will have my nuts. It's one thing to tell you guys, something else if I tell the rest of the team."

"Good plan. My sister might look sweet, but she's not. She's really not. You cross that woman and she's damn right evil."

"She's not evil." Pete rolled his eyes.

"Evil," Ryan stated, then looked at Gonzo. "So what's going on?"

"I'm not sure things are going to work out with Bailey."

Smitty's head snapped. "What? Why not? What are you talking about?"

He shrugged. "I don't know."

The server walked up and set the pitcher of beer and stack of glasses on the table. "Can I get you anything else?"

"No thanks," Gonzo replied. He grabbed the glasses and pulled the first one off the top, then the next until he had the four glasses lined up in a row.

"Talk," Pete ordered.

"You ever think about what happens when you get traded?" He grabbed the pitcher and started filling the glasses.

"What do you mean?" Ryan asked.

"I mean, like for Peyton, what happens for her when it's time for your next contract?"

Ryan's brow furrowed. "What do you mean?"

"Like how does she feel about potentially packing up her life and following you across country?"

Ryan shrugged. "I still have five years left in my contract, so it's not something we worry about too much."

Gonzo rolled his eyes. "Okay, fine. Smitty, how does Kia feel about it?"

"Fine, she's not too worried about it. She's moved around a lot doing tattoos, so to her this isn't really much different. She's looking forward to being near her sister for a couple more years, but other than that it's an adventure."

That was definitely not how Bailey saw things. "And Kendall? You guys gotta be thinking about it. You're a free agent like I am."

"Yeah, we've been talking about it quite a bit. Her boss is really open to her working remotely as much as possible, since she doesn't want to lose her. She wants to work from home a lot once the baby comes, anyway."

"Hold up." Ryan shifted in his seat. "The baby was planned? Why didn't you tell me?"

Pete shrugged. "I don't know. Wasn't sure how long it would take to get pregnant and didn't want the whole awkward conversation about us trying because trying means sex and you hate when I talk about sex with Kendall."

"Well yeah, cuz it's my sister and it's weird. But you could have said you were trying. You were so freaked out when she was late a couple of months ago."

"We weren't trying then. Now we are." That goofy grin popped back on his face. "I didn't know my boys would be beasts and I'd knock it out of the park on the first try." Pete held up his hand to be slapped.

Denying the high-five, Ryan shook his head. "Nope, could've done without that."

Pete snickered, then looked back at Gonzo. "I take it this is what the fight with Bailey was about?"

"Kinda," he replied. "So Kendall's cool with moving after this season?"

"I don't know that I'd say cool, but it is what it is. She's talked about doing her own thing if remote is too hard. She gets headhunted all the time, she's got lots of contacts, so she'll find work. What about Bailey?"

"She has no interest in moving." He hooked his thumbnail in the edge of the coaster.

"That's tough. She'll come around."

"No, she made it pretty clear she was not moving."

"Like end of discussion?" Pete asked.

"Yep."

Pete's forehead wrinkled. "But didn't she move here because of her dickhead ex?"

"Yep." He dug his nail deeper into the edge of the coaster, splitting apart the cardboard.

"Well, that sucks. How come she'd move for him and not you?"

Feeling vindicated, he threw up his hands. "Thank you. That's exactly what I said."

"And what'd she say?" Pete pressed.

"She went all feminist on me."

"What do you mean?"

"How she'd made the mistake of following a man once, never again. She was her own woman, blah blah blah." He shook his head. "Which I don't get. I don't see how it's any different from what's happening now. I don't charge her rent now, so I don't see how it would be any different if we moved someplace else and she couldn't find work."

"The difference would be that she might not be able to find work. She's got a pretty niche job, doesn't she?" Ryan asked.

"Yeah. Apparently professor jobs are thin on the ground, which is why I said she didn't have to work because I'd be making bank."

"You said that?" Smitty asked. The matching deer in headlights looks on Pete and Ryan's faces said they were all feeling the same thing.

"I wasn't a dick about how I said it. I said I wanted her with me and am happy to support her until she found the right thing. I don't see how that's a bad thing."

"I'm guessing she did?" Pete asked cautiously.

"Oh yeah." He picked up his beer and took a sip. "But she was planning on moving to San Diego with that asshat before she found a job. This professorship just came through at the last minute. She didn't have that when she said yes to him. So why would she move with him and not me?"

"I don't know," Smitty mumbled. "Did you ask her?"

"Yep, and that's when she went on about being her own person and all that shit. How does moving with me mean she's not her own person? I'm not some dick who's trying to control her life. And I'm fucking insulted that she thinks I am."

"Did she say she thought you were controlling?" Smitty asked. "Did you ask her to move with you, or tell her?"

Gonzo gawked at his friend. "In what world would I tell a woman she had to do anything?"

Smitty raised an eyebrow.

"Besides in the bedroom." Gonzo sighed. "Of course, I didn't demand she move with me. I'd just met with Brian." He rubbed his forehead with his hand. "Maybe I could have broached the subject differently. I don't know."

"Is he hearing talk?" Pete asked.

"No, he's speculating right now, but it got me thinking."

Ryan sighed. "I try not to think about the fact that you're both free agents after this season. That'll suck if the Hawks don't sign you both."

"I don't think the Hawks will be able to offer anything close to what'll be on the table for Gonz with the season he's been having," Pete said. "Me? We'll see. It'd be nice if they could."

"Brian's expecting some good offers." Gonzo didn't want to share with his friends yet what his agent had in the works for endorsements but if it went through it would guarantee teams wanted him even more. "You guys know how it is. We have no guarantee on how many seasons our body will hold up so you gotta take the best contract you can get." The money Brian was talking about was life changing, not just for him but for his family as well. "I don't have a choice. My parents sacrificed so much to give me this opportunity. I can just imagine how proud my dad would be if I signed a big contract."

"I've met your parents. They'd be proud of anything you did," Pete said.

"Yeah, but come on, me signing a huge contract, that's like the American dream. It doesn't get better than that."

"Wasn't their dream just for you to have the choice?" Smitty asked.

Was it?

"I don't even know what's gonna get offered, so it doesn't matter. What matters is Bailey uprooted her whole life for Brad and she won't even consider building a life with me. Fuck, I'm an idiot."

"You're not an idiot. Bailey loves you," Ryan said.

"Does she?" he asked. "Wouldn't she be at least willing to discuss options if she loved me? I'm not saying it has to be my way, but we should at least consider both sides, shouldn't we? How would you feel if Peyton said it didn't matter what the contract was, it's not up for discussion? You're staying here whether the Hawks' offer or not."

"The Hawks are gonna offer you something."

"Jesus, not the point," Gonzo growled. "How would you feel?"

"I don't know, cuz it wouldn't happen."

"How do you know? You guys haven't talked about when your contract is up."

"Well, cuz you can't date a ballplayer and not consider the fact that guys get traded."

"Exactly. So what does that tell you about Bailey and I?"

"Umm—" Ryan stammered.

"That I'm a fucking idiot. I'm over here thinking I'm gonna marry this girl one day and she's just passing time, fucking the friend with benefits." His eyes burned. "Sorry guys, I gotta go. I can't do this. It's not helping." He pushed against Smitty to let him out.

"Gonz, come on," Ryan pleaded.

Emotion clogged his throat. He pushed harder against Smitty's side. "Move," he growled. Finally, his friend slid off the bench and he could get out. "I'll talk to you tomorrow," he told them before he stormed away.

On autopilot, he walked back into the hotel and punched the elevator button for his floor. Once inside the room, he pulled his phone from his pocket and pulled up his message thread with Bailey.

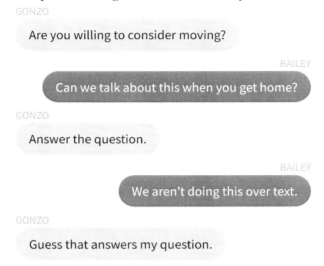

GONZO

Are you willing to consider moving?

BAILEY

Can we talk about this when you get home?

GONZO

Answer the question.

BAILEY

We aren't doing this over text.

GONZO

Guess that answers my question.

Three little dots appeared, then stopped. He waited. The dots appeared again, then stopped again with no message. It was almost like she was deleting what she'd typed. Then the dots stopped.

Fuck.

He chucked his phone on the bedside table. No reply. Looked like he had his answer.

Angry, he tore open the mini-bar fridge and pulled out the dozen mini-bottles of alcohol. If this night didn't call for getting drunk, he didn't know what did. He cracked the top of the vodka and downed it in one gulp. The liquid burned as it glided down his throat. He picked up the next clear bottle. Peppermint Schnapps? What the hell? Who drank that shit? He set the bottle down and picked up the remaining bottle with clear liquid. Vodka.

Perfect. He downed that bottle. He eyed the cluster of
bottles. Bourbon felt like the right next step.

The sound of his phone pinging with an incoming
message woke him up sometime later. He opened his
eyes. Jesus, why had he drank so much? Blurry eyed,
he leaned over toward the nightstand. Was that the
empty bottle of peppermint schnapps? Jesus. Fumbling,
he grabbed his phone. The screen flashed with an un-
opened message from Bailey.

BAILEY

> It doesn't answer your question at all. It says
> this is too big a topic to discuss when you're
> on the road. I lost myself with Brad. You
> helped me find me again. Now I just need
> to figure out what it means. And that takes
> time. Can you please respect that? We'll talk
> when you get home. Good luck at your game
> tomorrow.

Well shit.

He tossed his phone on the nightstand. He didn't have
much choice but to give her time. But when her time was
up, she better be ready to talk. Because he sure as hell
would have something to say if she thought she was the
only one who got a say in this relationship.

# CHAPTER TWENTY-SIX

B ailey glanced at the clock on the stove for the tenth time. God shouldn't he be home by now. She'd checked the airline four times and the plane had landed on time. She fidgeted with the belt of her robe. This better work because it was the only grand display she could think of. Maybe it was stupid, and she should come up with something else.

She heard the lock snick open on the front door. Gonzo was home. No time to rethink the plan.

She pulled the belt of her robe open and allowed the fabric to drop to the floor just as Gonzo rounded the corner.

"Holy shit." He stopped dead in his tracks.

She fought the urge to shift nervously. Bailey squared her shoulders and lifted her head higher.

"Ugh." Gonzo swallowed loudly. "Jesus." He rubbed his hand over his face and cleared his throat. "What's going on?" He quickly looked around the room, then his eyes honed back in on her.

She bit back a smirk. It was hard not to feel powerful when she'd rendered him practically speechless.

"Welcome home," she said.

"Umm...thanks." He flicked a look at her face, then his eyes trailed down her body. "I'm sorry. I have no idea what's going on here, and I can't form a coherent thought when you're standing here looking like that."

"This is my way of saying I trust you." She flipped her hair off her shoulder. "I trust us."

She took a step toward him, and he backed up slightly. Bailey bit back a grin. "You scared of me, Gonz?"

"What? No. I'm just trying to figure out what the hell is happening and my brain is seriously not firing. I can't believe I'm asking this, but can you put your robe back on so the blood can fire back into my brain?"

"What, you can't think when I'm naked?"

"Oh, I can think." His eyes darkened as his gaze slowly trailed down her body. "I can think about all the ways I want to fuck you, but I'm pretty sure, given how we left things, this whole naked thing means something else, and I'm not quite seeing it."

She scooped up her robe and draped it over her shoulders.

Gonzo let out a loud breath. "Bay."

She held up her hand. "Let me go first. I had thought being naked would be pretty clear, but I can see how you might have interpreted it differently." Having her robe back on should have made her feel safer, more comfortable, but strangely, it didn't. She missed the confidence she'd felt when Gonzo had been mesmerized. "Do you want to sit?" She gestured toward the sofa.

"Yeah." He followed her to the living room and sat down beside her. He bent his knee and turned so he was facing her. "Go ahead."

She took a deep breath. "I've been doing a lot of thinking since you've been away."

"Me too."

"I got scared. The idea of starting over again, giving up my job again to follow you terrified me. All of my insecurities flooded back and I couldn't think straight."

"Okay. Are you thinking clearer now?"

"Gonzo, I stood naked in your kitchen."

"So that's a no?"

Bailey laughed. She could see why he'd think that. "No, that's a yes. I'm thinking clearer. I realized I trust you. You've had my back my entire life. You've stood up for me. Championed me. Believed in me when no one else did. How could I not trust you'd have my back no matter where we were?"

He reached for her hand. "I would never hurt you, Bailey."

"I know that. I got scared and for a minute I let myself forget what kind of man you are. I know you aren't anything like Brad. If things didn't work out for us, it wouldn't be because some other woman caught your eye."

"That is not something you ever have to worry about."

"I know. I just let all my insecurities rise up." She clasped her hands in her lap. "I did a lot of soul searching while you were away. It might have taken jumping out of a plane to get me to realize it, but I'm strong and I can handle anything life throws at me."

Gonzo's mouth gaped open. "Hang on. You jumped out of a plane?"

"I did." She grinned as she remembered the way she'd felt.

"That's incredible. I wish I'd seen that."

"I got it on video, but that's not the point. What I realized these past few days is that because of you, I not only learned to trust you, but I learned to trust myself. So even if we don't work out, I know I'll be okay. I'm stronger than I thought."

He squeezed her hand. "First, I'm never going anywhere. You're it for me. Period. There isn't another woman in the world that could compare to you for me. I asked you to move with me because I can't imagine my life without you. But I get maybe it was selfish of me to expect you to move."

"No, it wasn't. It was silly of me not to realize it might be a possibility. Of course, you might have to move at some point."

He shifted closer to her. "I get how hard you've worked for your career, and it's not that I think mine is more important."

She cupped the side of his face. "I know that, Gonz. I do understand how it works. You just blindsided me the other day and I panicked. I'm not going to say I'm excited about the prospect of moving, but I'm willing to discuss it, which is more than I was willing to do the other day."

"That's all I ask." He trailed his finger down her palm. "We'll discuss any and all offers together, and whatever we pick will be what's right for both of us." He sighed.

"You aren't the only one who did some soul searching this week."

"No?"

"No. There isn't a deal big enough to make up for not having you with me. You being there is the deal, Bay."

"Gonzo, that's sweet of you to say but we both know if you're offered the deal of a lifetime, you wouldn't want to walk away from that. Yes, making the majors was a dream, but I remember that little boy who talked about making so much money he could buy his family all houses and cars and giving the big middle finger to all the people who didn't believe in you."

"Yeah, well, that was before my siblings got all greedy, demanding I buy them everything. Raul can buy his own house."

Bailey chuckled. "Still, I know you, Gonz, and whether you want to admit it or not, a huge contract means a lot to you."

"Well, sure it does. But so do you."

"I know that. I'm not saying I'm eager to follow you anywhere, but I'm willing to discuss any offers you get."

"Discuss meaning you might not move with me?"

"Discuss meaning we'll pick the best option for us both. I know your career is important, but so is mine."

He moved closer to her, sliding his leg underneath hers so she was practically sitting on his lap. "I can work with that." He rested his forehead against hers. "I love you, Bay."

She wrapped her arms around his neck. "I love you too, Ram."

Gonzo grinned at the use of his name. "So, can we talk about how fucking hot you look naked?"

Bailey snorted. So much for their sweet, romantic moment. "Sure."

"I damn near swallowed my tongue."

Bailey rolled her eyes.

"That is by far my favorite way to be welcomed home."

"Don't get used to it. I was making a point."

"So, like special occasions? My birthday?" he asked eagerly.

Bailey pushed her hand on his forehead. "You're such a goof."

"No, what I am is a guy with a sexy as fuck girlfriend." He pulled her closer and looked her in the eye. "It means a lot to me that you were willing to do that. I know how hard that must have been for you."

"It wasn't actually as hard as I'd thought it would be." And it wasn't. There hadn't been a doubt in her mind that he would appreciate the gesture. He'd proven to her every chance he got just how much he liked her body. He made her feel safe. "No one has ever made me feel as sexy as you do."

He shifted on the couch. "How about you let me show you just how sexy I think you are."

"You always have sex on the brain," Bailey teased.

"Can you blame me?" He squatted and pulled her with him as he adjusted his back against the sofa. Bailey straddled his lap.

"Not really no."

Gonzo grinned. "Right answer."

# EPILOGUE

Getting traded was bittersweet. He'd be lying if he said he wasn't stoked about the contract, but it sucked that he wouldn't be playing with his friends anymore.

Gonzo looked around the room at his teammates. They'd had a good run.

It was strange that this was the last time he'd be in this bar as a home team player. If he ever came in again, he'd be on the opposition. There'd be no more chanting his name as he walked through the place. Emotion clogged his throat.

Bailey rested her head on his shoulder. "You doing okay?" she asked.

"Yeah, yeah, I'm good." He kissed the top of her head. "It's just kind of weird, especially since Pete's staying. I'd expected him to go someplace else as well."

"The team won't be the same without you."

"It'll definitely be different." They'd been so close to winning the World Series again this year. It sucked that they hadn't been able to pull it out in the end. It would suck even more if they won it next year without him.

"Any regrets?" she asked.

"Fuck no. San Diego couldn't compete with New York." He pulled his attention off his teammates and focused on her. "What about you? You sad you won't be teaching anymore?"

"I'll still be teaching, just differently." Bailey's eyes sparkled with excitement. "I still can't believe I'm going to be working at the flippin' UN. That's insane."

"Meant to be," he replied. He still couldn't believe it had all worked out the way it had. When New York made the offer, he and Bailey had talked long and hard about taking it, even if she didn't have a job. There'd never been a contract in the league like what New York had put on the table. Only an idiot would turn it down.

As soon as Bailey put out feelers, she'd had multiple job offers in her area. When she'd said being asked to speak at that conference was like the World Series in her field, he hadn't really grasped the reality in terms of her career. The offers she received made it very obvious. His girl was a big fucking deal in the world of gender equality. And her being offered the UN job had been like a glowing neon sign that moving to New York was the right move for both of them.

"Agreed." She leaned in and pressed a kiss to his mouth. God, he loved this woman. He couldn't imagine making this move without her.

"All right, you two, enough of that," Pete interrupted. "You guys can play kissy face when you get home. This is our last night with the whole team together. We're not wasting it watching you two make out."

"Disagree, playing kissy face with Bay is never a waste," Gonzo replied.

Bailey patted his cheek playfully. "Awe, aren't you sweet?"

"Anyway." Pete rolled his eyes. "We all know how Gonz feels about his embarrassingly big contract—"

"My contract isn't the only embarrassingly big thing about me." Gonzo waggled his eyebrows.

"Gross." Pete pretended to throw up. "But how are you feeling about the move, Bailey?"

Bailey placed her hand on his thigh. "I can't wait. I know when the possibility of a trade first came up, I didn't handle it well. But now I'm really excited to see where this next chapter takes us."

He squeezed her hand. When she looked over at him, he smiled. "Me too, babe."

"Bailey," Kendall said, pulling their attention away from each other. "The girls and I were talking and thought we'd fly in with the team when the Hawks play in New York. Would you be down for skipping a couple of games and taking us to a show or something? Assuming it's baby friendly." Kendall rubbed her barely visible baby bump.

"Absolutely, I'd love that," Bailey replied.

"Good, then let's make it happen, girls," Kendall said to Peyton and Kia.

"Done." Peyton bounced on her seat. "Road trip."

"Do we get a say in this?" Ryan asked.

"Nope, but it's cute that you think you do," Peyton replied.

Brandon Sims walked up to their table. "Hey man, I haven't really seen you since you signed the big contract. Congrats. That's fucking unreal. I'm happy for you." He clapped Gonzo on the back. "It's gonna be weird not having you with us next season."

"Thanks" It was going to be really weird. A lump formed in his throat as he thought about playing against his former teammates. He cleared his throat and fought to lighten the mood. "It's gonna be fun catching you out of position and hitting the gap."

"Fuck you, you're not hitting the gap on my watch." Brandon laughed.

Gonzo grinned back at him. "Nah, you're right. I'll just hit it over your head and out of the fucking park."

"You can try," Brandon jeered.

"Oh, you better believe that's what's happening."

"Bring it on, bitch." Brandon flexed and postured like Gonzo knew he would. Man, he was going to miss these guys.

Brandon put his fingers in his mouth and let out an ear-piercing whistle, and instantly the bar went silent. "I want to make a toast," Brandon said, hoisting his glass in the air.

Everyone held their glasses up and waited.

"To Gonzo, I'm glad you're smarter on the field than you are about women. Thankfully, thanks to me you finally wised up with Bailey. You're welcome." Brandon toasted his glass toward Bailey, then turned back to him. "But seriously Gonz, I've learned a ton about baseball playing alongside you. You're a great teammate and an even better ballplayer. We'll see you next year in the World Series," Brandon toasted.

"Yeah, you will, when New York kicks your ass," Gonzo taunted and held up his glass.

Boos rang out around the room, and he laughed.

He pulled Brandon into a hug and slapped him on the back. "Thanks, man. You mock, but when you fall, you're gonna fall hard."

"Not happening," Brandon replied.

"We'll see."

Smitty stood with his feet on the rails of his stool so he could see above the crowd. "We aren't all as tall as this guy," he joked as he flicked a finger at Brandon, then held up his glass again. "My turn for a toast. To the next chapter for Gonzo and Bailey, and the Hawks."

Everyone held up their glasses. "To Gonzo, Bailey and the Hawks."

Gonzo turned to Bailey and clinked his glass against hers. "To the next chapter."

*If you enjoyed reading Gonzo and Bailey's story and want more I wrote an exclusive bonus scene. Download Here*

https://www.laurenfraser.com/hitting-the-gap-bonus-scene

Get ready for more in the Playing for Keeps Series. If anyone deserves love it's Grumpy Outfielder Brandon Sims. You can read all about it in **Catching the Fly.**

https://books2read.com/catchingthefly

# ALSO BY

**Playing for Keeps**
Too Far   Prequel- not sports romance
Everything to Me    Book 1
Throwing the Curve   Book 2
Sliding into Home  Book 3
Hitting the Gap  Book 4
Catching the Fly  Book 5

**Cowboy Code**
Rode Hard Book 1 Cowboy Code Series
Rough Stock Book 2 Cowboy Code Series
Round Up Book 3 Cowboy Code Series

**Best Things are Three Series**
Dani's Duo
Longing for Kayla

**Flirty Forties Series**
Sun, Sin and Surf
Aged to Perfection

**Standalone Books**
The Geek Next Door
Letting Go
Too Hot
Yielding for Him

# KEEP IN TOUCH

Want to stay up to date on everything Lauren's doing?
Join her newsletter for upcoming releases, exclusive
content, contests and giveaways,
Newsletter: http://www.laurenfraser.com/newsletter

**Let's be friends on social media**
Tiktok: @author_laurenfraser
Instagram: author_laurenfraser
Facebook: https://www.facebook.com/Author.Lauren.
Fraser/

Newsletter QR

# ABOUT THE AUTHOR

Lauren Fraser resides in British Columbia, Canada, with her husband, two children, and two dogs. When she's not busy writing, Lauren loves to spend time with her family outside—camping, hiking and paddle boarding.

Lauren writes about love and relationships in many different forms, but in the end, she's a sucker for a happy ending. She is multi-published and loves to hear from her readers. For the latest updates, visit her website.

For upcoming releases, exclusive content, contests and giveaways, be sure to subscribe to my newsletter http://www.laurenfraser.com/newsletter

Plus as a newsletter subscriber you'll get access to a newsletter subscriber-only FREE book.

Website http://www.laurenfraser.com/
Newsletter http://www.laurenfraser.com/newsletter